FINDERS KEEPERS

REBELS OF THE LAMP

FINDERS KEEPERS

BY
MICHAEL M.B. GALVIN
& PETER SPEAKMAN

DISNEY · HYPERION
LOS ANGELES   NEW YORK

Copyright © 2017 by Michael M.B. Galvin & Peter Speakman

First Edition, February 2017
1 3 5 7 9 10 8 6 4 2
FAC-020093-16358

Printed in the United States of America

This book is set in Bembo MT Pro, OCRB, Avenir LT Pro/Monotype; Aviano/Fontspring.
Designed by Tyler Nevins

Library of Congress Cataloging-in-Publication Data
Names: Speakman, Peter, author. | Galvin, Michael M.B., author.
Title: Finders keepers / by Peter Speakman and Michael M.B. Galvin.
Description: First edition. | Los Angeles ; New York : Disney Hyperion, [2017] | Series: Rebels of the lamp ; book 2 | Summary: "Twelve-year-old Parker Quarry and his friends are in a race to find the missing pieces of an ancient helm before the mad sorcerer, Vesiroth, does. If they lose, it's the end of the world as they know it"—Provided by publisher.
Identifiers: LCCN 2015042540 | ISBN 9781423180401 (hardcover)
Subjects: | CYAC: Magic—Fiction. | Wizards—Fiction.
Classification: LCC PZ7.1.S714 Fi 2017 | DDC [Fic]—dc23
LC record available at http://lccn.loc.gov/2015042540

Reinforced binding

Visit www.DisneyBooks.com

ACKNOWLEDGMENTS

Heartfelt thanks to Eddie Gamarra, Eric Robinson, Jeremy Bell, and Peter McHugh of the Gotham Group, Valerie Phillips at Paradigm, Jim Garavente, Russell Hollander, Faye Atchison, Kevin Lewis, Polly Watson, Tyler Nevins, Tracey Keevan, everybody at Disney • Hyperion, the one-and-only Ricardo Mejías, and of course our friends and our families. Your love and support mean everything to us.

*For my parents—the ones who
started this in the first place.
—P.S.*

*For Chelsea and anyone else who
likes magic and mayhem.*

—M.M.B.G.

MEMO

It took some legwork, but our agents have
finally pieced together the chain of events
that led to the carnage on the Cahill University
campus four months ago. Until the full report
clears the vetting process I'll just say it's
what we suspected: this was the first confirmed
confrontation between genies on American soil,
and it was a doozy.

We've established the involvement of New
Hampshire middle-schoolers Parker Quarry (case
file RX828), Marisa Lorden (case file RX830),
and Theo Merritt (case file RX829); the genie
Fon-Rahm (case file XX001); and Professor Julia
Ellison (case file KX471.1). Agents in the field
confirm that the genies destroyed were Xaru (case
file XX002), Rath (case file XX008), and Yogoth
(case file XX004). If we're to believe what we've
found in the ancient texts that means ten genies
are still out there. We have no way of knowing how
many are free and how many are still trapped in
their "lamps." Trust me, we're working on it.

In the meantime, Quarry and his genie continue
to operate virtually in the open. Fon-Rahm
has the ability to grant his master knowledge

and skill, albeit temporarily. Evidence also suggests that the genie can conjure up physical objects. Our drones have found trace remains of a high-powered sports car and even a "monster truck" near the Merritt farm. It's a wonder these kids haven't killed anybody yet.

That said, I still think it was a mistake to activate ████████ as a D.E.N.T. operative. ████████ lacks the training to carry out a mission of this importance and complexity. I have concerns, both for our new operative's safety and for a mission whose success is vital to the nation's security.

The department's history of quashing extra-normal threats and suppressing evidence of the Nexus's existence dates back to the Civil War, and this is the first time a civilian is being placed directly in the line of danger. I know ████████ is in a unique position to gain access to Parker Quarry and his friends. I'm still against it. You and I and every other D.E.N.T. agent who ever worked in the field went through a rigorous training program and withstood some of the toughest psychological testing the government geeks ever devised. ████████ is smart and resourceful, but our new recruit is no trained spy. The department has never lost an agent on duty and I'll do everything I can to make sure it doesn't happen on my watch, but that doesn't mean I have to be happy about it.

As for the mission, I prepared the brief myself. ████████ is directed to infiltrate

Parker Quarry's group and learn as much as possible about the source of Fon-Rahm's power and the genie's intentions. To aid the mission the operative has been issued a series of magical objects and has been given instruction in their use. It's risky to have these relics out in the field, but we can't send ██████ in empty-handed.

Under no circumstance is ██████ to engage. This is strictly an observe-and-report job. At the first sign that ██████ is stepping over the line we'll send in a cleanup team and the mission will be scrubbed.

One more thing: according to our research, energy released when the genies Xaru, Rath, and Yogoth were eliminated might have been returned to the wizard Vesiroth (case file KX256.1). As of yet there is absolutely no proof that he's been resurrected, but any reports of Vesiroth sightings should be taken very seriously. Everything we have on Vesiroth tells us he's incredibly powerful and without a conscience. He's the most dangerous man who has ever lived, and if he is back we're all in deep, deep trouble.

Sincerely,
E.C.

PROLOGUE

RONNIE GRIMMER STRETCHED OUT ON his floating lounge chair and let out a satisfying, stenchy burp.

He sighed as the smell drifted away. The sun was shining, the water was warm on his butt, and he was the richest guy in the whole town. Maybe even the richest guy in the whole country. There was a brand-new Ferrari in his garage, and that was next to a brand-new Bentley, and *that* was next to a sinister-looking Ducati motorcycle painted flat black everywhere but the lights and the tiny windscreen. The Ducati salesman had told him the bike would do a good hundred and eighty miles an hour, but Ronnie never rode it, mainly because he weighed almost three hundred pounds and could barely balance on the thing even when the kickstand was down. He didn't need to ride it. The bike was, along with the house and the heated pool and the state-of-the-art stereo system and the computers and the stainless-steel refrigerator, just a way to remind everyone in Mudgee that he was no longer just a fat bludger with a lousy job and bad skin. He was a new man. He had won the lottery, both literally and in a more symbolic way, and in the three weeks since it happened he had told off his boss at the carpet store, bought a restaurant just so he could fire a waiter who had made fun of the way he had mispronounced *fajitas* (how was he supposed to know? This was Australia, not Mexico), and lined up a date with a girl who had been ignoring him since grade school. Life was going pretty good for a guy who pretty much everybody agreed would never amount to anything, and it was all thanks to one very, very special new friend.

The church rummage sale seemed like a lifetime ago. Ronnie had been just about to leave when he spotted the weird metal cylinder poking out of a cardboard box filled with old TV remotes and broken desk lamps. Ronnie didn't have much use for gewgaws, but there was something about the tarnished metal tube that had appealed to him. It was covered in letters he didn't recognize, and when he looked closely he could swear he saw something glowing inside of it. He liked the way the bare metal had felt warm in his hands even though by all rights it should have been as cold as the business end of a sledgehammer. So he had dickered with the hardcase nun until she finally dropped the price from six bucks to three. As it turned out, throwing a little money into the pockets of Our Lady of Perpetual Sorrow was the single best investment Ronnie ever made.

He had been watching trashy TV in his shonky apartment and absently turning the end caps of the cylinder when the thing opened and Syphus first appeared. Ronnie was terrified at first, of course. Who wouldn't be? But it wasn't long until he realized just what he had lucked into. And look at him now.

From somewhere deep inside the house, Ronnie heard the doorbell ring. He turned his head and thought briefly about having Syphus answer the door. No dice. Ronnie laughed as he imagined the looks on his visitors' faces when they came face-to-face with whatever Syphus was.

Ronnie stuck his hands in the water and paddled his way over to the side of the heated pool. With as much grace as a wounded moose, he climbed out of the floating chair and onto his brick patio. He wrapped a blue-and-white-striped towel (the absolute best kind they sold at the mall) around his waist and walked through the sliding glass doors and into the mansion, leaving wet footprints on the marble floor behind him. He was always careful to note that Syphus, silent and staring, followed behind him, far enough to keep out of Ronnie's way but close enough to avoid the pounding headaches they both got when they split up.

Being so near Syphus all the time was a small price to pay, he thought, although sometimes just looking at him was enough to make Ronnie shudder. Ronnie had never given much thought to what genies were supposed to look like, but if you had asked him before all this happened he would have conjured up an image of a bald, blue-skinned man with harem pants and a booming laugh. Maybe a monkey would be involved somehow. He never would have come up with something like Syphus in a million years.

Ronnie walked by his new leather couches, a rec room stocked with full-sized arcade games and a pool table that once supposedly belonged to one of the guys in AC/DC, and a framed lotto ticket hanging on the wall of the hallway. He was particularly proud of that little detail. Instead of just wishing for a truckload of hundred-dollar bills he had ordered Syphus to rig the lottery. That way, nobody would come snooping when he started blowing cash all over town. Ronnie was a lot smarter than people gave him credit for. Would his sister, the big-shot lawyer, have thought of the lotto trick? Not a chance. She would have just started wishing for stuff left and right, never stopping to think about how it might look to other people. It took street smarts and imagination to manage something like this, not the kind of lessons you picked up in books or six years at a university.

Ronnie reached the cavernous atrium inside his front door. He made sure the genie was out of sight (Syphus had been trained to stay hidden until his master called for him) and opened the door.

"G'day," he said, before a skateboard smashed into his face and left him staring up at the ceiling in the entryway of his grand house, flat on his back and gasping for breath.

"Hi!" said the ten-year-old who'd hit him, admiring the chandelier that hung from the vaulted ceiling. "What a great house!"

Before Ronnie could even sputter out something supersmart like "What are you doing here?" or "Why did you hit me?" or even "Who are you?" the kid jumped over Ronnie's belly, landed on the board, and skated across the Italian-marble floor and into the den to the right of the atrium. "Come on in, guys!" the boy yelled. He was dressed in shorts, a neon-yellow T-shirt, and sunglasses with hot-pink frames. He spoke with an American accent and was chomping on strawberry bubble gum. "You have to check out the TV in here! It's as big as a bus!"

Ronnie craned his neck as two men in identical black suits

came through his front door. They didn't even glance at him. They were too busy assembling some kind of strange contraption made of old metal posts and what seemed to be chunks of green rock.

The shock was wearing off and Ronnie was starting to get angry. Who were these people invading his home? He didn't have to take this! He was rich! And besides, he had a secret weapon that would make these yobbos sorry they'd ever crossed paths with him. All he had to do was give the command and Syphus would do the rest. He almost felt sorry for the invaders. They would never even know what hit them.

He clambered to his feet, but before he could cry out for his pet genie, a hand reached around him from behind and covered his mouth. Ronnie looked over his shoulder to see who was holding him and froze with terror.

It was a man with piercing eyes as dark as black holes. He wore a fitted robe of shimmering black, and a silver pendant shaped like a spike hung from a string of leather around his neck. The right side of his face was horribly scarred. He was a man who radiated power and menace.

The man called out, "Duncan!" and the ten-year-old popped his head out of the TV room.

"Yeah, boss?" he said.

"Are your men prepared?"

Duncan stepped into the entryway and looked over the men in suits and their creations, which turned out to be elaborate metal staffs covered with branches sticking out at odd angles and topped with priceless jade globes. He popped a bubble with his gum. "Sure looks like it."

"Then we proceed." The man with the burned face leaned in and spoke directly into Ronnie's ear. "If you would be so kind, please invite your friend to join us."

The undying wizard known as Vesiroth removed his hand from Ronnie's mouth and took a step back.

Ronnie was scared. He was confused. He was still wet from the pool and somewhere along the way he had lost his towel. He had never felt more helpless in his life. "Sy...Sy...Syphus!" he cried. "Protect me!"

The genie appeared from out of the shadows with a terrifying hiss. Syphus was eight feet tall, with black hair that fell in scraggly clumps around his face and one oversized eye set right in the middle of his forehead. He wore tattered red pants and was covered with arcane tattoos of opposing armies that moved across his chest and arms in a battle that had been raging for thirty centuries. He was always surrounded by a glowing purple mist. The smell of old smoke that came off of him was so thick you could taste it.

Syphus screamed, "You leave Master alone!" and unleashed a torrent of psychic energy from his misshapen eye that distorted the air as it cut through the room. Duncan ollied out of the way but the men in suits were knocked across the atrium, their staffs clanging uselessly to the floor.

The Cyclops genie aimed another psychic burst at Vesiroth. The burned sorcerer wrapped his fist around his silver pendant and chanted something in a language lost for millennia. The attack from Syphus bounced off of Vesiroth and straight up, where it ripped a hole through the ceiling. The genie howled with rage.

Vesiroth called out, "Stand and wield your weapons!" and the men in suits scrambled to their feet. They grabbed their staffs and pointed them at the genie. The jade glowed and bright green beams struck Syphus, causing the one-eyed creature to writhe in agony.

"He doesn't seem to like that," said Duncan, watching in fascination.

"Genie!" said Vesiroth, staring at the tortured creature. "Third of the Jinn! You were created from my very life force, and I call upon the power of the Nexus to unmake you. Begone from this earth and exist no more!"

Vesiroth raised his hands in the air and brought them down as fists. Ronnie covered his ears and closed his eyes tight as the genie let out a high-pitched shriek so loud that the chandelier shattered and crashed to the floor. Then, with one final blink of his single eye, the genie imploded in a cloud of white ash.

Ronnie opened his eyes tentatively. He turned to Vesiroth and saw that the wizard's hands were shaking.

Duncan popped off his skateboard. "Um," he said, "I think it would be a good idea to, you know, let the big guy have a little alone time." The men in suits followed Duncan deeper into the house as Vesiroth began to convulse. Ronnie threw himself to the floor behind a thick table just as Vesiroth let out a scream of his own and released a blizzard of chaotic energy, uncontrolled and unfocused, as he reabsorbed the life force from the vaporized genie. The windows of the house shattered. Paint peeled from the walls. The staircase collapsed in a pile of gold and marble. The TV exploded, the arcade games burst into flame, and the water in the pool outside began to boil.

And then, as soon as it had begun, it was over. The silence

was deafening. Ronnie poked his head up. The men in suits had made their way back to disassemble their staffs.

Vesiroth, battered into exhaustion from his ordeal, was slumped against what remained of the staircase. Duncan bounced over and helped the wizard to his feet.

"I got you, boss," he said cheerily as he wrapped his arm up and around Vesiroth's waist. "Let's get out of this dump." As Duncan helped a stumbling Vesiroth toward what was once the front door, he stopped and considered the pudgy Australian in swimming trunks cowering on the floor. The kid held up his free hand and Ronnie gasped as a glowing knife as shiny as a mirror magically appeared, the point just a breath away from the tip of Ronnie's nose.

"I guess I should kill you," Duncan said. His eyes were so dead. How could a ten-year-old have such dead eyes? "But I kind of have a lot on my plate right now. I suppose I could always come back." He thought for a minute. "I'll tell you what. You just wait here and in a week or two I'll try to fit you into my schedule. See you then!" The knife vanished back into thin air and then Duncan, the spent wizard, and the men in suits were gone.

Ronnie slumped to the ground. He curled himself into a ball in the ruins of his massive house and began to cry. His luck had never changed at all.

1

THE MAGIC ACT WAS NOT GOING WELL.
The auditorium at Robert Frost Junior High was packed.
Parker's mom, Kathleen, was in the seats along with his aunt
Martha, his uncle Kelsey, everyone in his seventh-grade class,
and his math teacher, Mr. Rommy. The annual Spring Talent
Spectacular wasn't necessarily the Grammys, but Cahill, New
Hampshire, was a small town, and what kind of monster doesn't
like to see kids put on a talent show? The pressure was on and it
had to be said that Parker Quarry, late of Los Angeles, was tank-
ing. *Big*-time.

The metal rings that were supposed to lock together and then
separate at a magic word refused to come undone. The bit where
he poured a pitcher of milk into a rolled-up newspaper ended

with a soaked newspaper and a puddle of milk on the stage. The cane that was supposed to turn into a bouquet of flowers steadfastly remained a cane. By any objective measure, he was really, really terrible at magic.

Reese and Theo watched the fiasco from the side of the stage. Reese was wearing a newish blue dress that matched the streaks of color that ran through her dark hair and clunky black boots her mother absolutely hated. She had already gone on, playing part of Mahler's Symphony no. 5 on her viola. Reese practiced hard and had performed flawlessly, but Mahler was a tough sell to middle-school kids, and she was greeted with bored applause. Next time, she thought, she would go with something from this century.

"This totally isn't fair," said Theo, his arms crossed defiantly over his chest. "*I* should be the one doing the magic."

"I thought you said magic was for geeks."

"Magic *acts* are for geeks. I can do *real* magic."

"Yeah, but if it was you out there you wouldn't get to watch Parker eat it hard onstage."

Theo grinned. "That's true."

It sure seemed like Parker was in over his head. He swiped a hand across his forehead and tugged at his shirt collar. Underneath his cheap top hat his brown hair was wet with sweat. "Okay!" he said, picking a grapefruit-sized crystal ball and a white handkerchief off the folding table that held all his props. "This is just a plain, ordinary crystal ball, right? Just like the kind you use for—" Parker stopped. Nobody ever used a crystal ball for anything. "Um, just like the kind they sell at crystal-ball stores. I'm going to wrap it in this handkerchief, like so...." He did.

"And then, with just a wave of my hand and a hypnotic stare, I will cause it to float in midair!"

He pulled his hand away and the crystal ball that was supposed to levitate fell to the wooden stage with a clunk that echoed all the way to the fire doors. There was laughter and sarcastic applause through the crowd.

"Oh. Man. Okay. Okay, I got this. . . ."

In the audience, Parker's mom was dying along with her only kid. She cringed and occasionally muttered something that sounded like "Oh, jeez." No mother should have to be put through something like that.

"He should quit while he's ahead," said Parker's uncle Kelsey.

"When was he ahead?" asked his aunt Martha.

Through it all, Mr. Rommy sat, silent and impeccably dressed in a dark suit. If he had any opinions at all about the show he was keeping them to himself.

Parker chased down the crystal ball before it rolled off the stage and plopped it down on the table. "All right! Well, it looks like my time's almost up. I just have one more trick to astound and amaze you! I need a volunteer!"

No hands shot up. No one wanted their fingerprints on this particular disaster.

"Anybody! Anybody at all!"

In the wings, Theo sighed. "Break a leg," Reese told him.

"With my luck I probably will." Theo took a deep breath and walked out onto the stage to tepid applause.

Parker said, "Perfect! And what is your name, young man?"

Theo squinted up into the bright lights. "Um . . . Theo Merritt?"

"Theo . . . Merritt, did you say? And can you confirm that we have never met before this moment?"

"I've never seen you before in my life."

Groans and laughs spread through the crowd. There wasn't a person there who didn't know that Theo and Parker were first cousins.

"Okay! If you just give me a second, here. . . ." Parker fumbled on the table for a large red tablecloth (one of Martha's abandoned craft projects) and then realized he couldn't hope to hold the thing open by himself. "Oh. I'm going to need a little . . ." Parker gestured desperately to the wings for Reese to come out.

"No. No way," she said under her breath.

Parker gave her a pleading pout. Reese clenched her teeth and plodded sullenly onto the stage. Once again, Parker Quarry was dragging her into something she didn't want to do. It was the story of her life.

"Reese Lorden, everybody!" said Parker. She frowned and Parker handed her one end of the tablecloth. "Now, what I'm going to do is, Theo, could you move a foot to the left here, please? Okay, now my assistant Reese and I—"

"Your *assistant*?" Reese asked.

"Reese and I are going to hold up this cloth, like so . . ."

Parker and Reese stretched the cloth between them so that Theo was completely hidden from the audience.

". . . and then I'm going to give the magic incantation. . . ."

Parker met Mr. Rommy's eyes in the audience. The wannabe magician attempted a subtle nod, but nothing Parker ever did was subtle and his black hat toppled off his head.

Mr. Rommy waved his hand gently in the direction of the stage. If you had been looking right at him you might have seen that his eyes changed color slightly, going from a light blue to a stormy gray. A slight whiff of ozone could be detected in the air, the smell of a small electric charge.

"Akka! Makka! Za-zakka!" With sudden elegance, Parker dropped his corner of the cloth, snapped his fingers, and stepped away.

There was a collective gasp from the audience. Theo Merritt was gone.

Parker looked over the audience, now in complete control. "Ladies and gentlemen, if you will kindly turn your attention to the doors behind you." He gestured to the back of the auditorium. Everyone in the crowd turned around. A spotlight hit the doors. Parker shouted, "Ta-da!"

And nothing happened.

"Ta-da!" Parker's newfound confidence faded. "Um, Theo? You can come out now!"

Still nothing. As a confused murmur worked its way through the audience, Reese whispered in Parker's ear. "What did you do?"

"Nothing! I just—"

And then Reese's phone rang. She fumbled in her pocket and put the phone to her ear. "Theo?" she said. "Where..." She turned back to Parker with a look of panic on her face. "Oh no."

The crowd gathered below and cheered, astonished, at the sight of Theo. He was on top of the school's roof, safe but stuck.

"Come on, Parker, tell us how you did it!" Uncle Kelsey said, his eyes never leaving his son on the roof. "I mean, there's not even a staircase that goes up there! They have to get a ladder to get him down!"

"Sorry, Uncle Kelsey, but a magician never reveals his tricks."

Reese rolled her eyes so hard she thought Parker might be able to hear it. As Uncle Kelsey and Aunt Martha went with his mom to help Theo off the roof, Mr. Rommy leaned in to Parker and Reese. "I believe I explained to you that teleportation was a very bad idea."

"Come on, Rommy, he's fine! The trick killed!"

"Yes, but young Theo could just as easily have ended up a thousand feet over the school's roof, or in the middle of the Pacific Ocean. Teleportation is unpredictable and very difficult to harness."

"Theo was never in any danger. It was a controlled environment. Besides, look at him! He's having the time of his life!"

Theo was not having the time of his life. As the custodian and Theo's dad leaned the ladder onto the roof, Theo's face was the color of a fire truck.

"Well, you have to admit it was a memorable talent show," said Reese.

"We should be thankful it will not be remembered as the day Theo died," said Mr. Rommy.

"As always, you're a ray of sunshine, Fon-Rahm," Parker said.

The custodian and Uncle Kelsey finally got Theo off the roof, to the scattered applause of the teachers, parents, and students still gathered around. After his folks made sure he was okay, Theo stomped over to Parker, obviously displeased at the turn of events.

Before Theo could get within punching distance, Parker gave him a weak shrug and a comic bow.

"Ta-da!" he said.

Later, after Reese had gone with her parents and Theo, Kelsey, and Martha had piled into Kelsey's old work truck, Parker and his mom got into their secondhand (okay, thirdhand) Ford Focus and shut the doors against the night. Kathleen was always a little surprised when the car started right up. The Saturn she'd owned when they lived in LA was more temperamental.

She let the car idle.

Parker waited. "Are we going, or have you decided we're going to live in the school parking lot?" he asked.

She turned to her son. "Things are working out, don't you think? I mean, it's not perfect, but you like it here, don't you?"

Parker thought for a minute. He was as surprised as anybody to find that he *did* like it in New Hampshire. "Yeah. Why?" His face fell. "Oh no. Are we *moving*? That's not fair! I've got friends here! I've got a whole—"

"No. No! We're not moving! I swear. I wanted—" She stopped. "I have some good news, and I was waiting for the perfect time to tell you. . . ."

"You got a raise at the drugstore!"

"No. I *am* going to get a raise, just as soon as I can work up the courage to ask for one, but no. This is about Dad."

Parker's father, J.T., had been in prison for the last two years, convicted of convincing a group of senior citizens to invest in real estate in South Dakota and then charging outrageous fees for helping them buy land that turned out not to exist. J.T. always denied he'd done anything illegal. The federal prosecutor and the jury saw otherwise. Illegal or not, Parker knew what his dad had done was wrong, and he knew his mother knew it, too. J.T. was the reason they'd had to leave everything behind in the first place.

Parker shrank back in his seat. "What about Dad?"

"Parker, they're letting him out early."

Parker froze. "I thought he wasn't even up for parole until the summer."

"That's what I thought, too, but the DA made some kind of deal with him. He's coming home!"

"And by home you mean here?"

"Of course I mean here! He'll stay with us at your aunt and uncle's until we all get an apartment together. Or a house! How would that be, all the Quarrys together in an actual house with a yard and plumbing and everything?"

"I guess it'll be great."

"You *guess* it'll be great? This is incredible news! It's a new start for us, kid. And I don't believe for a second you're not excited about it. Come on. Admit that it's amazing. I'm not moving the car until you admit it's amazing."

Parker forced himself to smile. "It's amazing, Mom."

She reached out and messed up her son's hair before she put the car into reverse. "It's a new start for all of us."

As they pulled away, Parker looked out the window. Fon-Rahm was flying silently alongside the car, unseen by anyone but his master, blue lightning streaming down his arms as he continued his constant vigil.

2

REESE WATCHED THE CLOCK.
The last fifteen minutes of Mr. Nilmeier's seventh-period
photosynthesis lecture (come on, she had learned this stuff herself two years ago) had been excruciating, but in twenty seconds
the long school day would be a thing of the past and it would
be time for the single greatest thing ever: Historical Math Club!
The bell rang and she leaped out of her seat. In the hall she
exchanged cursory hellos with Erin, Alicia, and Jennifer. The
three girls were always together. For the millionth time Reese
thought about how cool it would be to have some friends who
were girls for once—just one would be fine, really—and for the
millionth time she packed that thought up and stored it alongside
other ideas that had merit (she had a great concept for a pop opera
based on the life of Marie Curie) but which she had no way of

currently implementing. This wasn't the time to be worried about things she couldn't control. Historical Math Club!

The Historical Math Club was the single least-popular after-school club at Robert Frost Junior High. Potential members were turned off not only by the unsavory combination of history and math but also by the fact that the club meetings took place in Mr. Rommy's classroom. Mr. Rommy was stuck with the worst room in the whole school. The heater was overbearing in the winter. The air conditioner was on the fritz when it was hot. The windows didn't close right, and the blinds were all tangled in a bunch near the ceiling. When you put it all together, you got something that did not in the least appeal to students trying to decide what to do with their precious moments between the end of school and the beginning of dinner.

Which was exactly the way the members of the Historical Math Club wanted it.

Parker had come up with the idea after Uncle Kelsey began asking questions about all the time they were spending in the barn. The truth was that the barn was where Fon-Rahm lived, but they couldn't tell him *that*. Parker's first instinct had been to order Fon-Rahm to remove the memories from his uncle's brain, but he knew Theo wouldn't like that and he wasn't sure if Fon-Rahm could actually do it, so he decided he and his friends needed an alternate place to hang out. Reese's house was out of the question because her parents had an annoying habit of showing up right when you didn't want them around, and the last time Parker had told his genie to build them their own clubhouse it had alerted Xaru, who nearly annihilated the human species. The next logical meeting place was the school.

The three members of the Historical Math Club (Parker, Theo, and Reese) had been meeting here two days a week with their adviser, Mr. Rommy, ever since. The particular genius of the name was that while it scared away other students, it reassured adults. Their children would not be exposed to anything dangerous or questionable in the Historical Math Club. Of course, *dangerous* and *questionable* are relative terms.

In the weeks since its inception, the club had trudged through exactly zero math problems and no history. They had, however, been rock diving in Cancún, shopping in Mumbai, surfing in Maui, and horseback riding in Argentina. On one of their trips, Fon-Rahm had piled them into his beiger-than-beige Toyota Camry and magically flown them all to a ski resort in Utah where Parker had the genie give them the skills of professional snowboarders. After they hitched a ride on a SpaceX test flight, Theo had puked on a multimillionaire boy-band star who had waited years for the trip. Reese thought Parker would never stop laughing.

And now, it was finally time for Reese to pick their activity. She was superexcited, but when she came into Mr. Rommy's room she found both Parker and Theo moping around like they were in pre-algebra.

Parker was usually bouncing off the walls at Historical Math Club, reeling off insane idea after insane idea, any one of which would prove irresistible to Theo while still causing the catastrophic failure of his digestive system. Instead, Parker was slumped in the noisiest and most uncomfortable of the noisy and uncomfortable desks, staring morosely out the window. Theo was absently scratching paint chips off a radiator. Fon-Rahm, still in what Reese liked to think of as his Mr. Rommy disguise, sat at his desk at the front of the classroom correcting math tests taken by seventh graders who had exactly zero idea that their boring teacher was really a genie older than history.

Instantly deflated, Reese turned to Fon-Rahm with a what-gives look that went right over the genie's head. Fon-Rahm was hopeless at reading body language.

"It's like a morgue in here. What's wrong with you guys?"

Nothing from Theo. Parker's desk squeaked.

"Wow. It'd be more fun to hang out with Vesiroth."

Fon-Rahm frowned. "I do not believe that to be an accurate statement. Although I have felt no changes in the Nexus, I feel we can expect an attack once Vesiroth has amassed the power required to ensure his victory."

"Yeah, I was being sarcastic, but thanks for reminding me we're always in constant danger."

Theo snorted. Parker stared out the window. His desk squeaked.

"Nobody? Wow. Okay. Great. Don't say anything, just sit there and pout."

"Leave me alone, will you?" Parker finally chimed in. "I've got a lot on my mind."

"Maybe if you told us about it we could help!"

"And maybe you would just make things worse."

Reese threw up her hands. "Fon-Rahm, can you please help me out here?"

Fon-Rahm took a moment before he answered. "I find that human emotions can be infinitely complex."

"Deep," Parker told his genie. "It's that kind of sparkling insight that makes me glad I'm literally forced to be within earshot of you a hundred percent of the time."

"Perfect," said Theo. "This again."

Parker said, "You don't know what it's like, buddy. You get all the benefits of having a genie without being chained to him. You can just walk away."

"I have problems, too, you know," said Theo.

"Yeah, like which Patriots shirt to put on in the morning."

Parker wasn't angry at Theo or Fon-Rahm, and he knew it. He was angry at his father. He had been angry with him since he went away. In Fon-Rahm, Parker had found an adult (kind of) who was there whenever Parker needed him, and now that J.T. was coming back into his life Parker didn't know how to feel about it. He wanted to give his father another chance, but he'd been burned before.

Reese said, "Guys? Can we just get past whatever this is and go do something fun? We have a magical genie right here, and it's my turn. . . ."

There was a knock and the door to Mr. Rommy's room swung open.

Reese stopped midsentence. Theo quit picking at the radiator. The distinctive, grating squeak from Parker's desk went mercifully silent.

"Hi, sorry. It's my first day here and they gave me this list of after-school programs with available spaces." The girl held out a creased list of clubs. "Is this right? Historical Math Club?"

The kids just gaped. This had never happened before.

Fon-Rahm was the only one who kept his composure. "Yes. We were just discussing Euclid's proof of the infinitude of primes and the effect early mathematics had on the politics of his time." The girl nodded. "Sounds like a real party." She was a cute, dark-skinned African American girl with shiny ringlets pulled back in a ponytail. She was dressed in light layers to fight the early-spring chill. "Nice place you got here," she said. "They run out of space in the boiler room?"

Parker and Theo just gawked, but Reese couldn't stop herself from giggling. The girl grinned at her.

"Robotics!" Parker cut in.

"Excuse me?" said the girl.

"I think they might have an opening in the Robotics Club." Parker knew they couldn't let anybody else in the club. They all did. "Or maybe Conversational Finnish. Anything is better than Historical Math. It's super boring. Really. It's the worst."

"Then why are you here?"

"Um . . . detention? Theo and I plugged up a toilet and they gave us a choice between getting suspended or doing this."

"I think we chose poorly," said Theo.

The girl nodded at Reese. "What about you? You don't look like the detention type."

"It's my mom's idea," Reese said. "Gotta pad out those extra-curricular activities for college applications."

"I know the feeling. My mom almost sent me to a summer computer camp."

"How'd you get out of it?" Reese asked.

"I told her it was a great idea because there was this really cute boy at computer camp and I wanted to spend *lots and lots* of time with him. After that she never brought it up again." The girl laughed. Reese tried unsuccessfully to avoid smiling herself. Parker jumped in. "Look, don't worry about us. We won't feel bad if you turn us down for something more exciting. Pottery! Meditation! Video Journalism!"

"What is your name?" Fon-Rahm asked the girl in an attempt to take control of the situation.

"Naomi Cook."

"Miss Cook, you are welcome to join us today, but you should know this will be our final meeting. As I was just about to tell my students, I am disbanding the Historical Math Club. I am sorry to say that it takes up too much of my time."

Naomi looked at all the empty desks. "Yeah, I can see how something like this would be a little overwhelming. Thanks for the invitation, but I just came down here to see if there really was such a thing as the Historical Math Club. You never know when you'll be seized by a sudden interest in math history." She looked at Parker, then at Reese. "I guess I'll try Robotics." And just like that, she was out the door and gone.

"Man, that was a close one," said Theo.

"We're gonna have to come up with a new name for the club," said Parker. "Maybe something with dulcimers?"

Reese looked at the closed door. She would have loved to have another girl to go on adventures with. The new girl seemed so *cool.*

"So." Fon-Rahm turned to Reese. "What exactly do you have planned for us today?"

Before Reese could answer, Theo stood up. "Actually, I just came to tell you guys that I can't hang out." He hoisted his backpack. "I have my thing today."

"Again?" Parker asked.

"Yes, again. I'm not crazy about it, either." Theo opened the door and took one last sad look at his friends. "Have fun."

Reese's heart sank. "So I guess there's no Historical Math Club adventure for today."

"He's going to do what he wants to do." Parker knew his cousin better than any of them. "I think we should go without him. Once he sees he's missing out, he might not abandon us so quickly next time."

Reese perked right up. She had always wanted to hike in the canopy of the Amazon rain forest.

3

FROM THE OUTSIDE, PROFESSOR Ellison's house looked like a house.

It was a modest place set back far from the road on a patch of carefully tended lawn, nice, if a bit on the small side. It was pine green with tan trim and brown shingles. There were lace curtains in the windows. Pillars surrounded a charming open-air porch, and flowers bloomed on both sides of the crushed-stone pathway that led to the front door. In the summer, hummingbirds flitted around a feeder hung from a birch tree in the side yard. A cast-iron weather vane in the shape of a farmer pushing a plow stuck up from the roof. It would seem to be the perfect home for an unmarried archaeology professor who didn't mind living by herself way out in the boonies. It was a quaint and pleasant little farmhouse.

At least, that's what it looked like from the outside. If the spell Ellison used to mask the place were to fall away, the locals would be mortified to see that it was in reality as big as a Walmart and about as aesthetically pleasing. It was constructed of concrete, metal, and high-strength glass, and it squatted on the property like a gray monster, sprawling in all directions. The professor had spent a small fortune building and updating the house. She used out-of-state contractors who moved in materials in the dead of night and were encouraged to keep their mouths shut with suggestions implanted by ancient magic directly into their subconscious minds.

It was less a house than it was a fortress. It needed to be. It was built to protect a collection of priceless books and the world's most powerful artifacts of magic.

"Pay attention, Theo! My time is valuable and I'd like to spend as little of it as possible watching you fail to master the simplest of tasks."

Professor Ellison was lounging on a silk sofa with a French fashion magazine in one hand and a cold Manhattan cocktail in the other. She was almost impossibly elegant, with long limbs, gray eyes, and meticulously styled hair. The professor was a very beautiful woman. You might have guessed she was around sixty. You would be off by about two thousand nine hundred and forty years.

Theo groaned and let his shoulders drop. He had been trapped in this ginormous living room for hours, trying without any success to knock down an empty wine bottle forty yards away using nothing but his own connection to the magical force called the

Nexus and an ancient amulet carved from the thighbone of a giant ground sloth.

"I can't do it!" he said. "I'm concentrating on the bottle, but I can't get this dumb thing to work. I thought it was supposed to shoot out fire or something."

"It would if it was used properly. You're waving it around like you're trying to swat a fly."

"Can't we try something else? Maybe I could practice my containment spells."

"Your containment spells certainly do need work, but right now this is more important. So if you would be so kind, please pretend you have some affinity for magic and knock over the bottle."

Theo let out a deep breath. He scrunched his eyes shut, pointed the piece of bone, and concentrated. A puff of green smoke appeared ten yards in the distance and dissipated pathetically into the air.

"Lovely," Professor Ellison said. "Perhaps Vesiroth will be scared off by the smoke and simply run away."

"I am so sick of this!" Theo threw down the bone in disgust. "I didn't ask to be connected to the stupid Nexus and I don't want to be a stupid wizard. I want to play football and video games and goof off like a normal kid and instead I'm trapped in a museum with . . ."

The professor's eyes lifted coolly from her magazine. "Oh, don't stop now," she said. "I'm dying to hear the end of that sentence."

"I want to have my own life! This isn't fair!"

"*Fair?* Who ever mentioned the word *fair?*" Professor Ellison set her drink on a side table and glared at her young pupil. "I for one would be more than content to spend my afternoons in blissful silence while you stared like a brainless dolt at a TV screen far, far away from here. You, Theo, are dim even for a seventh grader, and that's saying something. You're insolent, you're a slow learner, and worst of all, you mumble. I wouldn't bet on you to win a kindergarten spelling bee, but, for reasons beyond even my vast comprehension, you of all people have been given the ability to perform miracles, and while you stand there with a moronic look on your face and drool dripping down your chin, the most powerful wizard the world has ever known is preparing to enslave all of mankind." She flipped open her magazine again. "So we are going to stay here, my thick friend, until you pick up that amulet, summon every ounce of power from that wasteland you call a brain, and knock over that defenseless wine bottle."

Theo angrily picked up the fragment of ancient bone. He held it out toward the bottle and concentrated like he had never concentrated before. A sphere of roiling black fire as big as a basketball shot out of the amulet, missing the wine bottle and instead exploding a blue-and-white vase standing on a pedestal a good twenty feet away.

Theo lowered the artifact in horror.

Professor Ellison broke the long silence. "That vase was made in the Ming dynasty and at one point stood in the palace of the emperor himself. I bought it at auction for a little more than a million dollars."

Theo's jaw hung open.

"Oh, don't worry about it," Professor Ellison said. "I have three more. That was very good, Theo. You're making progress." Theo let himself smile, but his happiness was short-lived. "Um, Professor Ellison?"

"Yes, Theo?"

Theo pointed at the black fire slowly engulfing the distant corner of the room. "I think I set your house on fire."

While Theo trained inside, a black SUV came to a stop outside Professor Ellison's house. Five men wearing dark suits climbed out. Their leader gave them each orders in a strange language spoken only by the Path, a group of single-minded zealots from every nation on earth who devoted their lives to the goal of establishing genie rule over humanity.

One of the men opened the truck's liftgate, exposing a pile of assault rifles. The men each grabbed a weapon, checked to make sure the guns were loaded, and split up to approach the house.

The fire inside the house continued to grow and Theo's sense of panic grew with it. "Aren't you going to do something?" he asked as the strange black flames took over the pedestal that once held the vase and began to lap up a wall.

Professor Ellison flipped the page of her magazine. "Nope."

"But the house will burn down! We'll both be killed!"

"I survived Pompeii and the Great Chicago Fire. I'll be fine. Now, *you*, on the other hand..."

"You have to stop it!"

"I seem to remember teaching you a serviceable freezing spell. You are perfectly capable of stopping the fire yourself."

"That was weeks ago! I don't remember it!"

"Amazing. You can remember who won the football finals going back twenty years, but anything I teach you has a half-life of twenty minutes."

"It's called the Super Bowl, and it's . . ."

The fire latched onto an oil painting of a very unattractive Dutch woman. The professor watched the painting burn. "That's a Rembrandt, you know."

"Okay!" Theo said. "I learned my lesson. Please stop the fire. I promise I'll study harder. I'll pay closer attention. I won't complain anymore. Just please stop the fire!"

Professor Ellison picked up her drink. "Magic is a funny thing, Theo. Anyone—well, not *anyone*, but any one of *us*—can do amazing things when no one's looking. The real trick is to rise to the occasion when things get hairy. It's called grace under pressure. Now, if you have any intention of seeing the next *Super Bowl*, I suggest you pull yourself together and work a little magic of your own. I'd hate to have to explain to your parents why you never came home."

As Theo watched, aghast, the fire reached the wine bottle and knocked it over to shatter on the floor.

Professor Ellison said cheerily, "Oh, look, you finally got that pesky bottle!"

The Path members outside walked carefully, step by deliberate step, toward the house. One of the men in suits gestured with his weapon for another to get in closer. The scout raised his rifle into firing position and moved with hesitation to a window on the side of the house. Before he got within ten feet he hit something unseen and was knocked backward. It was as if there was something invisible surrounding the structure.

The leader, puzzled, picked up a handful of pebbles from the sidewalk. He threw them at the house, but they bounced off something in midair. The true dimensions of the house were making themselves known.

The living room was engulfed in flames.

Theo pointed a relic shaped like a brass key and spoke what he thought was an incantation that would douse the fire. Nothing happened. He tried again and this time every door leading out of the room slammed and locked itself. Wrong spell. "You have got to be kidding me!" he said. Sweat poured off of his forehead. He coughed up smoke.

"So close!" said Professor Ellison. "Maybe the next spell will make the walls close in. Won't that be exciting?"

Theo dropped his bag and held his hands helplessly in front of his face. The fire had backed him into a corner. He was going to be broiled like a chicken at a barbecue. Deep-fried. Sautéed. Fricasseed.

Right before the black flames reached him a high-pitched alarm sounded through the house. Professor Ellison dropped her magazine and clenched her fist above her head. Instantly, the fire froze into great stalagmites of hardened salt.

Theo dropped his hands. The flames were gone. The room wasn't even hot anymore. "Thank you thank you thank you," he said, as relieved as he had ever been in his twelve years on planet Earth. "Thank you!"

But Ellison wasn't paying any attention to him. She went to

what seemed to be a blank wall, brushed aside the piles of salt, and pushed a button on a hidden control panel. The alarm silenced and the wall lit up with screens that showed the outside of the house from every conceivable angle. Her high-tech security system had been activated.

Theo came to her side. "What's happening?"

The screens showed the five men in suits pointing their guns at the house.

"It appears we have visitors."

"Those guys are from the Path! They must have found out where you live!"

"I assumed they would drop by sooner or later. Of course, you don't live to be as old as I am without thinking ahead. Watch carefully. You just may learn something useful."

The men outside waited for their leader to return from the truck, their guns at the ready. He came back armed with a portable rocket launcher. He shoved a rocket into the cannon's barrel and balanced the weapon against his shoulder. He put the front door of the house in his sights and tightened his hand on the trigger.

Before he could loose the missile, the ground shifted. The men looked at each other with unease. The leader inspected the grass on which they were standing. It seemed solid enough. He gave it a good stamp with his foot and nothing happened. He shrugged the tremor off and put his eye back to the missile launcher's gunsight.

Suddenly, the grass beneath his feet exploded upward, thickening into tough green vines that wrapped tightly around him before he had any chance to react. The rocket launcher was wedged against his body in a cocoon of leaves and vines.

His men were similarly trapped. They called out to one another, but the creeping plants soon covered their mouths, leaving them wriggling and squirming and wrapped completely in green.

Theo and Professor Ellison watched it all on the security monitors. "Holy crap! You got 'em!"

"Language, Theo."

"Sorry! But what are you going to do with them now? We can't just let them go, can we?"

"I would think not. But I'm not going to do anything to them. I'm going to leave that up to you."

She went to the couch and returned with the Louis Vuitton bag that was her most faithful companion. Inside she kept a jumble of artifacts that might be useful in a world that hid dangers behind every corner.

She rooted around until she found what she was looking for. She handed a small stone pyramid to Theo. "Use this."

Theo turned the thing over in his hand. "What will it do?" he asked.

"It will turn our unwelcome visitors into sand."

Theo stammered, "I can't do that!"

"You can, and you will. We are fighting a war, Theo, and in a war people die. There is too much at stake to be sentimental."

He shoved the pyramid back at Professor Ellison. "I don't care what you say and I don't care what you threaten me with. I'm not going to kill those guys!"

"Very well. I suppose I'll have to do it myself." The professor held the pyramid up to the monitor and closed her eyes.

On the screen, the mummified men struggled against the vines that held them tight. Theo watched in dread as sand began to pour out between the leaves. When the plants drew back into the soil, all that was left of the men was five piles of sand on the manicured lawn.

Theo gritted his teeth. "You didn't have to do that."

"Didn't I? Should we have let them return to Vesiroth to report on what they saw here? Maybe they would have seen the errors of their ways and gotten jobs selling furniture." Her eyes grew cold. "I will do anything and cross any line to make secure the future of a free world. And by the time we're done, you will as well."

She put the bag over her shoulder and went back to the couch to pick up her magazine. She unlocked the doors with a cursory gesture and turned back to Theo.

"It would be best if you kept what happened here today between us. There's no reason to drag your friends or that genie into this. They'll just muck things up."

Theo didn't say anything. He just stared at the screens, watching as a gentle New Hampshire breeze scattered the sand into the air.

4

TEACHERS AT ROBERT FROST JUNIOR
High School were required to make themselves available for
twenty minutes at the end of the day to answer any student
questions.

For Mr. Rommy, this was the calmest time of the day. Nobody
ever came in for questions after school. He sat and graded papers,
and when twenty minutes were up he closed his door, let his
jeans and blazer dissolve into flowing silk robes, and began to
float. For Fon-Rahm, this was a time to look inside himself. And
not in a symbolic, hippie-dippy way, either. Fon-Rahm could
literally look inside himself. He didn't have a heart or lungs but
he did have a direct connection to the source of all power in
the universe.

As he meditated, Fon-Rahm saw that his magic was strong. His reservoir of power was full and his connection to Parker, including the tether that bound them to one another, was intact. But something was wrong. Since the battle at Cahill University, Fon-Rahm was no longer able to sense fluctuations in the Nexus the way he once had. Something had changed when Xaru and the other Jinn were destroyed.

Even if no other genies had been freed, Fon-Rahm should at least have been able to detect the waves Vesiroth sent through the Nexus as he gained strength. Yet the first of the Jinn felt nothing. It was like some part of his connection to the Nexus was broken.

If Fon-Rahm had been familiar with human concepts like worrying he might have recognized the sensation he was feeling. The genie was letting his doubts about the future cloud his judgment. He was getting sloppy.

He had to meet Parker by the side of the school soon, so he magically opened his briefcase (a Secret Santa gift from a fellow teacher, another concept that had baffled the all-powerful genie. He had gotten Mrs. Hernstadt socks). If someone were to open the door he had forgotten to lock, he or she would see the first of the Jinn, floating a foot off the ground, conducting a flow of airborne math tests into an open briefcase on his desk.

Someone like, say, Mrs. Pitt, the assistant principal who was standing on the other side of the door with her hand on the knob.

Parker Quarry sat and he waited. These were two of his least favorite activities.

He liked having Fon-Rahm around, he really did, but man,

this tether was getting annoying. Parker and Fon-Rahm had to arrange their schedules so they never got more than eighty yards apart and their heads didn't, you know, explode. The first day, before he had really thought everything through, Parker had wound up eating lunch in the parking lot.

So he sat on the metal bleachers, waiting for office hours to be over so he could stop watching the baseball team field grounders and get on with his life. Theo would've been out there, but he had stayed home sick. He hadn't said a word to Parker since he got back from the professor's place. Parker hadn't even had a chance to tell him about their Amazonian adventure yet.

Another dink grounder, another "Attaboy!" from the coach. Parker was bored, bored, bored, bored, bored.

His mind drifted back to the impending arrival of his father. See, this was why he didn't like to be bored. He knew that he should be happy that his dad was coming back into his life but he just wasn't. There was too much mistrust. Too much time holding on to it. And thinking like that started to make him angry again. He tried to turn it down.

And then he saw Naomi.

She was on the opposite end of the bleachers, engrossed in her reading. Parker moved a little closer to her. She didn't notice, so he moved closer still. He bent his neck until his head was at a ninety-degree angle to try to read the cover of her book.

"It's *Moby-Dick*," she said, never taking her eyes from the page.

"Right! Yeah, *Moby-Dick*. I read it last year."

"Really. Do you think the whale represents death or do you think it's symbolic of man's inability to let go of the past?"

"Um, the first thing?"

"Great. If I need any help with this paper I'll know who to call." She put the book away, slung her backpack over her shoulders, and started down the bleachers. Parker went after her.

"I'm Parker. I was at the math club yesterday?"

"I remember."

"So do I." Parker knew that was a lame thing to say before it got out of his mouth. He tried a change of tactics. "So, uh, where are you from?"

"Philadelphia. My mom got transferred here."

"A big-city girl! I knew it. I'm from LA, myself."

"Wow, that's fascinating." She started toward the back of the school.

Parker hesitated. She was going the wrong way, away from Fon-Rahm, pushing the limits of the tether. Still, the place was only so big. As long as Mr. Rommy stayed in his room, they should be fine. "Wait up!" he said before he chased after her.

Just as Mrs. Pitt opened the door to Fon-Rahm's room her attention was pulled away by two sixth graders tearing through the hall.

"No running in the halls! I've told you twice today already, Anthony Derkins!"

At the sound of Mrs. Pitt's voice the genie snapped out of his trance and became Mr. Rommy once more. The tests hit the ground in a riot of paper just as the assistant principal stepped into the room.

"Mr. Rommy, I was wondering if I could . . ." Mrs. Pitt trailed off as she looked at the papers covering the floor. The assistant principal was a no-nonsense sixty-five-year-old who had seen just about everything in her decades of work at the New Hampshire middle school.

"Mrs. Pitt. You . . . startled me." Fon-Rahm knelt down and began shoveling the papers into the case.

"I can see that. Are you busy? I need a little help moving some boxes and Mr. Coolidge is of course nowhere to be found. I swear that man sees me coming and ducks out the back door."

The genie frowned. He had to be at the side of the school to meet Parker in a matter of minutes. "I fear I have an appointment I must—"

"It won't take long." Mrs. Pitt stood in the open doorway, her glasses resting on the tip of her nose, staring at Fon-Rahm with a look every kid who had ever attended Robert Frost Junior High would recognize with a deep shudder.

Fon-Rahm took his briefcase and followed the vice principal out of the room and toward the front of the school. As long as Parker stayed still, they would be fine.

"Hold on a second!" Parker chased Naomi to the parking lot.

"Why?" she asked.

"I thought maybe we could talk. I know what it's like to be new here. It takes some getting used to, believe me. I mean, we are way out here in the boonies. All the trees and the nature and the open spaces. Don't worry. It's not as bad as it seems at first."

"Did you ever consider that maybe I *wanted* to move to the sticks?"

"Not really. Who would want to do that?" Parker took another step but stopped dead in his tracks. The low-level buzz in his head had just gotten worse. Fon-Rahm was moving in the other direction.

Naomi scrunched up her face. "You okay?"

"Sure! Sure, I'm okay. It's . . ." The headache was getting worse.

"Allergies?"

"Okay, I admit that New Hampshire would not be ideal for someone with hay fever. Is that why you can't play baseball?"

"What? No! I could play baseball if I wanted to."

"Of course you could! You don't have to let your physical challenges hold you back."

This was not going Parker's way.

Fon-Rahm followed Mrs. Pitt down the stairs and toward the front of the school.

"I really do need to keep this appointment, Mrs. Pitt. I would gladly help you with this task in the morning."

"No time like the present. It's just a few new textbooks. It won't take you ten minutes."

Fon-Rahm followed Mrs. Pitt around a corner and was confronted with rows and rows of sealed cardboard boxes in stacks that reached almost to the ceiling.

"Twenty minutes, tops."

Fon-Rahm closed his eyes. His head was really starting to hurt.

Parker tried to put on a brave face. He didn't know why he wanted to impress this new girl, but he knew he did. She didn't laugh at his jokes but that made her like just about every other girl on the planet. Why did he suddenly care about this one? Why was he so intrigued by the way one side of her mouth curled up when she was amused?

"Just hold on a second," he said. He bent over. His head was killing him now.

Naomi stayed where she stood. "I've heard that ninety percent of migraines are caused by stress. Are you stressed?"

"Stressed?" Parker looked up through the waves of pain. "Do I look stressed?" She started to smile. Maybe this would be okay, after all.

"Hey, guys. What's going on?"

It was Reese. Of course. Just when he was finally making some progress.

"Hey," said Naomi. "You're Marisa, right?"

Reese was thrilled. Naomi already knew who she was! She had an actual reputation!

"Yes! I mean, everybody calls me Reese. I mean, my friends do. Mainly Parker. And Theo. They're my friends."

"You're in eighth grade, too, right? Somebody told me you were the only one who got through the Mrs. Morrison's frog dissections without gagging."

"Yeah, we got a bad batch. They were sort of already rotting? Mrs. Morrison had to stick her head out the window to keep from puking."

"At least she stopped eating, right?"

"Oh my God! Have you noticed that, too? She keeps a bag of trail mix in her desk and she has M&M's in her purse."

"I saw her take a bite out of an M&M! It's like a whole one was too much for her so she only ate half! Who does that?"

Parker had to step in. He was losing Naomi to Reese. "Yeah, I saw her eating yogurt at lunch!"

The girls just stared at him. His headache got worse.

Fon-Rahm carried yet another box down the hall and into storage. His head was pounding.

"Oh, Mr. Rommy..."

The genie put his head down. "Yes, Mrs. Pitt?"

The vice principal approached with a pile of forms. "There's a problem with some of your paperwork. It looks like we don't have a valid address for you."

Of course they didn't. Fon-Rahm had thought it unwise to tell the school that he was living in a barn behind Theo Merritt's house. "I will review the forms as soon as is possible."

"No hurry. Just whenever you get the chance." She began to walk away but turned back. "Do me a favor please and leave that last box in Mr. Granson's office. He'll want to take a look at those books first thing."

Of course. Mr. Granson's office was the last one on the floor. This little trip would stretch Fon-Rahm and Parker's tether to the absolute limit. Fon-Rahm picked up the final box of books and staggered down the hall, the pain in his head so bad he feared he might pass out. He dropped off the box and hurried past Mrs. Pitt on his way to the side of the building where he hoped Parker would be waiting. As he rushed off, Mrs. Pitt reviewed his file and called after him. "Luc Rommy. What kind of a name is that, if you don't mind my asking?"

"It is Flemish. I am from Belgium. Originally." It was a story concocted by Reese, Theo, and Parker to cover any strange speech patterns Fon-Rahm might exhibit. Nobody knew *anything* about Belgium.

Mrs. Pitt nodded. "That explains *so much* about you."

"Listen," Reese said. "My dad just bought this huge TV and I was going to watch this old Carl Sagan DVD. I know it sounds lame, but..."

Naomi grinned. "Are you kidding me? Carl Sagan is hot!"

"Who's Carl Sagan?" asked Parker. This was really getting away from him.

Reese rolled her eyes. She turned to Naomi. "So, do you want to come over? My mom doesn't know it, but I have a stash of candy in my room...."

"Let's do it. My folks both work late, so I'm kind of on my own during the day anyway."

Parker looked aghast. "You're going to hang out with Reese? That'll kill your social life for the rest of the year."

"Shut up, Parker," Reese said. "Come on, Naomi. I can ride you double on my bike. It has an electric motor!"

"That's so cool!"

They started to walk away, excited by all the things they had in common. Reese stopped and turned back to Parker. She knew exactly why he couldn't follow them. "Are you going to be okay?"

Parker nodded. He would have to go looking for Fon-Rahm. "Yeah. You geeks go on ahead."

Reese smirked at him and Parker watched the two girls walk off. As soon as they were gone Parker sprinted back toward the school as fast as he could.

* * *

Parker and Fon-Rahm met at the school's side door. As soon as they were together, their headaches vanished completely. They were both out of breath. In between pants Parker asked the genie "And how was *your* afternoon?"

5

PROFESSOR ELLISON STIFLED A YAWN.

She hadn't slept since the sad attempt to break into her home. It's not like the old days, she thought. The Path never would have tried something that halfhearted when Nadir was in charge. Still, an attack was an attack, and it could not be overlooked.

She boiled down the sand that was all that remained of the Path assault team and brewed it into a tea. Then she fed the liquid to her Nevermind Flower and leaned in to listen.

Theo was right in one respect: it would've been easier to get usable answers from the intruders if they weren't dead. She knew they were from the Path, but she had no way of knowing what they were after. Oh well. There was nothing to be done about it now. She needed answers and she wouldn't get them by wishing she had made different decisions in the past.

The professor's immense library was quiet, but not quiet enough. When the flower began to whisper, she moved in closer.

The flower had been rare even thousands of years ago, when magic seemed to be everywhere—in the friends she kept, in the soil she stood upon, on the wind she breathed. As far as she knew, this lovely light-purple bloom was the last one in existence. When it died, another piece of the professor's world would die with it. Once, she and her kind strode the globe like giants. Now she stayed awake in her library, alone, trying desperately to learn what was meant in the pauses between the mystical words of a flower that could speak the memories of the dead.

There! A word, spoken softly but clearly, in that dead language the Path used to communicate with each other. She pulled an ancient tome from her shelves and looked for a reasonable translation.

She coaxed the Nevermind Flower to say it again, slower this time. The voice deepened and stretched, and at last sounded out a word that Professor Ellison had hoped never to hear again.

6

THE PATH MEMBER, NAMELESS TO
Vesiroth, gingerly placed a tray of hot tea by the wizard's side.
The servant was a thief and a killer. In order to prove his loyalty
and secure his place in the Path, the man in the suit had been
ordered to assassinate a random stranger in his native Brazil. He
did so without hesitation. He did not fear pain and he was not
afraid to die.

The only thing he was afraid of was Vesiroth.

The wizard's weird child servant was bad enough, but Vesiroth
was far worse. The undying sorcerer was known to fly into
uncontrolled rages. A servant who made even a small mistake in
Vesiroth's presence might have to go through the rest of his life
missing an eye. This man liked both of his eyes where they were,

and so he backed carefully out of the room, hoping against hope that he had given the wizard no reason to notice him.

Vesiroth never gave the man a second thought. When the wizard had come across the Path four months ago he had found an organization in complete disarray. It was shockingly easy for him to step in and seize control. Men like this needed to be ruled with an iron fist. Vesiroth was more than happy to provide that service.

He picked up his tea and took a dainty sip, favoring as always the right side of his face, which was an angry mass of burn scars. Vesiroth could have easily healed himself, but he opted to keep his face the way it was. It was a token of all he had lost and a constant reminder of mankind's capacity for cruelty.

Vesiroth was glued to the constant stream of information displayed on a collection of computers and flat-screen TVs set in a semicircle around him: news, movies, wiki entries, sitcoms, music videos, documentaries, sporting events, ads, cartoons, and everything and anything else the online world had to offer. So much had happened in the last three thousand years! He could sit here for weeks, for months, for *decades* and still only skim the surface. He was astounded that here, in an abandoned hospital in the middle of Siberia, he had access to so much knowledge. In the old days he'd been forced to search out books. The twenty-first century suited the wizard nicely.

"This is so *boring!*" Duncan threw his head back and moaned. He was poking halfheartedly at an iPad across the room, his chair leaned back and his legs propped up on a table, mowing down untold thousands of zombies in a first-person-shooter game. It was fun at first but it had gotten pretty dull now that he had beaten the game three times. "Can't we go out and do something?"

"We are in Siberia, Duncan." Vesiroth never took his eyes off of his flickering screens. "It is not a place known for recreational activities."

"I know that! I've been to Siberia before." Duncan went morosely back to his zombie slaughter. "I've been *everywhere* before."

Vesiroth simply tuned the child out. Duncan was a necessary evil. The Path was useful, but they were in essence cannon fodder with a small but handy fleet of planes, boats, and cars. Guns had their limits. If Vesiroth was to succeed he would need magic, and he had found that in his new world, magic was in short supply. Duncan was powerful and easily bought. Vesiroth was willing to overlook Duncan's... odd condition, but he would have preferred someone a little more conventional.

Duncan tossed the tablet onto the table, stood up, and hopped onto his skateboard. He did a kickflip and rolled over to his boss.

"Just so you know, those guys you sent after your old girlfriend never came back. I think they're probably toast."

Vesiroth turned his eyes to a monitor showing a commercial for some kind of cleaning product that promised miraculous stain-removing technology. "Yes, they are most certainly dead."

"What a waste. She saw that attack coming from a mile away."

"It was not an attack. Tarinn..." He stopped himself. She was not called Tarinn anymore. In this new age she was Professor Julia Ellison. He would have to remember that. "Professor Ellison is too strong for that at the moment. Those men were sacrificed to probe her defenses for weakness."

"Didn't find any."

"She was always clever. But there is no need to worry. Her time will come."

Professor Ellison was a threat to Vesiroth, and it galled him. For the past three millennia she had been growing more and more powerful while Vesiroth had been a living statue, aware but unable to move. The woman who was once his pupil was now his greatest enemy.

"Did you do what I asked?"

"Yep." Duncan hopped off of his board and manifested two gleaming chrome switchblades in each of his hands. "I went down there this week and cased the joint myself."

"The plan is sound?"

"I'm not sure I would call it *sound*, but it's doable." As Duncan spoke he juggled his knives. "I don't see why you're in such a hurry. You've been waiting three thousand years. What's a few more weeks?"

"A few more weeks is an eternity." Vesiroth's voice dripped poison. "Our journey to Switzerland will be the true new beginning of my ascension and inevitable victory."

"Whatever you say, boss." Duncan let his switchblades fade back into the ether and let out a loud yawn. "I'm hitting the sack. You going to stay up?"

"I have had enough sleep for one lifetime."

"I knew you were going to say something like that. See you at breakfast!"

Duncan mounted his skateboard and glided out of the room, leaving Vesiroth once again free to gorge on information undistracted. Footage from D-Day streamed on one of his screens. Explosions. Fire. Death. Nothing has changed, the wizard thought. Nothing will ever change until I am humanity's master.

7

"DUDE, YOU SHOULD HAVE BEEN there!" said Parker.

"Yeah, yeah," said Theo, bouncing a half-dead tennis ball against the wall. His dad was working at the university and his mom was out with his aunt Kathleen at a farmers market. That meant that Theo, Parker, Reese, and Fon-Rahm could hang out in the barn again.

"Seriously, I thought it was going to be super lame..."

"Hey!" said Reese.

"...but it turned out to be epic when I had my pal Fon-Rahm here search out a giant anaconda."

"It was supposed to be a *hike*, Parker, with walking and communing with nature. I wanted to see spider monkeys."

"We *did* see a spider monkey! He got eaten by the anaconda!" Reese shuddered. "That was really not what I had in mind." Theo threw his ball again. *Thwock.* He had always liked the barn. He had fond memories of playing here when he was a kid, when his dad would have Theo hand him tools while he tried (and tried, and tried) to get the engine in their ancient Farmall tractor to turn over. After they were done his dad would drink a beer and he would give Theo a bottle of orange soda. The barn itself had seen better days. There were exposed nails around the door and there was a hole in the roof his dad made a new promise to patch every time he came into the barn to grab a tool.

"How is it that we haven't talked about this? For crying out loud, how is this not an IMAX movie yet? This snake was huge. I mean, like, really big. Picture the biggest snake you ever saw and then picture a snake four times that big, and then picture a snake that could swallow *that* snake whole, and then you're getting close. Tell him, Fon-Rahm!"

The first of the Jinn nodded. "It was a very large snake."

The barn was the only place that was both private and close enough to the house so the genie could still be near his master. Fon-Rahm spent most of his time here, conserving his energy and trying to feel for changes in the Nexus. The barn smelled like apples. Fon-Rahm was beginning to associate the scent with looming disaster.

"I get the picture," said Theo. "You guys went and had a killer time while I rode my bike the eight miles to Professor Ellison's place and then got yelled at for two hours. Please, tell me more."

Parker said, "Nobody forced you to go over there."

"You just don't understand."

"What don't we understand?" said Reese. "Professor Ellison was going to let us die if we hadn't stopped Xaru in time."

"But she didn't."

"Sure, because Fon-Rahm stepped in. She was ready to let Xaru obliterate the entire town, including our friends and our families and everybody. She doesn't care what happens to us."

"She's training me to be a wizard! She's teaching me things that would blow your mind!"

"She's only training you because she's finally found somebody else with a connection to the Nexus she thinks she can control."

"You don't get it. I can be great at this, if I want to. I could be powerful and—"

"And what?" Parker asked.

Theo threw the ball again. "It doesn't matter. It's just something I have to do."

Reese shrugged. "Well, I don't trust her."

Parker was torn. He knew that Professor Ellison wouldn't hesitate to throw them all under a bus if it would help her stop Vesiroth. He also understood that Vesiroth was a threat to the entire world and they were just three junior-high-school kids in New Hampshire. "What do you think, Fon-Rahm?"

"I agree with the girl. Professor Ellison is not to be relied upon."

"You can call me Reese, you know."

"And yet," the genie continued, "the professor is correct that the world is in need of new wizards. The strength of the Nexus must not be concentrated in the hands of a very few. With power comes corruption, even to those with noble intentions."

"I knew I could count on you to make things even more confusing," said Parker.

"You will find that things are seldom either completely good or completely evil. We must all try to do what we think is right. We can do no more than our best."

Theo caught the ball and held it in his hand. "Something happened at Professor Ellison's house. These guys..." Theo stopped midsentence.

Reese said, "These guys *what*? What guys?"

"I can't tell you," Theo mumbled.

"What?" Parker said. "I can't hear you."

"I can't tell you!" Theo yelled. "Professor Ellison made me promise not to say anything!"

Parker stared at his cousin. "Oh. I get it. You two are keeping secrets from us now."

"No! It's not like that."

"Are you sure? Because it sure seems like it's like that."

"She has her reasons," Theo said glumly.

"Good boy, Theo."

At the sound of the unexpected voice, Parker, Reese, Theo, and Fon-Rahm looked to the barn door. Professor Ellison stood in the doorway with her Louis Vuitton bag and a look of cold contempt.

"Hello, children," she said. "And my dear Fon-Rahm. It's been far too long."

8

"PROFESSOR ELLISON!" PARKER SAID.
"Great! Now, if we can just get Xaru and that kid who beat me
up in third grade in here, we'll really have a party."

Professor Ellison smiled. "Parker. How I've missed that razor-
sharp wit! Of course, it might be more effective if your fly wasn't
open."

Parker looked down, mortified, but his zipper was fine. The
professor had gotten him with the oldest trick in the book. He
couldn't help but notice Theo fighting to suppress a grin.

"What are you doing here?" asked Reese, her tone as cold as
a snowstorm.

"Can't a person stop by to see some old friends? I thought New
England was famous for its hospitality."

"You're not our friend."

Professor Ellison strolled into the barn like she owned the place. "Oh, you're not still upset about that business at the college, are you? Really, Marisa, that was months ago. You'll find that you get farther in life if you learn to let things go." She cast a glance at Theo. "Theo certainly doesn't hold a grudge." Theo's cheeks burned with embarrassment.

Fon-Rahm watched Ellison as she walked through the barn, examining the tools and the outdated junk with bemusement. "What do you want here?"

"After giving the matter some thought I've decided it would be prudent to warn you."

"Warn us? Warn us of what?"

The professor cleared a space on Kelsey's dusty workbench for her bag. "My house was attacked. It seems I have again attracted the attentions of those charming fellows who make up the Path."

"Couldn't happen to a nicer person," said Reese.

Professor Ellison ignored her. She took a cube made of what seemed to be polished black glass from her bag and set it on the workbench. "I took care of it, of course, but I did have to wonder what exactly they were after. They already have the two lamps I collected before we met. There weren't enough of them to make a real go at killing me, and I doubt they were on a fishing expedition. They want something and they think I have it. But what could I have that Vesiroth needs? My amulets and talismans would just be trinkets to him. What else is out there that could really pique his interest? What could tempt him into showing his hand? What would be worth the risk? And then it came to me."

She waved her hand in front of the black box. The device came to life, and the projected three-dimensional image of an ancient, battered helmet appeared above the workbench.

"Whoa," said Parker. The helmet was so lifelike it seemed as if it was right in the barn with them. "What is that thing?"

"It's a magical projector my dear friend Lady Alisa Pembrook-Pendleton whipped up in England a hundred and fifty years ago. When her husband discovered it he had her committed to an insane asylum." She reached into the hologram and took the ghost helmet in her hands. "This is the Elicuum Helm."

"The what now?" asked Parker.

"It's a helmet," said the professor, turning the helmet over as if it were a solid object. "It's a simple thing, isn't it? No frills, no plumes, no fancy ornamental filigree. It's nothing but pounded brass. It would be useless as protection. Really, a half-solid swipe with a half-sharp sword would cut right through it." She stared intensely at the Helm. "Of course, it wasn't designed for defense. The Helm is a weapon."

She let go of the helmet and let it float out into the center of the barn. Parker, Theo, Fon-Rahm, and even Reese followed it as it went, captivated.

Professor Ellison continued. "It was created by the Elders before they even got the idea for genies. It was their first attempt at a superweapon." A raging battle of ancient armies appeared projected under the Helm. Horseback riders sparred with charging foot soldiers. Swords flashed in the sun and arrows found their marks across the battlefield. The detail was astonishing. The kids and the genie could practically smell the combat and hear the clash of steel. It was like watching an insanely intricate diorama come to life.

"All it required was a volunteer to wear it."

The helmet shrank down and set itself on the head of an unarmed man standing off to the side of the war. When it was set, the man waded confidently into the carnage. His own troops fell back, leaving him alone to fight an entire army of enemy soldiers.

"The Helm is an amplifier. It takes in all the negative energy that surrounds it, concentrates it, and then releases it back to the source."

A horseman came at the man in the Helm. As the soldier readied his lance to strike, the Helm let out a thick, oozy black tendril of pure negative energy that uncurled slowly. Suddenly, the tendril lashed out. It cut through the rider like a laser beam. He fell from his horse and was dead by the time he hit the ground.

"One man wearing the Elicuum Helm could defeat an entire army."

Hundreds of tendrils sprang from the Helm. They found targets all across the battlefield. Soldiers died without raising their swords. It seemed as if the man was an octopus whose tentacles were infinite and wholly without mercy. Then the arms of negative energy disappeared and the man walked off the battlefield. Every member of the opposing army lay dead in the dirt.

"It was very effective, but the Elders knew enough to use it sparingly. It was one-of-a-kind and they were afraid it might fall into the wrong hands. Of course, some things are too powerful to keep under wraps, and all it took to bollix everything up was one thief with more nerve than brains." She eyed Parker directly.

In the hologram, a thief snuck into a house and removed the Helm from a pedestal. He jumped from an open window and was gone.

"The Helm shows up sporadically after that. There are reports the three hundred Spartans used it against the Persians at Thermopylae. I know for a fact it was used in the Crusades."

"How can you be so sure?" asked Parker.

"Because I was there. Are you familiar with the story of Vlad the Impaler?"

"He was a Transylvanian prince," said Reese. "He was notoriously cruel. Vlad was famous for impaling his enemies on wooden poles. It would take them days to die. He's supposed to be the model for Dracula."

"Quite right. You always were the smart one."

The hologram flashed to a new scene. Vlad, wearing a mustache, a bloodred suit of armor, and a sneer, led a procession of men on horseback down a street lined with the impaled bodies of his victims. A man wearing the Helm stepped into the road.

"The Helm was never designed to confront inhumanity on such a sadistic level."

The Helm collected the negative energy, but instead of releasing it back to Vlad's army, the tendrils lashed out in a fury of confusion.

"It was overloaded with evil and irreparably corrupted."

Finally, the berserk tentacles wrapped themselves around the wearer of the Helm until he was bound by an inky-black blanket. The man jerked around like a mad marionette before he fell to his knees, screaming as every bone in his body was broken. He keeled over. The Helm bounced from his head, splitting into three pieces as it hit the ground. Vlad dismounted and held one of the pieces up to the light.

The hologram projector let out a sound like a dying eagle. The image in the barn flickered and then contracted into a single dot of green light.

Professor Ellison smacked the glass cube with the heel of her hand. "Lady Pembrook-Pendleton never did get this completely figured out. Well, I'm sure you get the general idea."

Parker said, "Vesiroth is after the Elicrom Helm."

"The *Elicuum* Helm. It's a very old word that means something like 'poetic justice.' The Elders were nothing if not whimsical."

"Is this weapon currently in your possession?" asked Fon-Rahm.

The professor paused. "No. I had a third of the Helm, but I traded it away somewhere around the time the black death took hold in Europe."

"What did you get for it?" said Theo.

"None of your business. The point is, I don't have it anymore." Professor Ellison returned to the matter at hand. "Even in pieces the Helm has tremendous power. Since it was damaged, anyone who has tried to use any shard of the Helm has found it to be dangerously unstable. It's impossible to control and the object itself has a corrupting effect on the user's mind. It will worm its way inside your thoughts. It will twist your will to its own ends. It will quite literally drive a person insane. Vesiroth, though . . . Vesiroth isn't human anymore. If anyone could withstand the Helm's effects, it would be him." She shook her head ruefully. "It was a mistake to let my piece of the Helm go. I was young and naïve."

"I can't picture you young," said Reese.

"I can't picture you naïve," said Parker.

Fon-Rahm was, naturally, all business. "Why would Vesiroth believe you have the Helm?"

"I honestly don't know. I can only assume he's searching for ways to speed his rise to power. Something like the Helm builds its own mythology through the years. Perhaps my name appears in some dusty old books. Perhaps the Path keeps better records than I thought. Either way, he's working with outdated information."

Parker said, "What's the worst-case scenario? Let's say he manages to get ahold of all three pieces of the Helm. What then?"

Fon-Rahm lowered his head gravely. "The end of civilization."

"Your pet genie is correct. If Vesiroth reunites all three pieces of the Helm, he won't even need to destroy the eight genies that are still out there. He can just put the helmet on and stroll into the Middle East, or Africa, or South America, or Chicago. If he was at full strength I believe that Vesiroth would be able to twist the Nexus itself to his own aims."

Theo gulped. "He would be unstoppable."

"So we'll have to beat him to it," said Parker. "It's three lousy pieces and we've got the first of the Jinn on our side. How hard can it be?"

Theo said, "We don't even know where the pieces are!"

"You're always worried about the details. Let's look at the big picture here. We're back! We'll fire up Fon-Rahm and kick some Path butt. Maybe this'll give you a chance to try out some of your new skills!"

"Oh my God." Theo put his hand to his forehead.

While the two cousins bickered, Reese was busy doing math

in her head. "Hold on. You said there were eight genies left besides Fon-Rahm. We destroyed Rath, Yogoth, and Xaru. That leaves *nine*."

Professor Ellison packed up her metal and slung her bag over her shoulder. "You haven't heard? Vesiroth bagged one in Australia. The Cyclops called Syphus, it's said, although there's no solid evidence. It's all the buzz in magic circles." She walked over to Fon-Rahm. "I'm surprised you didn't sense it."

"As am I," said the genie. "It is possible that with Vesiroth's resurrection my ability to feel the presence of my brothers has been dimmed."

Parker frowned. "That's not great news."

"It explains a lot, though," said Reese. "I mean, I never thought for a second that things were really this quiet. We're not that lucky."

"It certainly won't make it easier for us," the professor said. "All right. First things first. Theo, I'll need you to start scouring my library for references to the Helm. I've already put out the word that I'm in the market to pick up one of the pieces, and I'm confident someone will come forward soon. I'm constantly amazed at how pathetic most of my fellow conjurers are with money. You would think that with magical powers and multiple life spans they might be able to accrue some sort of savings. I would write a book on fiscal responsibility for magicians if I thought I could get any of them to read it. Oh well. Now, Parker. You and Fon-Rahm will have to put in some legwork. The last I heard, one of the pieces was—"

"You need our help, huh?" said Parker.

"If that makes you feel better, yes, I need your help. I'm trying to prevent a catastrophe of epic proportions."

"I understand that, I really do, and I would love for me and old Fon-Rahm here to jump right in and get our hands dirty, but here's the thing. We need you to do something for us in exchange."

"And how, pray tell, could I possibly be of service to you?"

"We want you to remove the tether that holds us together."

Fon-Rahm and Professor Ellison both looked surprised, and that's a feat. It's not easy to shock a genie or a three-thousand-year-old wizard.

The professor pursed her lips. "Can't be done."

"Of course it can. It's your spell. You can undo it."

"That seems right," said Theo.

"Not now, Theo." Professor Ellison turned to Parker. "All right. Even if I *could* do it I wouldn't. I built the tether in for a reason. It's a check on the genie's power. Binding one of the Jinn to a human at least slows it down. You think Fon-Rahm is your chum but he's not. He's a being of pure power. He has more in common with a god than he has with you."

"I would still control him, though, right? I just want the tether gone. It's getting harder and harder to always be within spitting distance of each other. People are going to get suspicious sooner or later. Besides, you know we'll be more efficient if we have a little more freedom."

Ellison looked the genie up and down. "Is your leash chafing you, Fon-Rahm?"

"As you say."

"Why should I allow you to roam the big bad world all by yourself?"

"I am Parker's to command, whether we are physically near or not. He has only to call me and I will come."

"So what do you say?" Parker asked. "Can you do it?"

"There's a way." Professor Ellison glared at Parker. "But you won't like it."

9

PARKER CRESTED THE TOP OF THE
water and took in a deep gulp of air.

Fon-Rahm surfaced next to him. He floated gracefully out of
the water and set himself down on the stone landing. "This must
be the place," he said.

"It better be." Parker pulled himself onto the cold stone. "I
don't think my lungs could handle another dip like that."

It felt to Parker as if they had been underwater for hours.
But that couldn't be right, could it? If they had been under for
any longer than a few minutes he would have drowned. Had
Fon-Rahm put an air bubble around him? Parker thought he had
been swimming on his own.

· Parker hadn't realized he was so cold. He shivered. His teeth
began to chatter. "I w-w-wish I was dry."

Fon-Rahm waved a hand in his master's direction and Parker was instantly dry. "Thanks. That's a lot better." That was when he finally took in his surroundings. He had to strain his neck to take it all in. "Whoa."

They were standing in a massive underground structure seemingly carved out of solid rock. If there was a ceiling at all, it was hundreds of feet above their heads. Pillars of stone extended from the floor of the room (could an open space this big be considered a room? Would you call Madison Square Garden a room?) up and up and up until they faded from view. He could see, but Parker couldn't find any source of light. The pool that had been their way in was in the center of absolutely nothing. There was an overwhelming sense of gray emptiness.

"Which way?"

Fon-Rahm nodded at the pillars. "There are faint markings on the pillars. I believe we are to travel in this direction." The genie set off, hovering a foot and a half off the ground. Parker followed.

"This is crazy," Parker said. "It's like a whole city down here. I can't believe this has been under our feet the whole time. This . . . whatever it is must be ancient, right? How do you think it got here?"

"I do not know. Perhaps Cahill has a history that has been hidden from us."

"Maybe. Still, it's weird. You'd think somebody would have stumbled across it eventually. How could they miss it? It's *huge*."

"It is puzzling."

They walked a little more. The muffled footsteps from Parker's sneakers were the only sound. "Are you sure we'll be able to find our way back? I'm having a hard time getting my bearings down here."

The genie rotated in the air to look back the way they had come. "Odd. It seems the pool from which we emerged no longer exists."

Parker spun and looked. Where the pool once sat was now just an expanse of empty stone. "Well, maybe we walked farther than we thought. It didn't just disappear."

"Perhaps you are right. Either way, our path is clear. We must continue on."

They started off again. Every two or three steps Parker shot a glimpse over his shoulder to verify that the pool was still gone.

The room was endless and the scenery never changed. Gray stone walls hundreds of feet to either side. Gray stone underfoot. Gray gloom above. With nothing to look at, nothing to touch, nothing to smell, and nothing to hear, Parker felt his mind wander. What was Theo doing now? Or Reese? Or . . . Naomi? He liked the way Naomi wore her hair. He also liked how she looked at him, really looked at him, when they were talking. Sometimes when you talk to people you can tell that they're just waiting until it's their turn to talk. Naomi was different. Naomi was . . .

Parker shook his head to wake himself up. This was no time to daydream. Professor Ellison had warned them not to let their minds wander. She had said there would be danger, and Parker had learned through hard experience that when it came to stuff like this she was almost always right.

They were here to retrieve . . . What was it, exactly? Some kind of object, right? Something to do with a ritual? It was so strange, but he couldn't quite remember what they were supposed to be doing. He knew that they had started at the old Conway quarry. He and Fon-Rahm dove off that cliff that everyone said not to dive off of and then they hit the water and...

"We come to a crossroads," said Fon-Rahm, his voice echoing in the vast chamber.

While Parker had been lost in his own head, they had come to a corner in the immense room. Corridors led off to the left and the right.

"I see no markings here. We must make a decision."

"What do you think?"

"I will as always follow your command."

Parker frowned. Of course it was up to him. The two corridors looked exactly alike. He picked a direction at random. "Let's go right."

The genie floated away, Parker alongside him.

The corridor tapered as they went. Soon, the walls were only fifty yards apart. Then thirty. Then ten. Eventually, they were so close Parker could touch them both with his arms outstretched. When the hallway narrowed even further Parker and Fon-Rahm moved ahead single file. After what seemed like another four hours of hiking they emerged into a dark and musty room.

This room was round and about as big as a baseball diamond. It was too dark to make out any details. After a few moments of walking, Fon-Rahm shot out his arm, stopping Parker from taking another step.

"Be careful where you walk."

Parker looked down. Underneath his outstretched foot was the edge of a great pit. One more step and he would have fallen in. "Good advice." His heart was racing. "It might help if we had a little light in here."

The first of the Jinn spread his arms to his sides. Pure electricity arced between his hands and created a flaring blue glow that illuminated the whole room. When he saw what was in front of them, Parker almost wished it was still dark.

"Oh, man."

An immense web of shimmering silver strands stretched over the pit. The threads were as thick as ropes.

Fon-Rahm cast balls of lightning around the room. They hit the floor in a fury of sparks and lit the room blue. The genie nodded to the center of the web, where a luminescent green orb as big as a kickball sat. "I believe that is the object Professor Ellison requested."

Parker nodded knowingly. "That seems about right."

"She did not say it would be easy."

"I know she didn't. It would have been a nice change of pace if it was, though, right?" He sighed. "Okay. Not a problem. You can fly. I command you to fly out there and grab that thing."

"As you wish."

Fon-Rahm lifted into the air. As he floated over the web, Parker heard a clicking sound behind him. He turned his head to look.

"Um, Fon-Rahm?"

Fon-Rahm hovered over the web. "Yes?"

"Could you maybe come back over here please?"

Fon-Rahm rotated in the air to see what Parker saw. "Do. Not. Move," he said.

A monstrous spider had emerged from the gloom behind Parker. It was hideously white, as if it had never been exposed to the sun. Its body was about as big as Fon-Rahm's desk at school. Its eight legs were angled spikes covered with fine hairs matted with grime. The spider stared with inky black eyes the size of Frisbees. Parker counted six of them, all staring directly at him. The clicking sound was coming from jaws that dripped green venom as they clattered.

Fon-Rahm landed in between Parker and the spider. "Find cover."

Parker looked around. There were walls, a ceiling, and a pit. "Yeah, cover seems optimistic."

The spider took a few tentative steps forward. It was clear it didn't appreciate the light.

Fon-Rahm said, "It is unaccustomed to visitors, and there are two of us. Perhaps it is too wary to attack."

He spoke too soon. The spider stuck its ghostly white abdomen into the air, hissed, and spit a thick stream of vile green venom directly at Fon-Rahm and Parker. A bolt of blue lightning sprang from the genie's outstretched arm, frying the poison in midair. As Parker shielded himself behind his genie, the spider reared up on its back four legs and charged.

Fon-Rahm pushed Parker out of harm's way and met the monster head-on in a flurry of crackling electricity. The lightning hit the beast square in the face. Parker thought it would put the spider down for good but the thing just lowered its head and glared.

"I think you made it mad."

The spider swiped at the genie with one of its front legs. The movement was so fast that Fon-Rahm barely had time to duck out of the way. Fon-Rahm countered with a blast of blue volts that tore the leg clean off. The ugly smell of singed hair filled the dank air.

"Yes!" cried Parker.

The spider backed up a step. Then, with the sickening sound of rending flesh, a new leg poked its way out of the white body. The spider tested its new limb, dug into the stone floor, and jumped at Fon-Rahm. The genie grabbed the demon spider's leading legs, one in each hand, and pushed with all his might. It was all he could do to keep the thing away from him. The spider snapped its dripping fangs inches from Fon-Rahm's face.

Parker hated standing uselessly by as his genie battled for both of their lives. He turned to the glowing orb in the center of the web. He had a job to do. He might as well do it.

He got down on his hands and knees and crawled to the edge of the pit. He reached out and gave one of the web's strands a good tug. It seemed solid. Parker had expected the fiber to be sticky, but it wasn't. The web had been there so long it was covered with a thick layer of gray dust.

"This might be a really bad idea," he said under his breath. Then Parker pulled himself onto the web.

Fon-Rahm had never faced anything like this creature. It kept coming no matter what the genie threw at it. As soon as he blasted off a leg, another grew to take its place. The thing was deceptively fast. More than once Fon-Rahm counted himself lucky to have evaded a river of venom coming right at him.

As he ducked another attack he saw that Parker was crawling onto the web. He would have called out, if he had thought he could change his master's mind. By now he knew that Parker was going to do whatever Parker was going to do.

That meant that Fon-Rahm needed to kill this spider, and he needed to do it soon. The balls of lightning that were keeping the room from total blackness were beginning to sputter out.

Parker's legs were shaking, and that meant that the entire web was shaking with him. He tried willing his legs to be still. It only seemed to make things worse. Nothing to be done about it, he thought. The sooner he could grab that glowing ball, the sooner he could get off the web and back onto solid ground. Sure, there was a spider the size of the *Titanic* to worry about, but at least you could *see* the thing. When Parker looked down, all he saw was a foggy darkness that filled him with dread.

There. He had made it to the web's center. The orb was within his grasp. He now saw that it was a giant egg filled with baby spiders that skittered around and over each other. There must be tens of thousands of them. It was vile, but strangely fascinating. A hypnotic pull of curiosity conquered Parker's revulsion and he reached out to touch it.

Before his fingers brushed the egg, Parker felt the web move. He froze. Directly underneath him, hanging upside down from the web and into the pit, was another spider.

A bigger spider.

* * *

Fon-Rahm threw a burst of fresh electricity at the spider. He was finally getting the thing to move back, but it was taking all of his energy.

He heard Parker scream and whipped his head around. Parker Quarry *never* screamed.

The genie saw the second spider pull itself onto the top of the web. It moved clumsily. This beast made the thing he was fighting look like a friendly puppy.

Fon-Rahm's eyes glowed blue. He put everything he had into one giant blast of lightning that started in his chest, radiated down his arms, and came off his fingertips with all the power of the Nexus the genie could summon. It hit the monster square in the face. Fon-Rahm feared it would have no effect, but when the blue haze of ozone dissolved, the spider was gone. It had simply vanished.

The first of the Jinn had no time to ponder the strangeness of what had happened. He threw himself through the air to save Parker just in time to watch the strands of the web snap one by one.

Parker looked very scared. "Fon-Rahm?"

The lights burned out. The room was cast into inky blackness. The last strand of the web broke and Parker, the mountainous white spider, and the glowing egg fell into the pit.

10

PARKER KNEW IT WASN'T THE FALL
that killed you. It was the landing.

He tumbled through the black air kicking spastically to fend off the slashing legs of the bloated spider that fell with him. The only light in the pit came from the glowing green egg that plummeted ahead of them.

So this is how I die, Parker thought. Clawed to death by a giant spider while falling into a bottomless pit. It would be a crazy story, if only there were someone left alive to tell it.

As it turned out, the shaft did have a bottom after all. The egg hit first. Instead of breaking, it bounced away into the gloom. Parker closed his eyes. His last thought was of his mother.

Just before Parker and the spider splatted to their deaths,

Fon-Rahm reached down from above and grabbed the seventh grader's collar. Parker let out a choked "urk" as he was jerked to a standstill in midair.

The kid and his genie floated above the stone floor and watched the fat white spider plunge to the ground. It waved its eight legs madly and managed to gain some purchase on the stone walls before it struck the floor with a loud thump. They hoped the fall had killed the thing, but it righted itself with a sickening display of flailing limbs and scampered off into the darkness to lick its wounds.

"Can you put me down, please? You're choking me to death."

Fon-Rahm drifted closer to the ground before gently dropping his master. Parker was glad to be alive but devastated to see that their situation was even worse than it had been before. A deep fog swept over the bottom of the pit. He couldn't see anything five feet away in any direction.

"Okay, I admit it. I'm a little freaked out here."

"It is an . . ." The genie searched for the right word. "*Ominous* place."

"Yeah, it's terrifying is what it is."

"We could abandon this mission. We could attempt to find our way out of this abyss and simply go home."

Parker shook his head. "No. We're not leaving without that egg." He knew that they needed the egg. He just wasn't exactly sure *why*.

"So it will be."

Parker and the genie stared out into the fog. Somewhere out there was a green egg worth more to them than diamonds and gold. Somewhere out there was a mother spider that wanted to feed Parker to her thousands of unborn children.

"We can cover more ground if we split up."

Fon-Rahm frowned. "That is not a wise course of action. Danger lurks here."

"That stupid egg can't have rolled very far. We'll stay within twenty feet of each other. If I need you, believe me, you'll know it."

"As you wish." The genie cast a light from his hands and began to search the ground.

It didn't take long for Parker to realize he had made a tactical error. It was too dim down in this hole to see much, and the fog cut his visibility down to about zero. Fon-Rahm could generate his own light. Parker was stuck with what he had.

"Um, Fon-Rahm? Buddy?"

From somewhere in the fog Parker could hear Fon-Rahm's voice. "I am here."

"You are where, exactly? I can't see you."

"As I cannot see you."

"Just follow my voice!"

"I am trying. My senses seem dulled in this place. I cannot locate you."

Parker felt a hot wave of panic flush over him. In the fog, he could hear the sickening clatter of the mother spider's legs.

"Fon-Rahm! A little help here!"

"I cannot find you!"

Parker was lost in sea of darkness. Fon-Rahm was nowhere and the spider was close. Parker could smell the thing's fetid stench. He could feel its hot breath on the back of his neck. Parker panicked. He broke into a run, pushing his way blindly through the fog.

He hit something in the smog. Parker braced himself for the worst.

"Hey, slow down, chief!"

Parker looked up, stunned, to find himself in the arms of his father.

Fon-Rahm waded carefully through the mist. It felt odd to have his senses so constrained. Not knowing what was ahead was a novel and wholly unpleasant feeling for the genie.

"Hello, my dear."

Fon-Rahm whirled to find Professor Ellison, dressed in the robes of magic she wore three thousand years ago when she was still a feared sorceress known as Tarinn.

"Professor Ellison . . . Tarinn," he said. "Have you come to guide me?"

"My goodness, Fon-Rahm," she said, amused. "You're *way* off." She waved her arm to the side. The fog parted and Fon-Rahm was confronted with the object of his deepest fear. The metal lamp that had held him captive for three millennia stood on the ground next to her.

And it was open.

Parker held his dad tightly. "What are you doing here? I thought you were still in jail!"

"Easy, champ. I just got here and you're going to crush me to death!"

Parker looked into his father's face. J.T. was exactly the same as when Parker had last seen him over a year ago. He had the same swept-back hair, the same sly eyes, the same I-know-everything-there-is-to-know grin.

"Dad, we have to get out of here! There's a spider, a really big spider, and I can't find Fon-Rahm, and I don't even know where we *are*."

"All right, all right. Don't worry. I've got you."

"Yeah, but we have to *go*. The spider..."

"The spider? Come on, buddy boy. The spider is the least of your worries."

"What do you mean? Why are you..." Parker tried to back away, but he was held tight.

His father's smile twisted into a sneer. "I never liked you, you little punk. You think I was sorry about going to jail? I was happy to get away from you."

Parker was stunned. He could only gape in terror as J.T. leered at him in the darkness.

Fon-Rahm fell to his knees. "No," he said. "Please. Not again."

"Oh, don't be such a baby," Tarinn said with knitted brows. "It'll just be for another ten thousand years or so."

"Please. Please don't."

"Look at you. The great Fon-Rahm, first of the Jinn, the keeper of a power great enough to level mountains, begging. I always knew that underneath it all you were pathetic."

She raised her hands and chanted words straight from the genie's nightmares. A hurricane wind began to swirl around her, clearing away the fog and pulling Fon-Rahm toward the open lamp.

J.T.'s eyes bored into his son. "It was all your fault. If you hadn't been such a spoiled brat I wouldn't have *had* to steal. But no, you needed toys and sneakers and video games."

Parker closed his eyes tight. *It's not real. It can't be real.* His father wasn't a monster. He wasn't holding Parker in a death grip.

"Your mother and I were *happy* before you came along."

Parker's father was in jail all the way across the country. He loved his son.

"I wish you had never been born!"

A calmness flooded over Parker. His dad might have made some mistakes but he would never say something like that. "You're not real," he said. "You're not real at all."

Of course he wasn't real. Parker opened his eyes. His father was gone.

Tarinn laughed as Fon-Rahm clutched at cold stone, desperate to avoid being sucked back into his metal prison by the gale-force winds that swirled around him.

"Don't fight it," she said. "Parker's a big boy. I'm sure he'll have no trouble defeating the most powerful wizard the world has ever known all by himself."

Fon-Rahm almost gave up. The forces pulling him into the lamp were just too strong.

"Fon-Rahm!"

Fon-Rahm craned his neck to see Parker. "Parker! Get back!"

"It's not real. Whatever you think is happening, it's *not real!*"

"The lamp..."

"You're not going back, Fon-Rahm, I swear, and if you did I would just free you again! You have to trust me. *There is no lamp!*"

All at once the winds stopped. The pit was quiet once more.

The genie was confused. He looked for Tarinn and her cursed lamp, but neither was to be found. He was alone with Parker in the fog. "I...I do not understand."

"It's some kind of an illusion. It's a trick to keep us from getting the egg."

Fon-Rahm got unsteadily to his feet. "I thought—"

"It doesn't matter. Look!"

Parker pointed. The glowing egg was just a few feet away.

"Let us take the egg and depart. I have had my fill of this place."

"I'm with you, big guy." Parker reached for the egg.

"No!" Fon-Rahm pushed Parker aside just as the mother of all spiders sprang from the gloom and swiped at the seventh grader with a razor-tipped leg. Fon-Rahm took the blow to his own left arm and screamed as he unleashed bolts of lightning that crackled with blue fury. When the smoke cleared, all that was left of the spider was an oily black outline on the cold stone floor.

"That," said Parker, "was intense."

The genie was exhausted from his battles. "Do you have the egg?"

Parker picked up the glowing orb. "Got it right here."

They each put a hand on the egg. They could feel the baby spiders moving inside.

"Um, what are we supposed to do with it?"

They didn't have to do anything. The egg began to rapidly expand in size, like a bubble growing out of control. Parker and Fon-Rahm were smashed against opposite sides of the ballooning egg and helplessly pushed away from each other.

"Fon-Rahm!"

"Parker! Hold on!"

In an instant they were at the limits of the tether that bound them to one another. The pressure inside their heads was too much for anyone to bear. Their skulls were on fire. Blood came from Parker's nose and ears and he heard nothing but the deafening roar of his brain exploding. His vision went red. This was the end for both of them.

"Fon-Rahm!"

Parker sat bolt upright, scaring the crap out of Theo and Reese.

Theo leaned in with his jaw on the floor. "Holy...! Parker, are you okay?"

Parker looked around. He was sitting on the floor in Professor Ellison's sprawling library. Fon-Rahm was a few feet away, bewildered by whatever had just occurred.

Parker ran his hands over his own head. He was dripping with sweat and out of breath, but he was very much alive.

"I think maybe he's got brain damage," said Reese with genuine concern.

"Just give him a minute!"

Parker blinked into the light. "What... what just happened?"

Professor Ellison strolled into his view. "Just a minor decoupling ritual of my own design. It's never been tried before and I was genuinely curious to see if it would work. It looks like you both survived, so there's that."

"But . . ." Parker said. "The spiders, and that egg . . ."

"Again with the spiders?" Theo said. "Dude, you've been babbling about spiders for the past twenty minutes."

Twenty minutes? That couldn't be right. They had been traveling for hours, for days.

"I do not understand. How did we escape the abyss?" asked Fon-Rahm.

Reese said, "Um, there was no abyss. You guys didn't go anywhere. You've been here the whole time."

"I suppose you could call it hypnosis," the professor said. "I put you under and made a few tiny suggestions and you two took it from there. The tether was a psychic bond and it had to be severed using psychic means. You created your own challenges and overcame your own fears."

Fon-Rahm began to understand. "You gave us a mission. What happened as we completed it was all up to us."

"Of course." She looked into the genie's eyes. "I would have loved to have been there to see what made you so very frightened. You were curled up on my floor like a scared toddler."

Theo asked, "What was it like? What did you think was going on?"

"It was pretty frickin' horrible. I had to face—" Parker stopped. Maybe what he had to face was no one's business but his own. "It's not an experience I would recommend to anybody."

With the help of Theo and Reese, Parker got to his feet. Fon-Rahm stood on his own. His reserves of energy were already being refilled.

Reese said "So ... did it work? Is the tether gone?"

"Only one way to find out." Parker started to walk away from Fon-Rahm. He got to twenty feet, and then fifty feet, and then a hundred. He could have kept walking forever. His head was clear. The tether was gone.

He ran back to his genie. "It worked! No more sneaking around and inventing jobs and worrying about staying within range all the time! We're free!"

Fon-Rahm nodded grimly. "Yes. We are ... free."

Parker got it. While Parker was alive, Fon-Rahm would never truly be free.

"Come on, buddy. This is a good thing! You don't have to watch me twenty-four-seven. You can see what life is like for regular people. And besides, you know I'm not going anywhere. We're a team!"

Parker grabbed Fon-Rahm in a bear hug, and the genie winced.

"What is it? What's wrong?"

Fon-Rahm rolled up the left sleeve of his flowing blue robe and revealed an angry red slash that tore through his arm. "I am afraid I have been injured."

Parker's face fell. "Oh, man. I didn't even know you *could* be injured."

"I was unaware of this fact myself. It appears I did not move quickly enough to evade the spider's final attack."

"But ..." Reese said, "There *was* no spider. It was all in your mind!"

"The girl is exactly correct," Professor Ellison said. "The spiders were a manifestation of your shared subconscious. I suppose

I should have warned you that breaking the tether might produce some unexpected consequences."

"Will it heal?" Theo asked.

"Hard to say." Ellison said. "Magic can be so unpredictable. But besides this little boo-boo you feel normal, yes?"

Fon-Rahm pulled his sleeve down. "I feel no different than before."

"Lovely." The professor smiled coyly. She was keeping something else to herself as well. Something she would keep in her back pocket in case she ever needed it.

11

FON-RAHM STOPPED HIS TAN CAMRY
in front of the Merritt farm. Theo jumped out of the backseat.
"Later, Mr. Rommy. Thanks for the lift," he said, just in case
anybody was watching. He slammed the door and jogged to the
house.

Parker undid his seat belt. As a general rule, Parker and the
genie tried to be seen in public together as little as possible,
but after their shared ordeal at Professor Ellison's, they were too
exhausted to care. Parker wanted nothing more than to crash out
in front of the TV for the rest of the day. And the next day. And
maybe the day after that.

"Well, I guess this is it," he said. He was well aware that this
might be the last time he and Fon-Rahm would be alone like
this. Everything was changing. "Where will you go?"

"I will as before disguise the automobile and secure myself in the barn, if that is your command."

"Well, yeah, I mean, you can do that if you want, but I was thinking maybe you would want to get out a little bit, take a look at the world on your own." Parker was torn. He wanted his freedom, but he also wanted the genie close enough to protect him if anything crazy went down. "You don't have to."

Fon-Rahm could feel the hesitation in his master's words. "You are concerned I will abandon you."

Parker just sat there. The smell of apples drifted by on a gentle breeze.

Fon-Rahm said, "You are my master. It makes no difference where I go. If you require my assistance, all you need do is wish me near. I will always come."

Parker's heart fell. He was glad that the genie was loyal to him, glad that Fon-Rahm would continue to be his sword and shield against Vesiroth and the Path. He was also disheartened to know that Fon-Rahm still thought of him only as his master. After all they had been through, Parker had hoped the genie considered him a real friend.

"Okay. Great! So, I guess I'll see you later, huh?"

"Yes."

Parker opened his door and climbed out of the car.

"Parker."

Parker turned back to Fon-Rahm.

"You need not worry," said the genie. "You are not rid of me so easily."

Parker smiled and nodded his head. As the Camry drove away he involuntarily braced himself for a searing pain in his skull that never came. It wasn't until Fon-Rahm was out of view that Parker understood he was truly alone. He wondered idly if he would miss the dull headache he usually felt when he and Fon-Rahm were more than a few feet away. It was a reminder of his bond with the genie and the price he paid for having his wishes come true.

As Parker approached the house Theo ran out, slamming the screen door in the precise way his father forbade him from slamming it.

"Dude," he said, a look of wonder in his eyes.

"What? What's going on?"

Theo just held the door open. Parker rushed in to find his mother, his aunt Martha, and uncle Kelsey sitting around the living room drinking coffee with a visitor. All eyes went to Parker. The visitor stood up nervously.

"Hey, Parker," he said.

Parker blinked. "Dad," he said.

Parker's mom stood. "He was released a little earlier than we expected," she said. "Surprise?"

"Come on, chief, aren't you going to give your old man a hug?"

Parker crossed the room slowly. Uncle Kelsey had his arms crossed over his burly chest. Kelsey never put much faith in J.T. Quarry. Aunt Martha's gaze went back and forth between Parker and J.T. like she was watching a tennis match. Parker's mother, Kathleen, had her hand over her mouth like she was witnessing something important. Theo watched leaning against the doorway.

Parker finally reached J.T. His experience in the pit was still raw in his mind, but Parker embraced his dad with as much strength as he could muster.

"I know, kiddo, I know," said J.T. "I missed you, too."

12

"WOULD YOU LIKE A LOLLY?"

The bank manager shoved a purple lollipop wrapped in cellophane across the desk. "Wow! Thanks, Mr. Muhleman!" Duncan smiled his best ten-year-old aw-shucks smile and took the candy. He and Vesiroth were seated in leather chairs in front of the bank manager's desk. Duncan was in a tie and he already missed his skateboard. Two Path members posing as bodyguards stood silently by the door.

"My secretary keeps a jar of these on her desk," Mr. Muhleman said, leaning in to speak conspiratorially to Duncan. He had a receding hairline and spoke with a thick accent. "When she is not looking I take one for myself."

Duncan unwrapped the candy and stuck it in his mouth. "Purple's my favorite flavor."

The bank manager winked at the kid and leaned back. "As I was saying." He straightened an already-straight computer monitor on a sleek desk made from blond wood and brushed aluminum. "You are sitting in one of the most secure financial depositories in all the world. We serve a very small, very select clientele with unique economic situations—"

"You cater to the obscenely wealthy." Vesiroth glowered. Duncan had convinced him to comb his hair and trade his black robes for a dark suit that cost more than Kathleen Quarry's used car, but there was no hiding the red scars that covered the right side of his face and no disguising the naked disgust in Vesiroth's eyes.

The bank manager huffed. "I prefer to think of them as well-off."

"Of course you do."

Duncan wished his boss would just shut up. It had been a long trip to reach the Swiss town of Lucerne and he had not been able to talk the scarred wizard into staying home. Duncan would have liked to do the talking himself, but it was no use. His physical appearance was simply too limiting. It seemed unlikely that a ten-year-old would gain entrance to a facility as secure as this one. There was nothing for Duncan to do now but hope that Vesiroth didn't make this any messier than it had to be.

"Well." Mr. Muhleman said, ready for the meeting to be over, "if there's anything else I can do for you . . ."

Vesiroth said, "I wish to see the vault."

"The vault? No, no, I am afraid this is out of the question. No one but senior management is allowed in the vault."

"I wish to see the vault." Vesiroth's eyes practically glowed with intensity. Duncan felt the bank manager scooch back in his chair.

"Um," Duncan said, "my father doesn't mean to be rude. It's just that these jewels have been in our family for hundreds of years and he's a little nervous about letting them out of his sight. He just wants to make sure our stuff will be secure. You can understand that, right?

"Well, yes, of course, but—"

"We get that you have security protocols you have to follow, but surely you could make an exception for someone of my father's stature?"

The bank manager relaxed slightly and turned to Vesiroth. "Your son is a very unusual young man."

"Yes. He is. Now." Vesiroth fixed the man with his gaze. "I wish to see the vault."

"I am not unaccustomed to dealing with the rich and the powerful. Princes and kings have sat where you are sitting now and, were they to ask, I would have told them the same thing. No one is permitted to see the vault." The bank manager smiled condescendingly. "I am sure you will understand."

Vesiroth turned to his second-in-command and drummed his fingers on his knee.

"Oh well," Duncan said, his mouth purple from the lollipop. "I tried."

Vesiroth sprang from his seat, knocked the computer to the floor, and pulled the stunned bank manager over the desk by his tie.

"What are you doing?" Mr. Muhleman choked. "Guards! Guards!"

Two heavily armed guards burst into the room and were immediately confronted by the two Path members and, more importantly, the two Path members' guns. The guards were forced to drop their own weapons and put their hands in the air.

"You really should have just shown him the vault," Duncan told the terrified bank manager.

Vesiroth pulled the man along by his tie as he strode out of the office and into the bank's clean, white lobby. Bank employees froze in their tracks. More guards appeared, but they backed off when they saw Mr. Muhleman desperately trying to keep up with a very scary-looking man with half a face and a look of grim determination that might as well have been a tattoo reading DON'T EVEN TRY IT.

The Path members held their guns on the cowering bank employees, and Vesiroth dragged the manager to the back room of the bank, where a steel door the size of a wall was the only thing in between the public and riches beyond comprehension.

"Open it," said Vesiroth.

"You don't understand!" Mr. Muhleman croaked, clutching at his own throat. "You cannot enter the vault no matter what you do. Even if I wanted to let you in I could not. There are measures and procedures to prevent this!"

Vesiroth swung the bank manager so that his face was pressed against the cold steel door.

"Open it."

"Please," the manager whimpered. "Please let me go. I can be of no help to you."

Duncan shrugged. "I suppose I could persuade him to be more

cooperative." He manifested a glowing butterfly knife from out of nowhere and swung it open in a chilling display of dexterity.

Mr. Muhleman gasped. Vesiroth looked down at the man and then simply tossed him aside. He crashed into a wall and fell to the ground, moaning.

"I guess we go with plan B," said Duncan.

Vesiroth had hoped to do things the easy way, but there was no avoiding what was sure to be a huge drain on his energy. Some things were worth a little sacrifice. He placed one hand on the vault door and one hand over the silver spike pendant that hung from his neck on a leather strap older than the Parthenon. He chanted a few words under his breath. The steel under his hand began to ripple, and then to soften. A weird groan came from the changing metal. Slowly but surely, the great door was melting.

"Coooooool," said Duncan.

The door fell off its massive hinges and began to spread hissing across the floor, now just a thick puddle of molten metal. Duncan jumped out of the way before the liquid steel burned his shoes.

Vesiroth took his hand off his pendant and sagged where he stood. The magic had taken a lot out of him.

"Do you need a hand, boss?"

"No!" Vesiroth stood as straight as he was able to. He could not afford the appearance of weakness. He set his foot down in the rapidly cooling metal pooled on the floor. The soles of his shoes sizzled, but if he felt any pain, the wizard didn't show it.

He entered the vault. With a wave of Vesiroth's hand, the lasers that guarded the riches went dead. The video cameras drooped in their mounts. The vault was his.

The room was lined with locked metal drawers. Vesiroth chanted a spell to himself and the drawers sprang open all at once, spilling their contents over the vault's floor in a riot of wealth. Vesiroth waded through the loot, ignoring the millions in stock certificates, cash, jewels, and gold bars at his feet until he sensed what he was after. He bent over, brushed away a blanket of thousand-dollar bills, and reached down to pluck a piece of old, dirty pounded brass off the vault's floor. He held in his hand the first piece of the Elicuum Helm.

He tucked it into the pocket of his hated suit jacket and strolled out of the vault. Duncan was leaning against a wall, waiting for him.

"You get what you wanted, boss?"

"Yes."

"The car's running. The cops will be here any second." He motioned to the Path guards to join them as he and Vesiroth marched to the bank's front door.

On the way, Duncan stopped and stared at a woman with dark hair cowering behind her desk. "You don't mind, do you?" He reached over and pulled another purple lollipop from a jar on her desktop. "I love these things."

And that's when Vesiroth froze.

"Nadja?" the wizard asked. "Could it be you?"

Vesiroth's eyes were locked on the woman. Duncan didn't understand what was happening. Vesiroth seemed confused and he looked as if he were in a trance. "Boss? Are you okay?"

Vesiroth paid no attention to his second-in-command. He threw the desk aside, leaving the petrified woman exposed.

"Nadja, my wife, I thought that you were lost to me forever. How can this be? I . . ." Vesiroth leaned in to touch the woman's face, but the moment his finger brushed her cheek, the hallucination was over. This was not Nadja. This was just some woman who worked in a bank. Nadja was long dead. But for a moment it had seemed . . .

There was rage in Vesiroth's eyes. The wizard began to tremble. He pulled the brass third of the Elicuum Helm from his jacket and held it against his head. Tentacles made of black air began to reach out from the Helm, searching with jerks and starts for negative energy it could feed on.

"Oooooooookay," Duncan said. "Well, if anybody here wants to live, they should get out of the bank. Like, *immediately.*"

No one had to be told twice. The bank employees joined the guards, the Path members, Duncan, and Mr. Muhleman in a mad dash out the front door.

The dark energy from the broken Helm had nowhere to go. Finally, the black tentacles lashed out at the walls and the ceiling of the bank itself. Vesiroth stood at the center of a furious tempest as the feelers ripped gaping holes in the plaster and stone. The building shook. Pieces of the structure started raining down on the mad wizard.

Duncan watched from outside as the building violently imploded, falling in on itself in a heap of dust and brick. No one could survive that, he thought. Not even a wizard of Vesiroth's power.

And then, there he was. Vesiroth walked out of the ruins and into the sunshine, brushing dirt off of his ruined suit. His anger had abated but he was clearly spent. As sirens wailed in the distance, Duncan pushed him into a waiting Mercedes limousine and told the Path driver to step on it.

Duncan was deep in thought as they sped down the highway. Vesiroth was getting more powerful by the day. Pretty soon he wouldn't need the Path, and he wouldn't need him either. Duncan would have to start looking for something to use as an insurance policy for when that day finally came.

13

THE FLUORESCENT-PINK GOLF BALL
rolled across the Astroturf bridge, squeaked past the swinging
blades of the windmill, went through the lighthouse, dropped
down a level, and headed straight for the cup. Then it stopped,
about two inches short. The grumbling in Parker's stomach got
louder.

"So close!" Parker's dad doubled over in mock pain. "Oh man,
I thought you had that for sure! A little more zing and it would
have gone in!"

Parker hoisted his putter. "Maybe next time."

Tramerville Fun Center was in the town next to Cahill. Along
with the mini-golf course there was a go-kart track, a set of
batting cages, a huge arcade, and enough junk food to make

everyone in China sick for a month. It was the kind of sensory-overloading circus divorced dads took their kids to when they spent the weekend together. Parker had been to places like this for parties, but it had never been just him and his dad. He hadn't actually been alone with his father since the night before J.T. left for prison, and even then they'd just gone to IHOP. The Fun Center was his dad trying *way* too hard, and it made Parker a little nervous.

He could tell his dad was nervous, too. On the drive over J.T. spent most of his time talking about two things. First, how difficult it was for ex-cons to find work in this environment ("Did you know sixty percent of ex-convicts don't ever return to the work force?") and second about the potential upside of helping people convert their apartments into condos ("It's like three hundred bucks a pop, just to file a little paperwork, and I'd be helping people out"). There was also a sidebar about the sorry state of the Dodgers ("All the hitting in the world won't help if you only have one starting pitcher!").

"All right, kid, move over and let your old man take a whack at this." J.T. wore a self-serving grin as he gave his son a pat on the back. "You know, I played on the golf team in high school. My coach told me I had the talent to go pro."

Parker knew that his dad was doing his best to regain his trust. One round of miniature golf wasn't going to solve anything, but you had to start somewhere. J.T. had already sat Parker and his mom down for a conversation about how this time things were going to be different. Of course he was innocent of everything he was charged with and prison was a nightmare, but his time inside had really driven home how much his family really meant to him. Everybody cried and hugged, but to Parker it sounded an awful lot like the speech J.T. had given them when he was first arrested. Parker wanted to be optimistic, but experience had taught him to take anything his dad said with a grain of salt.

J.T. lined up his putt. "Okay. If I make this, I pick where we get lunch. If I miss it, it's your decision. What do you say?"

"Sounds good, Dad."

"I mean it. I'm not going to tank this shot to let you win. And you should know that I've been craving beef tongue ever since I got out."

"Eeewwwww!"

"And liver, too. Do you think there's someplace around here that has *both*?"

"Just take the shot, Dad."

J.T. made a comically broad show of addressing his neon-yellow ball. Most mornings he joined Parker and Theo at the breakfast table, wearing a suit, scarfing down Cheerios, and running out the door chasing job interviews. Parker's computer time had to be limited while his father followed up on résumés and figured out his route for the next day. The job search sure seemed legit.

Still, Parker had his doubts. His mom had said his dad made a deal to get out of prison early. In exchange for what, exactly? It wasn't like J.T. had finally admitted he was guilty. And why now? It was good that his dad was cooperating, sure, but why not two years ago, when it might have really made a difference?

Parker desperately wanted to trust his father. He *needed* his dad to be telling the truth. Parker wondered if this was how the people living in that retirement home had felt when J.T. told them that the police and the federal investigators were just making a mistake, that their money was safely invested and they had nothing to worry about.

"Fore!" J.T. sent his ball rolling. It sped across the bridge and nailed the windmill vane with a solid smack. It wasn't even close.

"I was robbed! The whole course is rigged!" J.T. clutched his heart and fell to the ground in mock disbelief. Parker jogged over to give his dad a hand up.

"So I was thinking tacos," Parker said. "Lots and lots of tacos."

They turned in their putters and headed out, the arcade sounds fading to nothing when the door closed behind them. Parker felt like they were leaving some kind of alternate reality and heading back to the real world. He kicked at a rock as they walked through the parking lot.

"Hey, what's the deal with your math teacher?" J.T. asked. "Mr. Rommy, right? I can't place that accent. Where'd he come from?"

"Belgium."

"Are you kidding me?"

"That's what I heard. I don't really know him all that well."

"Really? It seems like you two are pretty tight."

Parker shrugged.

"Your mother thinks he's the second coming. I don't know. Something about him feels off to me. He doesn't seem like the math-teacher type. Maybe he's hiding some big dark secret." J.T. furrowed his brow in a show of over-the-top suspicion. "Maybe he's a communist spy."

Parker forced himself to laugh at the joke. "I guess he is kind of mysterious, but I think that's part of what makes him such a good teacher. I mean, he got me to care about math. That sure seems like a miracle."

"Can't argue with that. I'll tell you one thing, though. You have to keep your eyes open. You can't trust just anybody. I'm living proof of that. I've been locked up in a cell for two years for something I didn't even do. You know what my real crime was? I trusted the wrong people. My business partner lied to me, my accountant showed me cooked books, the cops said if I cooperated it would all go away, my lawyer said it would never even go to trial. Next time I'll do everything myself. Not that I'm going to get arrested again, just, you know, in general. I'm not getting railroaded anymore." He winked sagely at his son. They were two men of the world. "Just keep your eyes open, okay, buddy? People aren't always what they seem."

Parker just nodded. It was the kind of advice Fon-Rahm would have given him.

Reese and Fon-Rahm were already driving to see the place when Reese began having second thoughts about the whole thing. "I don't think this is going to work," she said. "Nobody's going to believe you're my father."

"You do not think we look related?" When he turned to Reese, his facial features softened and shifted until he looked more like her.

"Change it back! Change it back! Oh my God, that's the creepiest thing I have ever seen. I'll never be able to get that image out of my head."

Fon-Rahm let his face return to normal. "It would not be difficult to mold your face to resemble mine."

"No!" Reese flipped down the visor and stared in the mirror to make sure everything was the same. "Let's just go with what we've got."

They parked the tan Camry and walked to meet the manager in front of the building.

"I shall take it," said Fon-Rahm.

"Oh!" said the building manager, a fit woman in her mid-forties wearing head-to-toe Lululemon yoga gear. "Are you, um, sure you don't want to see the *inside* of the apartment first?"

Reese shut her eyes tight. She had made the genie swear to let her do the talking. He *promised*. "My dad's just kidding," she said. "Sometimes it's hard to tell."

With Mrs. Pitt asking questions, it was time for the genie to have a place of his own. Of course, Fon-Rahm couldn't be depended on to do it himself. His communication skills were improving but he was still conversationally erratic. He had spent the last three thousand years sealed in a metal tube, and before that the only people he knew had spoken a language that was now dead. Parker was busy with his dad and Theo was off doing who knows what with Professor Ellison. That meant that it was up to Reese to get things done.

She had searched online for an apartment that would keep him between Theo's house and the school, not so close that students would walk by it, but still close enough that he could get to Parker if he needed to. The perfect location turned out to be near Cahill University, which was convenient because the landlords would be used to dealing with immature college students and therefore more likely to overlook the idiosyncrasies that came with being an age-old genie.

Or at least that was the idea.

The building manager nodded knowingly. "My dad used to embarrass me with silly jokes, too. Come on, let me show you around." She unlocked the door, looking back at Reese and smiling. Reese didn't get it.

"It's just that the two of you look so much alike, sweetie," the manager said as she opened the door. "Here's the two-bedroom."

Reese and Fon-Rahm entered after her. The apartment was bright and clean, with worn brown carpet and fresh paint in the living room. It was simple and efficient.

"The light in here is good, and there are new fixtures in the kitchen. The refrigerator and the stove are less than two years old. Do you do much cooking?"

"I do not eat," said Fon-Rahm. Reese elbowed him in the stomach. "I mean, I do not eat *at home*. Very often. I do not eat at home very often." He looked to Reese for validation and got a weak shrug in return.

"Let me guess. Divorced, right?" The manager smiled at Fon-Rahm.

"Separated, actually," Reese pitched in. "They're working it out." She wanted to nip this little flirtation in the bud. Things were complicated enough.

"Okay," said the manager with just a hint of disappointment. "If you'll follow me, I'll show you the bedrooms."

The tour through the rest of the apartment was just a formality. Considering that the first of the Jinn didn't need much more than a place to store himself when he wasn't teaching or saving mankind or doing Parker's bidding, the unit was more than adequate.

Later, after the manager had filed the papers and Reese had

gone home, Fon-Rahm conjured himself up a complete set of furniture, including a TV, a microwave, and a bed. He filled the cupboards with food he would never eat and the closets with clothes he would never wear. He wished mediocre art onto the walls and, using the Merritts' home as a guide, placed a badly made quilt on his new futon couch. All the stuff would fade back into the Nexus within a day or two, but Fon-Rahm could always replace it with a wave of his hand.

When it was perfect, he sat in a chair at his kitchen table and waited. He was on his own in a new world.

Theo had spent four hours a day for the last three days in Professor Ellison's library, fuming the whole time. Back in the barn he had decided to keep the professor's secret. Then she'd sandbagged him by telling everybody about the attack on the house herself, and, just to make it worse, she'd called him a "good boy" for following orders. A good boy! What was he, some kind of pet? He had to fight off the temptation to let loose a magic fire to burn all of Professor Ellison's precious books to ashes.

But he kept at it anyway. The books were in weird languages and the pages were brittle. He was occasionally swept up into a story, but for the most part he was just skimming, checking words against the list the professor had left for him. "Something will jump out at you," she said, tapping him right on the temple. "Something will click."

Theo was hunting for any references to the Elicuum Helm or anything that looked like it might be the Elicuum Helm. He plugged whatever he found into a computer spreadsheet that plotted the date, location, and parties involved in each sighting of the

Helm or any of its pieces. It was sort of exciting when he actually found something. Which had been a whopping two times so far. Moving on.

At first, Theo thought it was only going to be one afternoon. Professor Ellison brought out four books for him to start out with. But, as with anything Professor Ellison–related, magic and trickery was involved. Every one of the books contained sub-volumes, each with hundreds of years' worth of collected knowledge. Theo wound up going back to the library's endless bookcases to check stories of unexplained phenomena that went back to the beginning of the written word. Sometimes having a teacher who was three thousand years old was a straight-up pain in the butt.

Theo squinted through the magical eyeglass that translated all languages into the reader's native tongue. Pieces of the Helm had been involved in some of the most famous battles of the last few centuries, but they always disappeared in the chaos that followed. The pirate Blackbeard was the last person seen with a piece of the Helm, and that was back in 1718. After that there were only rumors.

Theo yawned. He had managed to work backward all the way to 1900. That only left him another two thousand eight hundred years. He started flipping the pages as fast as he could. There was so much information! No one could ever get through it all!

He stopped at random and looked down. It was a chapter about burial rites in France. Who cared? He tried again and landed on the brutal and bloody campaign by Napoléon Bonaparte against the Egyptians. The French general encountered particularly strong resistance during the siege of Jaffa. At one point, the massive Napoleonic forces were turned back by a small contingent of Egyptian soldiers who had been surrounded on the outskirts of the city. It should have been a disaster for Egypt. Instead, the advancing French garrison was somehow massacred as they closed in for their final assault. The Egyptians carried their own leader off the battlefield bleeding from his nose and ears and whispered stories that he had used some kind of magic passed down directly from the Gods. The French eventually took Jaffa and executed the leader and his men, but disease and attrition cost the French their ultimate goal. When they finally left Egypt, soothsayers searched desperately for the artifact that had given the Egyptian leader such power. They tore up the city and its surroundings, desecrating graves trying to find the piece of the Helm.

It was that way for decades, but the piece was never found. And now, here Theo was, reading about French exploits in Egypt and burial ceremonies in Paris and . . . something clicked.

He could almost feel it in the spot Ellison had tapped on his temple.

14

IT WAS SO EASY. ALL THEO HAD TO DO was follow the script. "It's a research paper on the Abenaki tribe," he was supposed to say. "It's due on Monday." Just enough to show they were together to work on a serious homework assignment with a subject too dull for anyone to offer any help. It was a recipe to be left alone. Simple.

But, of course, Theo had gotten nervous. "We're just going to, you know, hang out?" he stammered. "I have this game *Echo Realms* on my desktop and Reese wants to play it?"

It was all Reese could do to keep from wincing. Martha Merritt and Kathleen Quarry observed the three seventh graders crashed out in Theo's room from the doorway and narrowed their eyes. Reese knew that look. It was a universal mother cue, meaning *I do not approve of whatever is happening right now.*

"I suppose that's all right," said Martha, looking to Parker's mom. "Isn't it?"

Kathleen nodded weakly. "I suppose so. I kind of wish you had let us know a little earlier. That you were . . . you know. Having Reese over."

"I don't see what the big deal is," said Theo. "We hang out with Reese all the time."

"I know, sweetie, but on a Friday night, in your room, it's just . . . different."

Parker and Reese were both squirming now.

"Mom," Parker said, "it's okay. I swear. We're just going to drink some sodas and play Theo's weird game. I guess if you wanted we could set up the computer in the dining room and do it down there. . . ."

Thankfully, she didn't call Parker's bluff. "No! No. It's fine. Really. If you need anything just call downstairs." Kathleen winked at Reese in solidarity before the moms closed the door (halfway) and walked down the stairs.

When they were gone, Parker turned on Theo with a *what-the-heck?* look.

"What? What's the problem?" Theo asked.

Reese fought the urge to bop Theo over the head with one of the now-useless books about the Abenaki she had hauled from the library to her house and then over to the Merritts'. Once again, they would have been better off if she had done the talking herself.

* * *

Kathleen and Martha joined J.T. and Kelsey at the card table in the living room. As Kelsey clumsily shuffled the cards, J.T. turned to his wife. "Anything we should be worried about?"

"No," she said with a shrug. "At least not yet."

"The *problem* is that now they're going to be checking up on us all night," Reese said, plopping down on the desk chair.

Theo mumbled, "They would have anyway. They're moms."

"Okay, okay," said Parker. He threw a protein bar and a bottle of Gatorade into his book bag and threw it over his shoulder. "It doesn't matter. I have to go and I have to go now."

"I still don't see why we can't all go together," said Reese. "It seems weird that you're doing this without us."

Parker said, "How would we explain it? The math club trips are one thing, but this has to happen tonight. It's easier for one of us to sneak out than all three of us. It might be different if we could have Professor Ellison magic us up some more doppel-gängers. . . ."

Reese frowned. She didn't want to go through anything like that again.

"Besides," Parker said, "Theo doesn't even *want* to go."

Theo didn't say anything, but Parker was right. He was still shaken from watching Ellison in action the last time. He had no problem sitting this one out.

Parker threw open the window and checked out the night. "Guys, this isn't a huge deal. I'll be back in a couple of hours. All you have to do is cover for me." He put on his blue Dodgers cap and climbed out onto the roof. "Wish me luck."

Reese and Theo stuck their heads out the window and watched Parker as he scrambled down the roof, dropped lightly onto the lawn, and ran off into the darkness.

"Good luck," said Reese under her breath.

"So, what do you think?" asked Theo. *"Echo Realm?"*

She sighed. "Why not?"

Parker found Professor Ellison's gleaming black Jaguar sedan parked under a canopy of trees far from the road. He climbed into the back and threw his book bag onto the tan leather seat. "Nice," he said. "Is this the XJ?"

"It is, and I'll thank you to treat it gently, please," the professor said from the driver's seat. "It was special-ordered from the factory in Birmingham and I am quite fond of it."

She looked from Fon-Rahm in the passenger seat to Parker in the back.

"What?" Parker asked.

"Just looking to see if there were any side effects to cutting the tether. You never know." Her eyes twinkled. "Perhaps you'll explode!"

"That's funny. Can we just get going, please? Some of us have to get back before anyone realizes we're gone."

Fon-Rahm remained sullen. "I do not understand why we could not make use of my automobile. It was carefully chosen for its ability to avoid attention."

"It does blend in, but I for one am not arriving in Paris in a beige Toyota. I have a reputation to protect."

"I thought our purpose was to arrive unnoticed."

"Come on, Fon-Rahm, live a little," said Parker. "This car is the *bomb*."

The genie frowned. "I was not aware this conveyance was also a weapon. Let us hope we have no use for it."

"Oh, for God's sake," said Parker. "Buddy, you know I love ya, but you have got to get with the times. Try to keep up, okay? Use your endless ocean of power to learn a little something about pop culture. Pick up a little slang. It'll make you seem less fussy."

"If you command it, it shall be so."

"I command it."

Fon-Rahm's eyes clouded. "I have absorbed one hundred years of your so-called popular culture and will now endeavor to assimilate this knowledge into my vocabulary."

"Yeah, see, that's a perfect example right there." Parker realized how much he missed poking fun at his genie. Did Fon-Rahm miss him when they were apart? Was he even capable of missing somebody?

"It seems as if you two have some deeper issues to discuss. Out of a spirit of cooperation and generosity, I'll offer once more to make this little trip on my own."

"Not a chance, Professor Ellison. It's not that we don't trust you. It's just that . . . You know what? It *is* that we don't trust you."

"How hurtful. In that case, do you think it might be possible to start our little treasure hunt? I'd like to be back before the sun comes up. I have delicate skin."

Parker nodded. "Take her up, Fon-Rahm."

Smoke pooled around the genie's eyes and a mist enveloped the big British car. The Jaguar lifted into the air.

"As you wish, daddy-O," said Fon-Rahm.

Parker grimaced. "I'm going to regret the whole slang thing, aren't I?"

Fon-Rahm pointed east and the black car took off like a rocket into the night sky.

15

PARKER HAD SEEN THE PICTURES IN
Professor Ellison's book and had read the entries Reese found
online. He thought he knew what to expect. He thought he was
prepared. It wasn't until he took his first steps into the catacombs
that he realized there was no preparing for something like this.

Fon-Rahm had landed the big Jag in a cloud of magic fog in
the shadow of the Eiffel Tower. They had followed the professor's
confident lead down Parisian side streets and into an alley behind
a cheese store that smelled to Parker like a house-sized pile of
wet gym socks. They went through a secret door with rusty
hinges and down a staircase illuminated by flaming torches they
lit along the way. The stairs ended and Parker once again found
himself in dark tunnels underground. This time, though, the

tunnels were lined with human skulls and Parker knew that it wasn't just in his head. Everything that was happening was actually real.

Professor Ellison took a flaming torch for herself and handed one to Parker to carry. "Are you all right, Parker? You look a little peaked."

"I'm fine. I'm just... I feel like I'm in a horror movie."

The catacombs that run underneath the city of Paris form a massive underground graveyard. Over six million of France's dead can be found there, their bones mortared into walls, their skulls in stacks and pyramids and built into altars. It's known as the world's largest cemetery and it attracts morbid-minded tourists from all around the world. Of course, not even the most seasoned tour guide knew about this hidden section of the catacombs, and even if they did, they would know better than to explore it at night. A sign at the catacombs' main entrance proclaimed ARRÊTE! C'EST ICI L'EMPIRE DE LA MORT. In English it meant "Stop! This is the Empire of the Dead."

"I can see how you might find it unsettling," said Fon-Rahm. "I have learned that humans have an uneasy relationship with their own mortality."

Parker shined his torch at a mosaic of bones set into the wall in the shape of a cross and shuddered. "If you mean we're afraid of death, then, yeah, that's true. Some of us aren't immortal."

"Immortality means eternal life. I am not immortal, as I am not what you might call alive."

"That's what I've been trying to tell you all along, dear boy," said Professor Ellison, shifting her bag full of magic amulets from one shoulder to the other. "It might seem as if Fon-Rahm cares about you and your friends, but it's an act. He isn't any more human than a cactus or a microwave."

Parker looked to Fon-Rahm, but the genie said nothing. Parker remembered the wound on the Jinn's arm. It was hard to know just how injured Fon-Rahm was.

They walked slowly down the dank tunnel, avoiding the puddles of standing water on the limestone floor. There was a stench of mildew and rot.

"It was the smell, you know," the professor said. "There used to be cemeteries all over the city, but they were overcrowded and the bodies began to pile up. Eventually the stink became so upsetting that they dug up all the bones and moved them down here." She peered thoughtfully at a skull. "I probably knew a few of these people." The professor looked around to get her bearings. "All right. I think this is the way. I haven't been down here in two hundred years. Aha. There we are."

She led Parker and Fon-Rahm into a shallow room and used her own blazing torch to light the torches set into the walls. The room was constructed entirely of skulls yellowed by age.

"Oh good," said Parker. "Skulls."

"I do not see any piece of the Elicuum Helm here. Are you certain your book is accurate?"

"I suppose we'll find out soon enough." Professor Ellison stared into the empty eye sockets of a skull covered with the flaking remnants of blue paint. She spoke as casually as if she were ordering croissants in a sidewalk cafe. *"Avez-vous ce que je cherche?"*

Parker held his breath as the skull, without a jaw or a tongue, answered her in a voice as dry as the dust in a desert. *"J'ai beaucoup de secrets. Quest-ce que vous cherchez?"*

"You see," said the professor with a smile. "The French aren't rude at all. You just have to know how to talk to them."

"What did you say to it? What did it say back?" Parker asked.

"Parker! Do you really not know any French? I'm shocked. Just what are they teaching in public schools?"

Parker turned to his genie. "I wish I spoke French."

Smoke pooled in Fon-Rahm's eyes and Parker felt the rush of an entire language flooding into his brain in the space of a millisecond. Parker shook his head to get himself straight and smiled back at the professor. *"Je en sais assez pour se en sortir."* I *know enough to get by.*

The professor spoke to the skull. "Are you the keepers of the Elicuum Helm?"

The skull answered, *"We are."*

"Relieve yourselves of your burden. Give the Helm to us."

"You must prove you are worthy to receive it. You must put forth a champion."

"What does this mean?" asked Fon-Rahm.

"They want one of us to step up and face some sort of test," Professor Ellison said. "It could be anything. A feat of strength, an impossible puzzle."

"Well," Parker said, "I mean, *I* could do it, but—"

"So be it," the skull rasped. *"Step forward and face your challenge."*

Professor Ellison put her hand to her forehead in pure exasperation. "Oh no."

"Who, me?" Parker spoke directly to the skull. "No! No, I was just saying that I'm probably *not* the best choice. Look, we have a genie right here—"

"Step forward and face your challenge."

Parker turned, panicked. "Professor, can you help me out here, please?"

"It's too late. You volunteered."

"I didn't really . . ."

"It *thinks* you volunteered. There's no use arguing with a skull."

"Fon-Rahm! Help me!"

"I do not think I can interfere. This situation is most puzzling." The genie shook his head. "It is a real lulu."

The seventh grader was at a loss. "What am I supposed to do?"

The professor shrugged. "Step forward and face your challenge?"

Parker took one last look at the Professor and Fon-Rahm and reluctantly took a step closer to the blue skull. The groan of shifting weight shook the room. With shocking suddenness, another wall of mortared skulls crashed to the floor behind Parker. When the dust settled, Parker saw that he was surrounded by empty eye sockets and completely cut off from his genie and Professor Ellison. He was on his own.

Kathleen loved pitch, and this was the first game she'd gotten to play with her husband in literally *years*, but she could tell J.T.'s thoughts were elsewhere.

"Maybe I should go check on the kids," J.T. said.

"What?" said Martha, half joking. "You don't trust your own son?"

"Sure I do. It's just that, you know, he's getting older. . . ." J.T. started to stand. "Maybe I'll just pop my head in."

"You stay here," said Kathleen. "I'll go and check on them."

Kelsey raised his eyebrows as Kathleen got up from the table and headed upstairs. "Those poor kids are never going to get a minute's peace."

"Well, I can't speak for you, buddy," said J.T., "but I was no angel when I was Parker's age."

Martha smiled. "Neither were me and my sister."

Parker's mother climbed the stairs and stood outside Theo's room, straining to hear anything beyond the blaring pop music and video-game sounds coming from within. Finally she poked her head through the half-open door.

"Hey, guys, do you need anything?"

"No thanks, Aunt Kathleen." Theo was on the bed reading a comic book.

Reese was on the computer battling an army of ogres. "Yes!" she cried. "Parker, look up what I'm supposed to do with orcs!"

Kathleen could only see the back of Parker's head sticking out over the top of the bed. He had the hood of his sweatshirt up and must have been bent over a guidebook of some kind.

"Okay. I'll leave you guys to it." She backed out of the doorway, leaving the door ajar. J.T. was just being paranoid. Theo, Reese, and Parker were responsible, levelheaded kids.

As soon as she was gone, Reese swiveled her chair around. "That was close! What if she comes back?"

Theo jumped up and stared at the stuffed sweatshirt he and Reese had propped against the bed as a substitute for Parker. "I don't know! I've never been good at sneaking around. That was always Parker's thing!"

"Okay. Okay. Let me think." Reese pulled out her phone. She didn't have to search through her contacts to find the number she needed. Besides her relatives and her various tutors there was only one other person in there. "Maybe we need to call in reinforcements."

Parker held his flickering torch to the blue skull set in the wall, bracing himself for whatever was going to happen next.

"Okay," he said. "So, uh, what do you want me to do?"

The skull spoke. *"To retrieve your prize you must only answer a child's riddle."*

Parker let out a sigh of relief. "That's it? Just answer a riddle? Jeez, I thought you were going to make me fight a skeleton or bend steel with my bare hands. I'm great at riddles! Lay it on me."

The empty sockets of the blue skull stared out into nothingness. *"I never was, I always will be. No man has ever seen me, nor ever will. No man dares believe me not, without me hope is lost."* Then every skull that made up the room spoke as one, a chorus of dead voices that shook Parker to his core. They said, *"What am I?"*

Parker took a deep breath. "Okay. That's easy. It's something that doesn't really exist, right? It's something we take for granted. It never was, but it always will be. Let me think about that."

The room groaned again. Then, in a cloud of bone dust and dried mortar, the stone ceiling began to drop down.

"Oh boy," said Parker. He needed to come up with the right answer, and he needed to do it, as the French say, *tout de suite.*

16

PARKER RACKED HIS BRAIN FOR THE answer to the riddle of the skulls as the ceiling dropped lower and lower. There was nowhere for him to go. If he didn't find a way to stop it he would be smashed flat.

Think, Parker! *I never was, I always will be.* It's something simple! It has to be!

The roof dropped, popping row after row of the skulls that made up the walls like they were bubble wrap. Parker coughed up ground bone.

No man has seen me, nor ever will. What's on the other side of a mountain, maybe? The back of your own head? It's got to be something like that.

The falling ceiling reached the torches in the walls. They were extinguished and smashed, just like Parker would be if he didn't land on the answer PDQ.

No man dares believe me not, without me hope is lost. Love? Could it be love?

The only light in the room came from Parker's flaming torch. He felt the roof touch the top of his Dodgers cap. The ceiling was close enough to make Parker scrunch down. In another few seconds the blue skull would be crushed and Parker would be next.

He started to blurt out answers the second they came into his head. "Um, your shadow when it's dark! What's in a mirror when you turn around!"

Come on, Parker! *I never was, I always will be. . . .*

Reese checked a text and rushed to the open window. She saw the glowing screen of a phone waving from the dark yard outside.

"Hey!" someone yell-whispered. "How am I supposed to get in?"

Theo ran over and pointed to a trellis leaning against the house. Naomi bounded up the trellis and was on the roof in no time. She climbed to the window and swung herself gracefully into Theo's bedroom.

"So." She grinned. "How are we getting in trouble tonight?"

The ceiling took out another row of bones, including the blue skull. Parker threw himself faceup on the ground. The ceiling was now just a foot away and still falling.

Parker's answers got more desperate. "A ghost! Glass! Bigfoot! An invisible cat!"

No man has seen me. I never was. Without me hope is lost.

The roof filled Parker's vision. Right before he was crushed, his mind was flooded with the thought of pancakes. Thick, golden pancakes dripping with rich butter and way too much maple syrup. His mom had promised to make him pancakes in the morning. Parker loved pancakes, but morning was hours away and it was looking like he wasn't going to live to see . . .

"Tomorrow!" he cried. "No one has ever seen it, but it's always there! It's always a day away!" The ceiling kept on in its relentless descent. It was inches from Parker's face. Parker screamed out again, this time in French. *"Le demain!"*

Parker shut his eyes tight, sure he was about to be smashed as flat as a DVD. He heard the roof come to a grinding halt. When he opened his eyes, he saw the ceiling somehow rising back to where it belonged.

Parker stood on shaky legs and picked his still-burning torch out of the dirt. A hole opened in the mortar behind the pulverized blue skull. Parker reached his hand in, hoping against hope that it wasn't filled with spiders. He hated spiders.

Naomi sifted through the junk in Theo's closet while Reese and Theo explained their situation.

"It's not a big deal," said Theo. "He just went to an R-rated movie with some high school guys he met, that's all."

"We're covering for him," said Reese.

"We didn't think he was going to be gone this long, that's all."

"He'll be back, like, any second."

"That's all?" said Naomi.

"Yeah, that's all," said Theo.

Naomi threw a half-deflated football out of the closet. "We're sitting ducks up here. We need to get somewhere we have some room to maneuver."

"There's the basement," Theo said. "There's a Ping-Pong table down there, but we hardly ever use it. It smells kinda funny."

"The Ping-Pong table smells funny?"

"The *basement* smells funny."

"Okay. So. Is this all we have to work with?" Naomi held up a lacrosse stick and a catcher's chest protector. "Because I have to tell you, it doesn't look promising."

Theo said, "Yeah. Well, I mean, there's some crap under my bed, but it's just old toys and stuff." He turned red. "I just haven't gotten rid of it yet."

Reese bent down and pulled a cardboard box out from under Theo's bed. Naomi leaned in and cracked it open. "Oh, yeah," she said. "This'll do just fine."

The wall separating Parker from his genie and Professor Ellison rose and Parker emerged into the hall of skulls, burning torch in one hand and a third of the brass Elicuum Helm in the other. "Piece of cake," he said, tossing the fragment of the helmet into the air and catching it like this was stuff he did every day.

Professor Ellison eyed the helmet. "Nicely done, Parker. I must admit I had my doubts."

"You should have a little more faith in me, Professor. I feel like I'm getting pretty good at this."

"Let us not let success go to our heads," said Fon-Rahm. "We should split the scene as soon as possible."

"Split the scene?" asked Parker.

"Yes. I fear this place is bogus."

"The genie's right, you know," said the professor. "This place is rather bogus."

"Hey, I'm all for getting topside. I'm as sick of bones as you guys are. Lead the way."

Professor Ellison said, "I'd feel better if you handed the Helm over to me."

"Yeah, I'm sure you would, but I'd just as soon hang on to it for now."

"A stalemate! How exciting!" The professor stared at Parker in the flickering light. "However shall we resolve our differences?"

Fon-Rahm cocked his head to one side, listening to something neither Parker nor Professor Ellison could hear. "Get behind me," he said. "Get behind me *now!*"

They ducked behind the first of the Jinn just as he raised his arms and created a force field crackling with blue electricity to block the tunnel ahead of them.

For a moment, nothing at all happened.

"I don't get it, Fon-Rahm," said Parker, peeking past the genie. "What's out there?"

"Annihilation," Fon-Rahm said just as Duncan skated around the corner, accompanied by a suited member of the Path and a figure cloaked in black.

"Oh, hi guys," said Duncan, cheerfully. "We didn't expect to find anybody here. Looks like we have company, boss."

The figure lowered his cloak and Parker saw the scarred face of the ancient wizard Vesiroth for the first time. Parker heard Professor Ellison gasp. His blood ran cold and he remembered what his mother used to say about someone walking over her grave.

17

"VESIROTH," PROFESSOR ELLISON SAID, and then, more softly, "Vesiroth."

She had not seen the scarred wizard in more than three thousand years, but just being near him brought her back to the days when she was a child clinging to life in the gutters of Mesopotamia. She had begged him to take her in and teach her the ways of magic, only to betray him when his dreams of world conquest drove him to madness.

Vesiroth stared at his former pupil through the crackling blue lightning of Fon-Rahm's force field. "Tarinn. I had hoped to put off this confrontation until later, but here you are. Surely fate has a sense of humor."

The sound of his voice made Professor Ellison shiver. It sang to her of death and destruction.

"Hi, Professor," said Duncan, chomping on pink bubble gum. "Long time no see."

"Duncan." Professor Ellison tried to maintain her cool, but she could hear the shakiness in her own voice. "Aren't you out a little late for a school night?"

Duncan's smirk disappeared. "Watch yourself. I could slice you to pieces without batting an eye."

"So cranky. Perhaps you'd like a juice box?"

Duncan took a step toward the force field but Vesiroth held him back. The wizard spoke directly to Professor Ellison. "I suppose it's a waste of time for me to try to convince you I'm right. You must have noticed that mankind's penchant for killing each other has not abated. From what I've seen, it's only gotten worse. Humanity spends most of its time devising newer and ever more horrific ways to create sorrow. I could put a stop to all of that. The world could finally know true peace."

"Sure, as slaves," Parker said.

Vesiroth turned his steely gaze in the direction of the seventh grader. "You keep company with an actual child. This surprises me. Is he to be a sacrifice of some kind?"

Parker flushed red. "You wish."

"He is with me," said Fon-Rahm. "I am bound to do his bidding."

"Ah, Fon-Rahm. My firstborn. Do you not bow to your creator?"

"I have never bowed to you."

"Of course not. You only obey your *master*." Vesiroth got on one knee and fixed his eyes on Parker. "A dream come true, isn't it? A genie to fulfill your every wish. Tell me, why are you traipsing through this endless tomb instead of sitting on a throne of your very own? You could rule over all you survey."

"I don't want to rule over anything."

"No? You lack imagination, boy."

Parker bristled. "Don't call me boy."

Vesiroth smiled. "When Tarinn was your age she had dreams of becoming a great wizard. She wanted revenge on all the people in her life who had wronged her. She has a dark heart, no matter how she presents herself. She can't be trusted." He shifted his gaze to his onetime student. "But I suppose you know that already. You have enemies on both sides of this barrier, *boy*."

"Check it out." Duncan jutted his chin at the piece of brass in Parker's hand.

The wizard stood. "You have something I want, so I'm willing to make a deal with you. Give me that shard of the Elicuum Helm and I'll let you live, for now. Who knows? You may even survive long enough to see a world without war."

"Get stuffed," said Parker.

"Excuse me?"

"The boy told you to get stuffed," Fon-Rahm said. "I will second his sentiment."

Vesiroth locked eyes with Professor Ellison. "Tarinn! You will take that object from this brat's hand and you will give it to me. Do you hear my command?"

Professor Ellison shuddered. She opened her mouth to tell the wizard no, but nothing came out. Even now, after all this time, she felt the pull of obedience to the man who saved her life. Something inside her still wanted to please him.

It took all of Fon-Rahm's energy to maintain the force field, but he saw Ellison was struggling. "Professor Ellison!" She didn't answer. "Tarinn!" he shouted, and the professor finally snapped out of her trance.

"You can't have it," she told Vesiroth in a whisper. "You're right that nothing has changed. I still stand against you."

"Why even bother? I already have one piece of the Helm."

Professor Ellison paled.

"Ah, you didn't know that, did you? You can't stop me, woman. Every time I destroy a genie I regain a piece of my old strength. You'll see it when I kill Fon-Rahm."

"Enough of this talk!" When Fon-Rahm yelled, the force field surged with blue power. "This conversation serves no purpose. You are far too weak to face both Tarinn and me at once. Begone, creator, back to your hole and your dreams of death!"

Vesiroth grinned. It was an evil sight among the skulls of the dark catacombs.

"You're right, Fon-Rahm. I couldn't take you both on. Not yet. That's why I brought a secret weapon."

He held his hand out to the silent Path member. The man threw his gray duffel bag to the ground. It landed with a clang.

"Oh no," said Parker, as the Path member reached into the bag and pulled out a glowing cylinder made of metal and carved with intricate runes. It was one of the lamps stolen from Professor Ellison. Vesiroth had brought a genie of his own.

Reese looked over Naomi's disguise and groaned. "This is never going to work."

"Of course it'll work," Naomi said, her voice muffled. "Believe me, parents only see what they want to see."

"I don't know," said Theo. "This whole thing seems nuts."

Naomi shrugged. "We don't have to do it. We could just tell Parker's parents he's at the movies. What's the worst that could happen?"

Theo and Reese exchanged a knowing look. The worst that could happen? Well, Parker's mom and dad could go to the movie theater, for one thing, and when they saw Parker wasn't there they could search for him, and then they could call the hospital and the police station, and then they could discover that their only son was in France with a three-thousand-year-old sorceress and an actual real-life genie, and that would be, you know, bad.

"No, we should do this," Reese said. "Maybe we'll even pull it off."

Naomi said, "Okay then! The key to this whole thing is going to be speed. The less time we spend in the open the better. You guys ready?"

Theo nodded without enthusiasm. Reese got out her phone and trained the video camera on Naomi. "If we're going to do it we might as well do it," Reese said. "Let's go!"

Theo screamed and tore out of the room and down the stairs, Naomi stumbling behind him, moaning as low as she could get her voice to go. Reese followed them filming the whole thing from the back. They were headed straight toward the living room and a card table filled with parents. Reese had faced homicidal Path zealots with machine guns, a building-sized genie with rats for hair, and the prospect of being burned to cinders by Xaru, but this was somehow worse. It was a plan so crazy that it was hard to believe Parker hadn't thought it up himself.

* * *

"Lower the shield!" yelled Professor Ellison.

Fon-Rahm kept the shimmering force field in place. "No! I cannot place my master at risk!"

"He'll certainly be at risk if we let this maniac free a genie!"

"She's right!" said Parker. "Once the genie's out we're in trouble. Either the genie wins and we're done or we kill it and all its power goes back to Vesiroth. We have to stop that guy *before* he opens that lamp."

On the other side of the blue energy field, Vesiroth smiled. It did not improve his appearance. "You never could think strategically, Tarinn. I've bested you before we've even started."

"You have to lower the shield!" the professor repeated.

"Do it, Fon-Rahm," said Parker. "I command you to lower the shield!"

Fon-Rahm closed his fists and the incandescent lightning crackled away into the ozone. The instant the shield came down, Duncan conjured a mirrored dagger and sent it zinging toward Parker. Fon-Rahm blasted it with a bolt of pure electricity milliseconds before it could embed itself into the seventh grader's throat. The genie threw another blast at Duncan, but by the time it got to him the ten-year-old was gone, spinning away on his board like a pro skater. The lightning exploded a wall of stacked skulls instead.

"Who is that kid?" asked Parker.

"He's no kid," replied Professor Ellison. "He just *looks* like one."

Duncan slammed to a stop in front of the Path member and let loose a string of ninja stars at Parker. The genie threw balls of lightning that melted the deadly spinning blades in midair.

Duncan was never going to kill Parker, but every second he kept Fon-Rahm occupied was another second the nervous Path zealot could use to twist the ends of the metal canister, first one way, now the other. The zealot's hands were sweaty and shaking. He knew that when he completed his task his life would be over.

As Fon-Rahm and Duncan traded magic attacks, Vesiroth and his one-time protégé stared each other down, neither making a move. After what seemed like an eternity, they began to take slow steps toward each other.

"I have been waiting a long time to see you again," the undying conjurer said above the din of electric jolts.

"And I've been ready," said Professor Ellison. With sudden swiftness she raised an amulet shaped like an ankh from her bag. Dust from the floor of the catacombs swirled around Vesiroth's feet and the dark wizard grabbed at his throat.

"Like it?" Ellison said as she took a step toward him, the amulet held high. "It was carved from a piece of the Great Sphinx of Giza. I searched for it for years and years and I don't even want to tell you how much it cost."

Vesiroth struggled for breath. His eyes began to bulge.

"It's sucking the air out of your lungs. Even an eternal wizard has to breathe."

Vesiroth sank to his knees.

"It's time, Vesiroth. Let go. Leave this world behind and find peace."

The wizard's eyes bored into Ellison, his hatred fueling his mad desire to survive. His fingers found the spike around his neck. With a thrust of his arm the wizard used his magic to snatch Ellison off of the ground and hurl her against the wall of the catacombs. The ankh was knocked out of her hand to vanish in the dark.

Professor Ellison could feel the bones on the wall digging into her back as Vesiroth took a deep breath of stale air. Finally he got to his feet and approached her.

Parker saw Vesiroth moving slowly toward the professor. "Help her, Fon-Rahm!"

The genie turned his attention away from Duncan. In the split second the genie wasn't attacking him, Duncan saw his chance. "Nice meeting you, Parker," he said as he spawned a razor-sharp battle-ax and heaved it straight at Parker's face.

18

FIVE MINUTES AGO PARKER HAD
thought he was going to be crushed to jelly in a room filled
with talking skulls. Now he was pretty sure the lethal ax slicing
through the air was going to be the last thing he'd see before he
died. He couldn't decide which was worse.

But right before the blade cleaved Parker's head in two,
Fon-Rahm grabbed it and swung it at Vesiroth. The scarred
wizard turned his attention away from Ellison just in time to
catch the speeding battle-ax between his hands. It didn't cut him
but the force of the blow sent Vesiroth flying.

Ellison dropped off the wall. She hit the floor hard, gasping
for breath. Parker and Fon-Rahm ran to her.

"Are you injured?" the genie asked.

"No, I'm...I didn't realize he would be so strong. Even at a fraction of his full power he's strong."

"Hold it together, Professor," said Parker. "We're going to need you if we want to survive this."

"I fear we are in for more trouble," said Fon-Rahm, holding his wounded left arm by his side.

Parker and Professor Ellison followed his gaze. As Vesiroth staggered to his feet, the Path member collapsed, one of Duncan's gleaming knives protruding from his chest. The sacrifice had done his duty. He had opened the lamp and been killed to ensure the released genie could act with free will.

The open canister pulsed with light. A green fog rolled out one end. The damp air of the catacombs was filled with the scent of sulfur and rotting flesh.

Duncan knew danger when he saw it. He took a step back from the lamp.

Vesiroth took a step forward.

The scarred wizard peered into the canister. All at once a swarm of wasps erupted from the lamp and filled the air around him. Fon-Rahm threw a protective electric dome over Professor Ellison and Parker as the flying insects took over the tunnel. They choked the empty eye sockets of the skulls in the walls and covered the ceiling of the catacombs. Parker put his hands over his ears and screamed. The droning sound alone was enough to drive a person mad.

Vesiroth cried out, "Genie! Eleventh of the Jinn! You were created from my life force and I am your master. Obey me!"

At the sound of the wizard's words the buzzing insects gathered around him in a swirling vortex of wings and stingers.

"You know, Fon-Rahm," said Parker, clutching the broken piece of the Elicuum Helm to his chest, "I'm really glad I stole your lamp instead of that one."

Fon-Rahm nodded grimly as the wasps formed themselves into the shape of a man. This was the genie Qen-Noh, a monster made completely of stinging insects.

The three kids hit the Merritts' living room with their energy turned up to eleven. The adults looked up in confusion as the parade ran around the card table in a ball of roiling weirdness.

"Come on, kids, we're trying to play cards here!" said Martha.

J.T. said, "I knew it was too quiet up there."

"What the heck do you guys think you're doing?" asked Kelsey.

"We're making a movie!" said Reese.

Naomi held her arms up and moaned some more. She was wearing Parker's sneakers, his jeans, and his sweatshirt with the hood pulled over Theo's old latex Frankenstein mask. Her fingers were hidden under oversized green Hulk hands. Any evidence of a twelve-year-old girl was well hidden.

"Parker, you're looking a little green," said his mother.

J.T. added, "I think he looks better than normal."

"Come on," said Theo. "You guys have to act scared! You're being terrorized by a monster!"

Martha, Kathleen, and Kelsey were game to play along with halfhearted shrieks. J.T. just shook his head and watched what was supposed to be Parker jump around.

Theo wished Naomi would take it down a notch. But she was having a blast. She even tried to pick up a bowl of chocolate-covered peanuts with her clumsy Hulk hands.

"Okay, okay, don't get carried away," said Martha, gently taking the candy away from her. "I don't want to be vacuuming crushed chocolate out of the rug for the rest of my life."

"Go downstairs! We'll use the basement as a dungeon," Reese said, hoping to move things along.

Naomi-as-Parker let out a low grunt and loped toward the stairs that led to the basement. Theo was right behind her, doing his best to get in between her and the card table.

"Try not to make too much noise down there," said Kathleen, going back to her cards.

We did it, Reese thought. We got away with it! She trailed her friends to the stairs.

And then J.T. spoke up. "Wait," he said. "Parker. Get back here. Now."

All three kids froze in their tracks. They'd known it was too easy.

Naomi turned slowly around and did her best Frankenstein walk back to the living room. Reese and Theo had no idea what they were going to say when J.T. ripped the mask off Naomi's head. They could only hope that Naomi was better at talking her way out of trouble than they were.

Naomi stopped just a few feet from J.T. He squinted at the mask and leaned back in his seat.

This is it, thought Reese. This is how it all comes crashing down.

Then J.T. reached into his pocket for his own phone. He took a picture of Naomi and beamed. "That's my new wallpaper," he said.

Naomi gave one last monster grunt before she limped straight-legged after Theo and Reese.

When they were safely in the basement Reese let out a sigh of relief. "I thought we were nailed for sure!"

Naomi shook off the huge green foam hands and pulled off her monster mask. Her face was dripping with sweat and she was wearing a huge grin.

"We have got to hang out more often. You guys are so much fun!"

Theo groaned and collapsed on the Ping-Pong table.

The wasp genie Qen-Noh was a horrifying image in the torchlit catacombs underneath Paris. It held a human shape, shaking with the vibrations of countless beating wings and the clatter of insects crawling over each other. It had been trapped for thousands of years in its metal lamp and now that it was out it was restless and ready to move. It was torture for the thing to wait for the weakened wizard Vesiroth's command. But Qen-Noh was not like his brother genies Fon-Rahm, or Xaru, or even Syphus. Every genie created was a paler and more distorted version of its original creator, Vesiroth. Fon-Rahm, the first of the Jinn, had an intellect and a will of his own. Qen-Noh was one of the last created. It was a mindless horror born to follow commands and created simply to obey.

Vesiroth raised his open hand to his new ally. When he pointed at Parker, Fon-Rahm, and Professor Ellison, the wasp genie took one look at his prey and swarmed after them.

"Run!" Fon-Rahm didn't have to tell Ellison or Parker twice. They were already on their way down the dark tunnel.

Fon-Rahm followed behind them. His left arm hung useless at his side so he used his right to throw bolts of blue lightning backward at Qen-Noh. The blasts went right through the cloud of wasps, doing more damage to the skulls lining the catacomb walls than to the enemy genie.

Duncan was fascinated by the wasp genie. It was magnificent, the ultimate magic weapon. He wanted desperately to run after Qen-Noh, but Vesiroth was barely standing and Duncan was forced to help the wizard along.

"I am not certain Qen-Noh can be stopped," cried Fon-Rahm as he ran with the professor and Parker down the bone-lined corridors. "I cannot assure your safety."

"Yeah, I don't feel particularly safe," said Parker. "What happens if they sting us?"

"Nothing good, I assume. I have no choice but to make my stand here. Prepare yourselves." As the wasps swarmed around them, Fon-Rahm planted himself in the middle of the tunnel and became the world's largest bug zapper. He killed as many flying insects as he could, but no matter how many were burned alive, there were always more. The smell of fried wasps was acrid and horrible.

Vesiroth and Duncan finally caught up to them. Fon-Rahm's time was running out. "Vesiroth comes!" the genie said. "You must find a way out of this tomb!"

As Fon-Rahm reduced the endless waves of flying insects to ash, Professor Ellison turned to a wall weakened by a stray bolt of lightning and began to bash at it with a loose brick. "A little help, please!" Parker joined her, digging at the wall with his bare hands. Professor Ellison squeezed through the ragged opening and pulled Parker in behind her. Parker turned back for his genie. "Fon-Rahm, come on! This way!"

The genie heard his master's command. Leaving a net of crackling lightning behind him, he climbed through the wall and collapsed at Parker's feet.

Parker's heart sank. "This is no good. We're trapped!" They were in a sealed crypt with no exit on any side. Robed skeletons roped to the walls stood watch over more skulls and bones. They were cornered.

A manic buzzing drew their attention to the hole in the wall. It was Qen-Noh forcing himself through. For a moment, the tornado of wasps gathered themselves into human form again. The buzzing insects shaped themselves into a twisted version of Fon-Rahm's face and screamed an insect drone.

"Fon-Rahm, buddy, we need you!"

"I ... I am not ..."

The genie was clutching his left arm to his chest. He was clearly in pain and confused. Parker was shocked. He had never seen Fon-Rahm so helpless. Parker stared in horror at the wasp genie. No one was going to save them now. It was up to him.

He raised the shard of the Elicuum Helm to the side of his head.

Professor Ellison barely had time to blurt out "Parker, no!" before Parker seized up. A black tentacle sprang from the broken helmet, searching the vault for a source of negative energy. The wasp-eyes of Qen-Noh's face followed the black arm as it wove through the air and finally lashed out. It surrounded the swarm of wasps in an oozing black cocoon. The never-ending buzzing stopped as the inky goo absorbed the life from the genie.

When it was over the tendril returned to the broken shard of the Helm. Parker pried it off his head and threw it aside, but the damage was done. He collapsed onto the dirt.

"Parker!" Fon-Rahm tried to rouse his master. They needed to get out of the catacombs while they still could.

In the corridor, Duncan felt his boss start to convulse. He had seen this movie before. He knew that the wasp genie had been destroyed and that its life force was returning to Vesiroth. He dropped the wizard and dove through the hole in the wall just as Vesiroth lost all control and released a shock wave of pure energy that ripped through the tunnels shattering skulls and bone into dust.

Fon-Rahm looked up to see Duncan enter the vault. Ellison was clutching her bag to her chest and Parker was shaking from his experience with the Helm. They were sitting ducks.

Duncan saw his chance. Hatchets appeared in both of his hands. He had Parker dead in his sights.

19

PARKER SQUINTED UP INTO A BRIGHT light. It was round, and it was coming straight toward him. He found it mesmerizing.

"Look out!"

Professor Ellison yanked Parker out of the way just before the motorcycle smashed right into him.

Parker blinked in amazement. They were out of the catacombs and plopped down in the middle of a riotously busy, insanely dusty street. Horns blasted and engines roared as a stream of buses, motorbikes, scooters, trucks, and yellow taxis swerved around them. Professor Ellison, Fon-Rahm, and Parker had to Frogger their way through the impatient traffic and to safety.

When they reached the side of the road Parker gawked at the chaos of machines and pedestrians. After the murk of the catacombs, the lights were blinding. There were billboards advertising Coke and signs for telecom companies in a language Parker didn't even recognize. Weird smells hung in the air. He was dumbfounded. "Where *are* we?"

Professor Ellison barely glanced at the bedlam that surrounded them. "If I had to guess I would say Calcutta."

"We're in *India*? But how—"

"I warned you that teleportation is dangerous," said Fon-Rahm. "I have little control over the outcome of such a desperate gamble. In my condition I suppose we should count ourselves lucky we are on the correct planet."

"Your arm!" Parker cried. "Are you okay?"

"I fear I am not." Fon-Rahm carefully pulled open his robes to reveal a pulsing mess of blue-black lines that spiderwebbed from the angry wound on his arm up his shoulder and onto the side of his neck. "My injuries grow more severe."

"Magic wounds can be tricky business." Professor Ellison stared at the damage on Fon-Rahm's side. "The infection is a by-product of your broken bond with Parker. If I had to guess, I would say it spreads when you use your magic. You'll have to be more careful from now on."

"I cannot afford to be careful." Fon-Rahm winced as he pulled his robes closed. "None of us can."

"Vesiroth is as scary as you said he was. That face..." Parker shuddered. "And that kid really has it in for me. What did I ever do to him?"

"Kid?" Ellison snorted. "Duncan Murloch is almost as old as I am."

"But he—"

"Duncan was once a very cunning wizard. He was also obsessed with the idea that he could make himself young again. But something went wrong with his spell and when the smoke cleared instead of being twenty again, he was ten. He's been trying to put himself right for two or three hundred years."

"Yeah, well, whatever that kid is, he's bad news."

Professor Ellison frowned. "There's worse news. In all the excitement we seem to have left the shard of the Elicuum Helm behind." She glared at the genie. "Your all-powerful friend here decided your safety was more important than securing one of the deadliest weapons the world has ever known."

"Parker's security was my primary concern."

"Of course it was. How rude of me. What's the fate of humanity compared to one seventh grader's well-being?"

"Guys, I don't mean to . . ." Parker stopped mid-sentence.

"What is it? What's wrong with you now?" Ellison snapped.

"I don't feel great."

Fon-Rahm caught Parker as he collapsed to the sidewalk. He was pale and sweating. His eyes were unfocused.

Ellison watched with an air of ambivalence. "It's an effect of the broken Helm. If he had kept it up for another twenty seconds it would have killed him."

"I want to go home," Parker said.

"What a shame my lovely car is five thousand miles away." Professor Ellison hoisted her bag and began to walk. "We'll have to make do with something else."

Instead of killing Parker, Duncan's hatchets shattered the skull of one of the skeletal guards in the vault. One second Parker, the genie Fon-Rahm, and Professor Ellison were there and the next they were simply gone. It must have been the genie. Even Vesiroth didn't have that kind of power.

And then something caught his eye in the dust. It was the shard of the Elicuum Helm. The night wasn't such a loss after all. He bent over to pick it up but before he could even touch it he heard a voice behind him.

"Stand aside."

Duncan stood up and stepped away so Vesiroth could reach down for the brass relic himself. He picked up the shard with a shaking hand.

"Only one piece more." His eyes glowed with new energy. "Soon the world will be mine."

"As long as you remember our agreement," Duncan said.

"I have not forgotten. When this is over I will make you twenty again. I am a man of my word."

"If you say so, boss."

Vesiroth barely glanced back as he took his prize and crawled out through the hole in the wall. The Elicuum Helm was a waste of time, his second-in-command thought. The real power was in the Jinn. Duncan wondered what kind of damage he could cause with a genie of his own.

20

PARKER USUALLY ENJOYED BLASTING through the air with Fon-Rahm.

The genie could make anything fly. The first time he took Parker, Reese, and Theo up he used a kitchen-floor-sized piece of linoleum. Lately they rode in his Toyota, looking out the windows at the oceans and mountains and cities below them in all the luxury provided by a mid-priced Japanese sedan. Now they were flying the friendly skies in a rickety Hindustan Ambassador sedan that someone had attacked with lime-green house paint. Parker was laid in the car's stained backseat. He was as sick as he had ever been in his life. Cold sweat covered his face. He shook uncontrollably. He was nauseous and weak. If he made it out of this alive, he thought, he would never make fun of Theo's motion sickness again.

Professor Ellison turned around in the driver's seat to take a look at Parker. She wasn't really controlling the Indian-made car anyway. "How is he?"

Fon-Rahm had not taken his eyes off of his master since they got in the car. "He is not well, and my power does not extend to healing."

"I'm well aware, Fon-Rahm. It's almost as if you were designed as some kind of a weapon." She began to dig through the bag in her lap. In a moment she handed Fon-Rahm a small glass vial filled with a pretty amber liquid. "This is an elixir I keep for emergencies. Give him a sip, but not too much."

Fon-Rahm uncorked the vial and smelled the potion inside. "Is it dangerous?"

"No, it's expensive. I don't want to waste it."

The genie pressed the vial to Parker's lips. Parker coughed but finally managed to take in a few drops of the stuff.

"It does not appear to be working."

"Give it a second. You would think that all those years in the lamp would have taught you something about patience."

Parker put his hand to his forehead and groaned. Fon-Rahm reached back to help him sit up. "Are you feeling better?"

Parker blinked at the genie. "Sure! I feel great!" He looked out the window. "Are we in a plane?"

"We are in an automobile. The power of the Nexus keeps it aloft."

Parker nodded knowingly. "Cool. One time? I went to a park and I saw a dog."

Fon-Rahm narrowed his eyes and spoke to Professor Ellison. "He seems to be confused."

"Ah. That could be a side effect of the potion."

"A side effect?"

"He might be a little . . . loopy."

"Well," said Parker, "thanks for driving me! I am so late for the candy parade!" Then he opened the door to the Ambassador and stepped out into thin air. Fon-Rahm dove into the backseat and used his good arm to catch Parker's ankle before the seventh grader plunged seventy thousand feet into the Atlantic Ocean. Parker didn't even seem to realize he was dangling from a car speeding at over eight hundred miles an hour. "I'll see you guys at the garage sale!" he yelled over the roaring wind.

Fon-Rahm pulled him back into the car and managed to slam the door.

"Maybe we should have gone with ibuprofen," Professor Ellison said.

"How long will he remain in this state?"

"Oh, not much longer than an hour or two. Just keep him inside the car and he should be fine."

Parker gave his genie a sincere smile and gently ruffled his hair. "You look just like my math teacher."

Fon-Rahm frowned. Nothing in the world of humans was ever simple.

The genie put the car down just out of sight of the Merritts' house. Anyone watching would have seen a bank of fog roll in and leave an Indian car the color of a toad sitting on the grass when it evaporated.

"Home!" cried Parker. "I love this place. I wish I had a lion."

Fon-Rahm's eyes filled with smoke. Before he could materialize a live lion in the Merritts' lawn Professor Ellison stopped him. "For God's sake, Fon-Rahm, he doesn't mean it. You're going to have to control your urge to make this child happy until he's himself again. Otherwise we'll be swimming in lions and submarines."

"Submarines are *dope*," agreed Parker.

"Just drop him home and let him sleep it off. We'll get back to work in the morning. There's still one more piece of the Helm out there somewhere and we have to assume that Vesiroth has at least one other lamp in his possession already. We don't have time for nonsense."

Fon-Rahm climbed out of the car and opened a back door for Parker, who stumbled out, slammed his door, and waved to Ellison. "Bye, Professor! You always say mean things but I know you're a good person on the inside!"

Professor Ellison couldn't help but smile. "Thank you, Parker. What you did in the catacombs was very brave."

"You hear that, Rommy? I'm brave?"

"It is true," said the genie. "You have real moxie."

"You're so weird."

Professor Ellison putt-putted the little Indian sedan away, leaving Fon-Rahm and Parker to walk to the house in the dark. "Could we stop for ice cream?" Parker asked as he stumbled ahead leaning on his genie. "Or boxing lessons?"

"Perhaps later."

"I hope Theo's up. He's so cool."

"Yes, he is very cool."

"Fon-Rahm?"

"Yes, Parker?"

"Why do I have the French national anthem running through my head?"

They reached the trellis on the side of the house. Parker stuck his foot in and began to climb up to Theo's window. "Theo!" he yell-whispered. "Hey, Theo!"

"You must be quiet, Parker. We do not want to alert Theo's parents, or your own."

"Good point!" Parker loudly whispered.

"Parker! I'm over here!"

Parker heard Theo's voice and looked up. His cousin was not at the window.

"Look down!"

Parker looked down. Theo's head was sticking out a basement window. Parker got off the trellis. He was so unsteady on his feet Fon-Rahm was forced to prop him up.

"Hey, buddy! What are you doing down there?"

"We had to—"

"You're back!" Naomi stuck her head out of the window, too. Thinking fast, Fon-Rahm made himself unseen. Since she couldn't see Fon-Rahm, Parker looked to Naomi like he was leaning at an impossible angle. "Whoa."

"Get back inside!" said Theo. "We're making too much noise!"

"Nope." Naomi squirmed her way out of the high window and onto the side of the house. "I have to get out of here before my folks notice I've been gone all night. They're clueless, but they're not *that* clueless." She pulled off her sweatshirt and threw it to Parker. He made no attempt to catch it and it landed hung up on his face.

"What's wrong with him?"

Theo had no idea. "Nothing's wrong with him. Thanks, Naomi! We'll see you at school!"

"Yeah, thanks, Naomi! We'll see you at school!" Parker's voice was muffled by the sweatshirt. "You smell nice."

Naomi just stared at Parker. "Okay." She started to walk away, but then turned back. It seemed as if she was looking directly at the genie. "I'll see you guys later."

Theo held his breath until she was gone. "What happened to him?" he asked Fon-Rahm as Reese helped them lower Parker through the basement window and down the wobbly wooden chair they were using as a stepladder.

Fon-Rahm said, "Parker was injured and required a magic potion to revive him. He is suffering a side effect that should diminish with the passage of time."

"Wait a second," said Reese. "Are you saying Parker's *drunk*?"

The genie nodded. "Exactamundo."

J.T. Quarry left the game to pour himself a glass of water in the kitchen. "Does anybody want anything?" he yelled into the living room.

The card players all said no.

J.T. took a halfhearted look inside the refrigerator and then locked his eyes on the basement door.

Theo, Reese, and Fon-Rahm propped Parker up against a wall in the basement.

"His condition will improve at any moment," the genie said. Parker's eyes were half-shut, his movements were slow, and a goofy grin was plastered on his face. "That seems optimistic," said Reese.

"What's up, guys?" Parker said. "You missed this thing where there was a genie and then it was, like, a bunch of bees."

Fon-Rahm used his good hand to hold Parker's arms above his head so they could get the sweatshirt on him. "They were wasps, actually."

"Did you find the piece of the Helm?" Reese asked.

"Yes!" Parker exclaimed. "But then we lost it again. It had something to do with a motorcycle."

Theo's shoulders sagged. "So Vesiroth has a piece of the Helm now?"

"He sure does! Two, I think. Didn't he say he had two?"

The genie nodded. "He did. Our trip was not successful."

"It was tight, though! A whole bunch of things tried to kill me and I talked to a skull!" He looked puzzled. "That can't be right. Hey, Reese! I totally speak French! *Combien de salles de bains sont sur ce bus?*"

Theo asked, "What'd he say?"

"He asked me how many bathrooms were on the bus."

"What bus?"

"I don't know, Theo! I've been here with you!"

Theo said, "Let's take a look at him."

They stepped away from Parker. The sweatshirt was on. His eyes were open.

Reese nodded. "He looks okay!"

Parker gave her a thumbs-up and then slid slowly down the wall and fell asleep on the floor, passed out cold.

"This could be going better," Reese said.

They heard the door at the top of the stairs open and Theo's eyes went wide with terror. "What are we going to *do*?"

Fon-Rahm grimaced. "Take a chill pill," he said. "I have a plan."

"Did you just tell me to take a chill pill?" Theo asked.

J.T. reached the bottom of the stairs. To the left was the unfinished half of the basement the Merritts used for their washing machine and extra storage. To the right was the junk-filled playroom.

He went right.

"Hey, guys! What's happening down here?"

"What's up, Uncle Jay," said Theo as he blasted a Ping-Pong ball to the other side of the table where Parker, in the Frankenstein mask, easily volleyed the ball back. If his movements seemed a little jerky, that's because Fon-Rahm was propping him up and guiding his movements with his one good arm. J.T. couldn't see the genie but Theo and Reese could. The whole thing was very strange.

J.T. said, "You okay, Reese?"

Reese sat against the wall, petrified but trying hard to look like she was just playing on her phone. "Sure, Mr. Quarry. I've got winner."

"It's getting pretty late. I think maybe someone should drive you home."

Perfect! A way out! She jumped to her feet. "I'm ready! See you, Parker, see you, Theo!"

"Bye, Reese!" Theo didn't stop playing. "We'll see you Monday!"

Reese hurried to the stairs. Before J.T. took her up, he turned to his son. "Parker, aren't you going to say good-bye to your guest?"

Parker (Fon-Rahm, really) took a swing at the ball but missed by a yard. It bounced noisily across the room.

"Parker? You in there, kid?"

J.T. stepped toward his son. Theo and Reese held their breath as J.T. grabbed the plastic hair on the latex mask and pulled.

The mask came off. Parker blinked. Then he looked at his dad and smiled. "Bye, Reese! Thanks for hanging out with us!"

J.T. seemed satisfied. He chucked the mask onto the Ping-Pong table and followed Reese as she ran up the stairs. "Go to bed, guys. I'll see you in the morning."

When J.T. and Reese were gone, Theo and Fon-Rahm gathered around a finally clearheaded Parker. "Do you think he knows something's up?" Theo asked.

"Hard to say," said Parker. "He's not dumb. Even when I got away with stuff with my mom, my dad always knew about it. He plays it cool, but he *always* knows more than he lets on."

"What do you think we should do?"

"We shall keep our present course," said Fon-Rahm. "It is all we can do."

"And what about Professor Ellison?"

Parker shrugged. "Well, as far as I can remember, she didn't kill anybody, so that's something."

"Parker..." Theo paused. "Was he there?"

Parker nodded.

"What's he like?"

Fon-Rahm said, "He is the father of the Jinn and the most powerful magician the world has ever known. He has not wavered in his desire to hold mankind in his fist."

Theo looked to Parker.

"He's the scariest guy I have ever seen, Theo. Just being in the same room with him is..." Parker shivered. "He's worse than Xaru. Theo, he's worse than anybody."

21

FON-RAHM HAD VISITED CAHILL'S TINY
Main Street with Parker many times before, but this was the first
time he had gone alone. It was the first time really he had gone
anywhere alone.

He took a few tentative steps. Were people looking at him
funny? Did they sense he was not what he appeared to be? The
genie briefly considered making himself unseen, but that would
have defeated the whole point. He was making an effort to fit in.

What did humans do all day? He knew that children went to
school, of course, and he knew that adults usually had jobs. But
this was a Saturday and TV had taught Fon-Rahm that week-
ends were reserved for movies and mowing the lawn. Fon-Rahm
didn't have a lawn and he didn't see the point of movies. Life in

modern America was confusing enough without throwing fiction into the mix.

He walked past a bar filled with TVs blaring some kind of sporting event and paused briefly to look at the clothes in the window of a small department store. He was free to do whatever he wanted and yet nothing appealed to him. He was resigned to the idea of returning to his apartment when he saw the diner and remembered that he did have one hobby worth exploring.

He sat down at a booth by a window. "I would like a pie, please. Apple, I would think."

The waiter nodded. "A slice of apple pie. Gotcha."

"Not a slice. An entire pie."

"Wow. Um, okay," the waiter said. "Can I get you anything to go with that?"

Fon-Rahm thought for a second. "An extra-large order of French fries."

Reese tried to keep a straight face but Naomi was making it impossible.

"It ees not qvite right," Naomi said in a fake accent that seemed to be an unholy mix of German, Russian, and straight-from-a-vampire-movie Transylvanian. "Vould you have this in, how you say, vlack?"

The jacket was made of bright red sequins and it looked ridiculous on Naomi. The increasingly frazzled salesclerk gave the girls a weak smile. "Let me check in back."

As soon as she was gone Naomi and Reese burst into laughter. The store was way out of their price range and the clothes it sold were more appropriate for fifty-year-old rich ladies than for middle-school girls. Naomi had claimed to be the daughter of a diplomat visiting the college from Europe, shopping for a new dress for an embassy ball.

"Naomi, we're going to get caught!" Reese said.

"What are they going to do, send us to mall jail? The next store you're going to be a princess from the Republic of Bulgrania. You talk in, like, weird gibberish and I'll pretend I'm your translator!"

Reese shook her head wildly. "You're out of your mind!"

"Come on, nobody cares what you do as long as you don't hurt anybody and you get good grades. Straight A's are a license to do whatever you want."

"Yeah, well, you've never met my mother. She sent me to an SAT prep course when I was in fifth grade."

"My mom's no picnic, either." Naomi looked over Reese's shoulder. "We should get out of here." Reese turned around and saw the salesclerk heading right for them with a man in a suit in tow. Naomi quickly took off the jacket and laid it over a nearby rack.

The two girls hurried for the door. "Good-bye!" Naomi yelled back. "Your store is qvite lovely!"

The girls ran giggling arm in arm back into the mall. Reese had traveled the globe and arguably had saved the world from total annihilation, but this was a new kind of thrill. For the first time, she was hanging out with a cool friend who thought she was cool, too.

Parker yawned as he trudged up the stairs, still wiped out from his adventure in Paris. Almost getting killed took a lot out of a guy. He had been looking forward to kicking back on his bed, cranking some music, and just zoning blissfully out.

He swung open the door to his room and froze. J.T. was looking through a pile of Parker's clothes heaped in a corner.

"What are you doing, Dad?"

J.T. looked up, his eyes wide. "Nothing, I . . ." He trailed off. What could he say? He was caught red-handed.

"You're looking through my stuff."

"Yes, I was looking through your stuff."

"Why?"

"Because there's clearly something going on with you!" J.T. took a deep breath. "Look, I don't know what you're up to and you won't tell me anything and I . . . I thought that maybe I could find some clues."

Parker stood in the doorway, his face red with anger. "Like what, exactly? Did you think you were going to find *drugs?*"

"No! Maybe! I don't know, Parker. You and Theo are always sneaking around. I don't know what you two have in common with Reese. And that weirdo Mr. Rommy . . . What kind of kid would rather talk to his math teacher than his own father? I'm worried about you."

"Yeah? *Now* you're worried about me? You can't just show up here after more than a year and start poking through my life. You don't *get* to be worried about me."

J.T. held up his hands to calm Parker down. "This isn't a big deal, Parker. Maybe I made a mistake coming in here. I should have left this to your mother."

"Yeah, you should've. You let her do everything else."

"Watch it, pal." J.T.'s voice was cold.

"It's not fair. You're the one who went to jail and you don't trust *me?* Maybe I should be looking through *your* crap!"

On the other side of the wall Theo stopped typing on his computer to listen to Parker and his dad fight. He hated it when people yelled at each other. His parents had gone through what they called a "rough patch" two years ago, and he'd had his fill of raised voices in the house.

It was bad enough that J.T. was snooping around where he didn't belong (and had already come *this close* to catching them with Fon-Rahm), but he was also bringing tension back into the house.

Theo put his headphones on and went back to his game. He couldn't wait until his cousin and his aunt and uncle moved out.

22

USUALLY, RIDING HIS BIKE WOULD HAVE a calming effect on Theo. The cool air would blast past his face as he coasted through town, blowing away whatever had been holding him back. He wasn't trapped in a car. He wasn't stuck at home or in school, where there were authority figures up the wazoo.

The bike was freedom.

Today, though, it wasn't doing the trick. From the minute he got up in the morning Theo had been snapping at everyone and everything in his path. He was mad at his aunt for running out of bacon. He was mad at his uncle for spending all morning in the bathroom. He was mad at Parker for...just about everything.

Then, when Theo's mom was doing her last-second make-sure-you've-got-everything bit she did every morning (with Theo ducking and dodging as she tried to reshape his bedhead), all she could talk about was "is Parker okay" this, "is Parker okay" that. As if Theo wasn't sick of it already.

So, after school, on his way to his off-campus meeting with Professor Ellison, Theo stood on his pedals. But instead of his pain dissolving into the wind every time he drove his feet down onto the crank and chain, Theo thought about how angry he was and what he wanted to do about it.

Theo dumped his bike and sloughed off his backpack. Professor Ellison was waiting. She didn't have to be a mind reader to see he was in a foul mood.

"You found the place," she said, the Givenchy scarf over her hair blowing in the breeze. "I thought a little fresh air might do you some good."

The professor had chosen the woods near the Merrimack River to see how Theo would respond outside of a controlled environment. The tall, skinny pine trees filtered the light into a mosaic of sunspots on the forest floor and sparse underbrush. The sound of rushing water drowned out any outside noise. It was all very bucolic, with the added bonus of accessible parking.

"Today we'll be working on holding spells. Simple things you can do without any outside gadgets to help you. Nothing earth-shattering, just a little Magic 101. We know that you have a connection to the Nexus, but it would be nice to know exactly how strong that connection is." Professor Ellison walked to the water's edge. "We can test that today. The closer you are to the Nexus, the easier is should be for you to control your environment. Take this river, for example."

Where they stood, the Merrimack was forty yards across and

lined with sharp-looking rocks. The water flowed freely and frothed with white over the stones.

"It's not exactly Victoria Falls, but it will have to do." The professor plopped her bag down at her feet and put her hands on her hips. "Now. I myself have a very strong connection to the Nexus. Over the years I have used it to master many forms of magic." She held her hands with her palms facing the river. "And I never tire of showing Mother Nature who's boss."

Her eyes narrowed as she concentrated her thoughts on the rapids. Theo watched openmouthed as the water began to calm. Soon the waterway itself slowed. It was a river, then a stream, and then a creek. Fish flopped on newly exposed rocks. Brownish-green crayfish scuttled for safety.

"I was about your age when Vesiroth administered a similar test to me. I failed, of course. I was too flustered to properly access my own skill. Vesiroth was not pleased. He pushed me aside and with a wave of his hand he stopped the river altogether. It was the greatest show of pure power I had ever seen."

The professor brought her hands down. The water came rushing back, sweeping the fish and mudbugs away.

"There." Ellison let out a deep breath and turned to Theo. "And now it's your turn. Let's see what you can do."

Theo walked tentatively to the water's edge. "You haven't asked me to study anything like this. All I've been doing is shutting doors and starting fires."

"And now you're doing this. Magic isn't a hobby, dear one. Do you really want to be a wizard, or are you just making a show of it to impress your friends?"

Theo frowned and looked out over the rapids. He raised his hands the same way that his mentor had. Nothing happened. He tried again. Still nothing. Ellison could tell the boy was getting frustrated. At this point, she put the odds at seventy-thirty that Theo was going to crack and quit right there. Then he began to talk to himself, under his breath, through clenched teeth. Eighty-twenty. What a waste.

"Theo. Close your eyes and picture the water slowing. Imagine that the current doesn't exist. There's nothing making this river run. All you have to do is tell it to slow down. The water will obey you."

Theo shut his eyes tight and shoved his palms at the river. He was concentrating so hard he was actually shaking but still the water rushed on. Ellison couldn't understand his mutterings, but Theo looked like he was exorcising some demons (not literally, of course. Ellison had seen that in real life and it was a much more violent proposition entirely).

"Are you even trying, Theo? I'm getting tired of you wasting my time."

Theo's eyes popped open. He turned away from the river and stared daggers at Professor Ellison.

"All right, Theo. I suppose that's enough for . . ."

The ground shook. It was all Professor Ellison could do to keep her footing. She looked up and saw that the trees were bending down, straining toward Theo. One broke loose from its roots and came crashing to the ground. Dirt exploded all around them.

"Theo! That's enough!"

Theo spun and jutted his palms at the river. In a matter of

seconds the water stopped flowing entirely. Theo cocked his head and the Merrimack became a roiling wall of water that towered above him.

Then Theo stretched his hands out to his sides and the whole river exploded. The wall of water became a roaring cyclone that shot hundreds of feet straight up. The tornado whipped through the air, sucking in wood and rocks and pulling entire trees out of the ground, roots and all.

Professor Ellison hit the dirt and held on tight to avoid being pulled in herself. She grabbed the strap of her Louis Vuitton bag just in time to stop it from flying into the cyclone and being lost forever.

"Theo! Stop!"

The boy turned his head but didn't respond. His eyes were looking through her and into someplace that didn't exist. She had seen that look before.

"For God's sake, Theo! Look at what you're doing!"

The water funnel bore down on her. Ellison held out her open hand, closed her eyes, and chanted a spell to match the one her student had cast. But when she opened her eyes, the cyclone was just feet away and still coming. After more than three thousand years Professor Ellison was going to die, covered in mud and crushed by a wall of water in the middle of the New Hampshire woods.

She made one last desperate attempt to reach her pupil. "Theo! Please!"

Theo blinked. He looked at the wild cyclone tearing through the air and then down at his own hands. Had he really created this thing himself? He dropped his hands and the waterspout came crashing down. He stared in stunned silence with his mentor as the Merrimack rushed back into its banks.

After a moment, the professor stood and made an unsuccessful effort to brush the mud off of her clothes. "Well," she said. "I believe that will be all for today."

"Professor, I—"

"Not now, Theo. There will be plenty of time to discuss this later."

"But—"

"Ah, there you are!"

Theo and Professor Ellison turned at the sound of the voice and were dumbfounded to see a bloated, unshaven man in a wrinkled suit panting near a tree. He took in the wreckage of the woods around him. "And here I thought it might be hard to find you."

The man reeked of sweat and vodka and his eyes twinkled with sly mischief. "Come now, Julia," Maksimilian said. "No kiss for an old friend?"

After Theo had been sent pedaling home, Maks and Professor Ellison walked through the woods, two old friends on a pleasant hike.

"The boy's coming along nicely. I had no idea he had that much power."

"Neither did I." Theo's power was greater than she had ever dared believe. If he couldn't control it, Theo could someday be as big a threat as Vesiroth. "Although I fail to see how Theo's progress is any of your business."

"Oh, let's not bicker. You know you can't stay mad at me forever."

"I can try. Why exactly are you here, Maks?"

"The word on the street is that you're looking for the missing pieces of the Elicuum Helm," he said casually. "For the right price, I just might be able to tell you where to find one."

"Oh, really? And where would that be?"

Maksimilian scratched his butt and winked at his old friend. "Right where I hid it."

23

MAKSIMILIAN SQUARED UP HIS
shoulders and let loose a mighty burp. "You might want to roll
down the window a tad," he said. "That one's been brewing all
day."

Reese said, "Eeeewwwwwww," and covered her face with
her hands while Maks roared with laughter. Theo broke out
into a broad smile. He was more than happy to have something
to distract him from what had happened with the river in the
woods. The big wizard with the bad suit and the five-day beard
was gross, sure, and he took up way more than his share of the
Camry's backseat, but you couldn't help but like the guy. At least
he had a sense of humor.

"I can't believe Professor Ellison wanted to miss all of this,"
said Parker from the front passenger seat. They had all been

surprised when Professor Ellison had told them she wasn't going to go with them to get the last piece of the Elicuum Helm. The professor had said that she had complicated preparations to see to at home, but Reese had a sneaking suspicion that she just didn't want to be cooped up in a flying Toyota with Maks.

"Julia and I have a complicated relationship." Maks sighed. "That's what happens when you've known someone for a very long time. Resentments build up, slights are amplified."

"Well, yeah, but you did sell us out to the Path last time," said Reese.

Maks waved his hand in the air. "Pah. I came to your rescue eventually. Besides, what's a little betrayal among friends?"

"We approach our final destination," Fon-Rahm said from the driver's seat. They were cruising through cloudy skies at over forty thousand feet.

"That's too bad," said Maks as he put a meaty arm around each of his backseat companions. "We were just getting to know each other back here."

Fon-Rahm began their descent. When they broke through the clouds Parker looked out in awe. "Maks, are you absolutely positive this is the place?"

"Of course I'm positive." Maks unscrewed the top of a silver flask he kept in an inside coat pocket and took a mighty swig. "I'm old, I know, but I'm not senile."

Reese crawled over Theo to take a look out the side. "Wow," she said. Then, after she took a moment to collect her thoughts, she said, "Wow," again.

The first of the Jinn landed the car amidst a swirling storm of ice and wind. The Camry bucked a little in the maelstrom but finally settled with a crunch into the snow, and just like that they were on top of Mount Everest, the highest mountain on Earth and one of the most deadly places on the planet.

Fon-Rahm said, "This is a desolate and unforgiving place. The air is too thin for humans to breathe and the cold will freeze your blood solid. I have created a shield to surround you. I remind you to stay within its borders."

"You don't have to tell me twice," said Parker.

The mountain was a freezing nightmare but they were warm inside the shimmering blue force field. The snow that hit Fon-Rahm's dome melted and slid away.

"How are we supposed to find the piece of the Helm up here?" asked Theo. "We can't even see anything!"

"The whole point was to hide the thing," Maksimilian said. "The Helm is serious business. I was foolish enough to try using it once, and it wiped away an entire village. It's been five hundred years and I'm still not welcome back in Prague."

"Wait!" said Reese, pointing. "I see something!"

They looked where she was pointing and could just make out the dark gash of a cave opening in the side of the Himalayan mountain.

"I knew it was around here somewhere," said Maks. "Now all you have to do is go in and get it."

Theo said, "Wait. Why do *we* have to go in? You're the one who stashed the Helm!"

"I got you here, didn't I? I've fulfilled my part of the bargain." Maks took another sip from his flask. "If it's all the same to you, I think I'll just stay here and keep Fon-Rahm company."

"It must be sixty below out there," Reese said. "The cold will kill us."

"It would if we didn't have a genie!" said Parker. "Fon-Rahm, I wish we had some cold-weather gear. Like, the absolute best cold-weather gear there ever was. Money is not an object."

"As you command," said Fon-Rahm. He closed his eyes and a pile of equipment manifested in a swirl of mist in the center of the dome.

"Handy," said Maks. "All this time I've been fooling around with spells and amulets. I should have been opening lamps."

Fon-Rahm raised an eyebrow. "If you had opened the wrong lamp you would, I am afraid, have been toast."

"Too true, my friend."

Parker, Reese, and Theo struggled into their new gear. It was all made of space-age material and included full-body mountaineering suits with zippers and hoods, cumbersome mittens, helmets, goggles, face masks, socks, boots with metal cleats, pickaxes, flashlights, and bottled oxygen. They would need everything if they wanted to survive for even a few minutes at twenty-nine thousand feet above sea level.

When they were suited up, they looked each other over and laughed. The only way you could tell them apart was that Parker's suit was bright red, Theo's was neon green, and Reese's was highlighter yellow.

"We can barely move in these things!" said Reese.

"The cave's right there," Parker said. "We'll go in, grab the thing, and come right back. No problem."

Reese groaned. Things tended to go very wrong whenever Parker assured her that there was "no problem."

"We're ready, Fon-Rahm. Make a hole for us, please."

"Do be careful. Remember that your safety is my responsibility." Smoke drifted from the genie's eyes.

Parker, Reese, and Theo left Fon-Rahm and Maks behind as they stepped through the new gap in the shield and into the reality of life at the summit of Everest. Reese gasped. Even in their state-of-the-art climbing gear the cold was bitter and biting. She had to will herself to move forward with Parker to the mouth of the cave. Breathe, she thought to herself as she took a hit of the oxygen through a mouthpiece that dangled by her neck. You can do it. Tenzing Norgay and Edmund Hillary did it in the 1950s with no oxygen at all. And they were wearing wool pants.

They took labored step after labored step until they were at the mouth of the cave. They yelled to hear each other over the roar of the storm.

"Wait," Parker said, holding his two friends back. "Take a look around!"

Reese and Theo did. There was nothing to see but swirling snow.

"This is the top of the world!" Parker said. "We'll remember this for the rest of our lives!"

Reese couldn't argue with that. She held out her mittened hand.

Theo asked, "What are you doing?"

"I'm giving you guys a thumbs-up!" She looked down and realized that with her mittens on, you couldn't tell. "You'll just have to take my word for it!"

Parker grinned and stepped into the cave.

And that's when the yeti attacked.

24

PARKER WAS SO SURPRISED THAT HE stumbled and fell over backward. It was a good thing, too. If the snow beast had connected with his razor-sharp claws Parker would have been ripped to shreds. The yeti cocked its head as he regarded the fallen seventh grader.

"Parker!" Reese took a step toward her friend but stopped when the monster whipped its head around to face her. It was nine feet tall and covered with white hair frozen into matted clumps. It had the face of a pale ape, with pink eyes that glared in anger. Reese withdrew and the thing turned its attention again to Parker, who was lying flat on his back in the snow.

"Oh, right, the yeti," Maks yelled out from Fon-Rahm's force field. "Forgot all about it. I whipped him up as a little deterrent for anyone who might want to take the Helm."

Reese was incredulous. "Wait. Are you telling me you *invented* the abominable snowman?"

"An ancient book, a little vodka, a little more vodka, and voilà." Maksimilian smiled, a wistful look in his eyes. "I was really something in those days."

Blue electricity crackled off Fon-Rahm's arms. "At your command, Parker, I shall match myself in combat with this monster of snow and ice."

"No!" Parker said, his breath visible in the frigid air. "Stay there! Keeping that shield up is already screwing with your injury, or whatever it is. If you fight, it'll just get worse!"

Maks looked the genie over. "Injury? Not possible."

"It is, as they say, a long story."

Parker held his hands up slowly, showing the thing he meant it no harm. "Easy, fella. It's okay! We're your friends!" The yeti seemed to consider this for a moment before it leaned down and let out a bellowing roar that exposed jagged teeth and black gums.

Reese said, "Parker, I think it would be a good idea for you to lie very, very still."

Parker nodded. "I'm with you on that one." He could feel the ice ape's hot breath on his face. The wheels frantically turned in Parker's brain. He didn't have much time. "Fon-Rahm!" he yelled. "I wish I knew parkour!"

Smoke misted from the genie's eyes and Parker felt the knowledge and skill of years of practice and study flood into his mind. He rolled away just as the snowman took a swipe with his claw that sliced through the Everest ice like it was made of paper. Parker popped up, executed a perfect standing front flip, and set himself in a crouch. A smile spread over his face. "Yeah, this'll do nicely."

"What good is parkour going to do against a yeti?" Theo said. "Are you going to backflip it to death?"

"We don't have to kill it. We just need to get around it so we can snag the Helm." The snowman swatted at Parker. But the seventh grader somersaulted out of the way. "It's big, and it's strong. I wouldn't call it *fast*, though..." The snow beast leaped. Parker ducked to the side and watched the yeti hit the ice and slide on its face. "...and I've fought *smarter* monsters. Reese, you and Theo go in and grab the Helm." He grinned. "*I'll* keep Icy here busy."

Theo rolled his eyes. Of course Parker was playing the hero.

"On three," Reese said. "One. Two. Three!" She took off for the mouth of the cave with Theo right behind her. The thing scrambled to its feet and lunged after them. Theo and Reese were running as fast as they could but the gear made it hard to move. If Parker couldn't distract the monster, they would be yeti food.

"Hey, Bigfoot!" The yeti turned its pink eyes to Parker Quarry. "Come and get me!" The beast bared its crooked fangs and charged. Parker bounced to the yeti's left and used his leg to push off the side of the mountain. Shaking with rage, the snowman clawed the air where the seventh grader was supposed to be. Parker was already gone, a bright red blur against the white snow, as Reese and Theo vanished into the black maw of the cave.

The walls were lined with ice and Reese's flashlight made the whole space glitter like it was filled with diamonds. She pulled her face mask down and was assaulted by the stench of wet yeti.

"Wow," she said. "It's even worse than Maks."

Theo's flashlight picked up bones piled in a heap against a wall of the cave. "I hope those are bear bones and not..." He let the sentence trail off.

Reese took a quick look. "Not unless bears have horns. I'd say the yeti eats yaks." Her light lingered on what looked like a torn ski parka. "Well, *mainly* yaks."

"Um, I think I found the piece of the Helm."

"Great! Where?"

Theo pointed his light. High up and well out of reach was a dark piece of metal embedded in the frozen cave wall.

Reese screwed up her face. "I'll rock-paper-scissors you for it."

Theo shrugged. "We'd have to take off our mittens and I'd just lose anyway." Theo squatted down and made a step for Reese with his hands. "Try not to step on my head."

The yeti was getting really, really frustrated. Why wouldn't this meat thing just stand still and get eaten like all the others? The beast brought a hairy claw down but its prey rolled away.

"Is that all you got, Snow Face?"

If the snowman couldn't kill the thing in red, maybe it could at least get the creature to stop making so much noise. The yeti took aim and brought both of its arms down like a massive club. It missed and knocked a new hole in the ice.

In the force field, Fon-Rahm watched his master's antics with dismay. The snow beast was built for the cold and the thin air. Parker was not. He was for the moment the most skilled parkour athlete in the world, but he was also still just a twelve-year-old used to a less hostile climate. New Hampshire wasn't Los Angeles but it was certainly warmer than this.

Fon-Rahm turned to Maks. "You created this thing. You must hold the key to its destruction."

Maks scratched the top of his head. "What do you want from me? It was four hundred years ago!"

Fon-Rahm glared at Maks.

"Okay, okay, I'll give it a shot." Maks stuck his flask back into his pocket and cracked his neck from side to side. He narrowed his eyes and concentrated. Then he let out a deep breath and thrust his hands toward the monster with a low grunt.

The yeti didn't even flinch.

Maks looked at his hands and scowled. "I could have sworn that was the right spell." The ground started to quake. A low rumble that he felt in his stomach rather than heard came from above. Maks and Fon-Rahm looked up the mountain to see a wall of snow bearing down on them. "Oops."

"Avalanche!" Fon-Rahm's urge to protect Parker overrode anything else in his mind. He dropped the force field and used every bit of magic power he had to create a crackling net of blue energy to catch the rampaging onslaught of snow and ice. The force of the avalanche actually pushed Fon-Rahm back, but his shield held. Snow slammed down all around them, obliterating everything else on the mountain.

"Nicely done, friend," Maks said.

Fon-Rahm looked down to see the disheveled wizard holding him tight around the waist. "You don't mind, do you?" said Maks. "I'd rather not freeze to death up here."

As he struggled to hold his ground, the genie hoped against hope that Reese and Theo would shake a leg.

* * *

Theo was sure his knees were going to give out any second.

"Just a couple more hits should do it!" Reese said. She had been perched on Theo's shoulders, using her ice pick to hack away at the frozen cave wall for what seemed like hours. "This thing is *really* in there."

Every blow of the pick sent a shock that ran through Theo's entire frozen body. With one last jab, the ice finally surrendered the last piece of the Elicuum Helm to Reese.

"Yes!" She dropped off of Theo's shoulders, the Helm clutched in one of her giant mittens.

"Awesome!" said Theo, his shoulders throbbing. "Next time I'm getting on *your* shoulders."

Parker jumped a chasm right in front of the yeti and made it by the skin of his teeth. He was fading fast.

"Fon-Rahm! I can't hold this thing off much longer!"

"I cannot come to your aid!" Holding back tons of ice and snow was taking its toll on the genie. Although the air around him was well below zero, the pain in Fon-Rahm's arm was as hot as a pizza oven. The crisscrossing web of blue-black bruises reached up his neck and to the bottom of his jaw. "My injury worsens."

Parker could feel the yeti bearing down on him for one last attempt at dinner. The twelve-year-old was out of breath and completely spent. He didn't think he would survive much longer. "Fon-Rahm! When I tell you, drop the shield!"

The genie shook his head. "I cannot put you in such great danger."

"I'm already in danger!"

"He's right about that," muttered Maks.

"I command you to drop the shield..." Parker waited for the snow beast's charge. "...now!"

Fon-Rahm had no choice. He let his hands fall to his side, letting tons of frozen rock and ice charge down the mountain.

Parker timed the avalanche and used every ounce of strength he had left to rush the snow beast, ducking under its swinging claws and climbing the yeti with carefully placed steps and handholds. As the snowman lashed out, Parker stomped on the very top of its head and launched himself onto the side of the mountain and to safety.

The confused yeti turned just in time to be buried by the freight train of snow.

Reese and Theo ran out of the cave with the final shard of the Helm. "We got it!" Reese shouted. But the landscape had changed. Everything was covered with a fresh flood of ice. There was no sign at all of Maks or Fon-Rahm, and Parker was gone.

"Parker?" Theo asked.

"Up here," he said. Reese and Theo looked up to see Parker clinging to the mountain high above them.

"What happened?"

"Oh, we almost got wiped off the world's tallest mountain." Parker climbed wearily down from his perch and collapsed melodramatically onto the ice. "You know. The usual."

Theo searched the desolate landscape. "Where's Fon-Rahm? Where's Maks?"

He heard a loud *hissssssss* and jumped aside as a steaming sinkhole melted itself into the ice. Fon-Rahm rose stoically through the steam and floated above the new hole. Maks was cradled in his arms. "That is an experience I do not wish to repeat," the genie said.

"Me either," said Maks, climbing gingerly down to the snow. "I almost lost my flask!"

As Fon-Rahm rescued the Camry from the tons of ice that had covered it during the avalanche, Reese, Parker, and Theo took one last look at the mountain. "Well, Parker was right about us remembering this for the rest of our lives," Reese said. "We battled the abominable snowman on the top of Mount Everest!"

"Yeah. Good times," said Parker. "I'm gonna be sore for a month."

Fon-Rahm whirled on his master and spat his words. "Your plight is your own doing. Only a half-wit would take such foolish risks."

They all stared at the genie.

"That's a little harsh, don't you think?" said Theo.

"I am sorry." Fon-Rahm blinked, trying to clear his head. "I did not mean to lash out like that."

"You're just tired, buddy," Parker said, looking at the snow. "It's okay."

"I am not sure what came over me."

Theo snorted. "Don't worry about it. Parker's enough to make anybody lose his cool."

"We're all wiped. I think we should—" Reese stopped. Something was shaking in the ground beneath her. "Guys?"

The yeti burst from the ice right in front of her. As she stared in terror, it rose to its full height and bellowed at the top of its lungs. Just before it brought down a claw to tear Reese's head from her body, the snowman was hit from behind. Parker pulled Reese out of the way just as the yeti fell like a dropped redwood onto the ice. Its back was smoldering with embers and ash.

Reese and Parker looked to Theo. He was holding a glass trinket from his bag. It was so hot he dropped it and it melted its way deep into the snow.

"Not bad!" Maks nodded in approval. "For someone so *young*."

Theo felt a wave of relief wash over him. He *could* control his magic. All he had to do was have faith in himself.

They all climbed back into the car and lifted off. Before they left Mount Everest behind for good, Reese looked out the window and saw the yeti stumble to its feet and lumber back to its cave to lick its wounds. It would have to find something else for dinner.

25

WHILE MAKS PLAYED WITH THE
projector cube on the workbench, Fon-Rahm, Parker, Reese, Theo,
and the professor stared at the final shard of the Elicuum Helm.

They were in the Merritts' barn. By a stroke of sheer luck,
both Theo's and Parker's parents had been called to the school
for a hastily arranged parent-teacher conference. A little shuffling
of papers on Fon-Rahm's part *might* have had something to do
with the revised schedule.

The third piece of the Helm was encased in a glass box atop the
tractor's rusty engine cover. The professor had commissioned the
glass case in advance. She didn't want anyone touching the Helm
unless it was absolutely necessary. "It wants to be used," she said.
"It wants to reach out and it needs to meld with someone's mind
to do it. If it can, it will suck the life right out of you."

"I can vouch for that," said Parker. "I can still feel that thing wriggling around in my brain."

"If we can't use it, what are we supposed to do with it?" Reese asked.

Ellison sat primly on the tractor's seat and looked over the group. "We're going to use it as bait."

"Bait?" asked Theo. "Bait for who?"

"Vesiroth." Fon-Rahm crossed his arms over his broad chest. "The professor is suggesting we use the Helm to attract Vesiroth."

The kids looked to Professor Ellison in the hopes that she would tell Fon-Rahm he was wrong. She did no such thing.

"You're going to try to lure Vesiroth *here*?" asked Theo. "That's insane. We *live* here!"

"Not *here*, Theo," the professor said. "We're going to lure him to *my* house."

Theo let out a humorless laugh. "Oh, well, in *that* case . . ."

Maks hit a button on the projector and a startlingly realistic life-sized hologram of a high-stakes chariot race suddenly filled the barn. Theo actually jumped out of the way before he was run over. Parker smiled.

"Lady Pembrook-Pendleton," Maks muttered. He pushed the button once more and the scene collapsed into a single blue dot that faded away into nothingness. "She was always a bit *off*."

Reese ignored him. "I don't get it. Even if we do manage to get Vesiroth to Cahill, what then? Are we going to try to kill him?"

"Can he even *be* killed?" Theo asked. "It seems like the guy's not even human anymore."

"You don't want to kill him, do you, Professor?" said Parker.

"You want to capture him. That's what you've been working on. Some kind of wizard trap."

"It's tricky," Professor Ellison said, shifting her weight on the tractor. "But I believe it can be done. Vesiroth is not without weaknesses. He's vain. He's impulsive. He's insane. I know for a fact he's prone to hallucinations."

"Hallucinations?" Reese asked. "Really?"

"He sometimes sees his dead wife and daughters." Reese blanched at Ellison's words. "Seeing your family slaughtered is enough to drive anyone over the edge, dear. So I'm told."

"Well, *I* can't believe we're even talking about this." Theo paced by the old apple press. "He almost gutted you guys in the catacombs and now he's got two pieces of the Helm *and* he absorbed the strength of the wasp genie, right? That means he's even *more* powerful."

"No one ever said life was without risk, dear one."

"I don't know." Theo sulked. "This seems like a really bad idea."

Parker said, "She may be right, buddy. We all know we're going to have to fight him sooner or later. We're better off doing it on our turf. At least we'll have the home-field advantage." He looked to his genie. "What do you think, Fon-Rahm?"

The genie thought for a moment. "It will be difficult. Vesiroth must be enticed to come to us before he has regained his full strength. The allure of the Helm may prove irresistible to him..."

"It will," said Professor Ellison. "The Helm is his key to world domination and Vesiroth was never one to deny himself."

"If we succeed in drawing him here, he will not come alone. He will bring the Path with him."

"And that other lamp he stole from Professor Ellison." Theo shook his head. "For all we know, he has *all* the other lamps."

Ellison shrugged. "That's a risk I'm afraid we'll have to take."

"So." Parker leaned against the wall of the barn. "It'll be three kids, one genie, and one, um..."

"Enchantress, dear. Today I feel like an enchantress."

"*Enchantress* against Vesiroth and the Path and whoever else he decides to bring with him. I like the odds."

"And Maks," said Theo, hopefully eying the sloppy wizard.

"Me?" Maks leaned against the workbench. "A fight with the most powerfully evil wizard the world has ever known is tempting, but you'll have to do it without me. I have other responsibilities."

"Like drinking until you pass out?" asked Reese, disdain burning in her eyes.

"Like saving my own skin." Maks clunked the projector onto the bench. "I may look like I'm in prime physical condition but the truth is, I'm not quite as strong as I once was. I know my own limitations."

"Or maybe you're just scared," said Theo.

"Of course I'm scared. If you had any sense you'd be scared, too." He walked over to Professor Ellison. "I did my part. Do you have something for me?"

The professor retrieved a small velvet purse from her Louis Vuitton bag and tossed it to the grimy wizard. Maks snapped it out of the air, loosed the purse's strings, and peered inside. "Yes," he murmured. "Yes, this will do quite nicely."

Theo peeked over his shoulder in an effort to see what was in the bag, but Maks yanked it away. "Not for you, I'm afraid." He stuck the purse into his pocket and winked at Professor Ellison. "Always a pleasure doing business with you, my dear."

"Until next time, Maks," she said.

Maks snorted. "Let's hope there *is* a next time." He straightened his filthy suit jacket, opened the door to the barn, and walked away.

"We're really going to do this, aren't we?" wondered Reese out loud after a moment's silence. "We're really going to bring Vesiroth here."

Parker said, "And we'll be ready for him. I don't care if we're outnumbered and I don't care if we're outmatched. I would bet on us against anybody, anytime. If there's any team in the world that can stop Vesiroth, it's us!"

The projector fell off the edge of the workbench. When it hit the ground, it sprang to life and spat out a hologram of two steam trains smashing into each other headfirst at full speed. The carnage when they hit was brutal.

"I don't think that's a great sign," said Theo.

Later, when everyone had left, Parker and Theo straightened up the barn. They didn't want any evidence of the meeting left behind.

"I don't know why I even bother to say anything to her," said Theo. He boosted himself onto the workbench while Parker gave the barn floor a once-over. "She never listens to a word of it. I mean, would it kill her to ask me for my opinion once in a while? I feel like I'm as invisible as Fon-Rahm."

"Yeah, I don't envy you, Theo. If I had to spend a lot of time with her I'd—"

"You'd go insane, is what you'd do. I could count the number of nice things she's ever said to me on one hand. She—"

"Theo, what is this?"

Parker held up a brick-red stone the size of a nine-volt battery. Theo jumped off the workbench and grabbed it from Parker's hand.

"Weird," he said, turning the stone over in his hand. "It's made out of clay. These markings look like letters. You know, this looks familiar to me. When I was going through all those stupid books in Professor Ellison's library I saw—" He stopped mid-sentence.

"What? Theo, what is it?"

"Parker, I saw this in a book of magical objects. It's part of the Babel Stone."

Parker closed his eyes. "Do I even want to know?"

"The Babel Stone is...Look. There's *this* part, right?" He held up the stone. "And it's like a microphone. And then there's another part, like a big clay tablet, somewhere else. And whatever you say into this part gets carved into the other part. When that part gets filled up it starts over again from the top. It's been rewriting itself since, like, for thousands of years. It's an ancient magical tape recorder."

"But what's it doing here? I mean, somebody must be..." Parker instantly stopped talking. He took the stone and set it on the old apple press and motioned for Theo to follow him out of the barn. When they were clear of the stone Parker turned to his cousin. "Somebody's spying on us."

"It's gotta be Vesiroth! But who could he use to spy for him? The only one who makes any sense is your—" Theo stopped before he finished his sentence.

"Go ahead," said Parker. "I already know what you were going to say."

"He showed up out of nowhere, Parker," Theo blurted. "He's not even supposed to *be* here. He's supposed to be in jail. In *California*."

"There's no way. He would never do that to me!"

"Sure, he wouldn't. Just like he would never steal money from old people."

Parker felt the anger rise up in his throat. He reared back and shoved his cousin as hard as he could. "Shut up, Theo! You don't know what you're talking about!"

Theo's eyes darkened and his hands tensed into fists. He might have actually punched Parker if he hadn't seen how hurt his cousin really was. "Okay." Theo unclenched his fists and held up his hands. "Okay, I take it back."

Parker turned away so Theo wouldn't see the pain on his face.

Theo said, "All I know is that *whoever's* on the other end of the Babel Stone knows everything we said today. If they're working for the Path, Vesiroth's going to know he's walking into a trap. We have to tell Professor Ellison right now!"

"No." Parker let out a deep breath. "There's too much at stake. Professor Ellison barely puts up with us as it is. If she finds out about this, she may cut us out of the whole deal, and I don't think she can pull it off without our help." He looked to the barn. "Let's just carry on with what we're doing for now. Grab the Babel Stone and put it somewhere safe. Somewhere it can hear us talking but not about anything important. We'll decide what to do about the spy later."

Theo frowned and dashed back into the barn to get the stone.

Parker didn't like the thoughts that were racing through his own head, but he couldn't stop them. Finally, he went into the house. He walked through the kitchen and into the enclosed porch his parents were using as a bedroom until they could find a place of their own. Then he locked the door behind him and began to systematically search through every bag his father had brought into the house.

If the other part of the Babel Stone was here, Parker would find it.

26

DUNCAN GAZED OUT AT THE EIGHT
thousand Chinese warriors gathered before him. He had always
wanted his own army. Too bad they weren't real.

Duncan and his men were in China's Shaanxi Province,
underneath a massive hangar that protected the famous Terracotta
Army from the elements. It was a force of life-sized statues—
soldiers, horses, generals, and wagons, all made of fired clay. They
were created sometime in the third century and buried with the
emperor Qin Shi Huang to provide protection in the afterlife.

Qin Shi Huang was long gone but his army was still here,
uncovered by archaeologists and standing at attention in deep
trenches broken up by dirt walls. Duncan doubted the clay warriors did the dead emperor any good, but they sure were impres-
sive to look at.

"Make sure to grab all your crap," the ten-year-old told one of the Path henchmen. "We don't want to create an international incident."

The man in the dark suit nodded brusquely before joining his two brothers in collecting the excavation gear. Duncan left them to their work and jumped onto one of the clay walls. As he walked he looked down on the terra-cotta warriors in their sculpted helmets and armor, waiting patiently for an attack that would never come.

The satellite phone clipped to Duncan's belt beeped. He didn't have to check the caller ID. There was only one person on earth who had the number.

"Hiya, boss," he said as he answered the phone. "What's shakin'?"

Vesiroth was blunt on the other end of the line. "Did you find the lamp?"

"Nope." Duncan kicked a rock into a trench as he strolled. It bounced off a clay soldier's head and vanished into the dirt. "We looked everywhere, but zero, zilch, zippo, nada. It's not here. This was a wild-goose chase."

"That is most disappointing."

"Yeah, as much as I enjoyed digging through literally tons of dirt, I have to admit I was a little bummed myself."

"Very well. You will assemble your men and bring them back to headquarters."

"Will do." He stepped over the body of a dead Chinese guard. You couldn't just stroll in and start digging through the grounds near the Terracotta Army. It was a national treasure. "So. What's the new mission?"

"You will be told in good time."

The phone went dead. Duncan clipped it back to his belt and walked back to the men. "Where is it?" he asked.

A Path member brushed dirt off of his suit and nodded to a small crate. "It's here. The box has official government labels from three provinces. We should have no trouble getting it out of the country."

"Good." Duncan nodded, satisfied. "You guys do fine work." Then Duncan conjured up three razor-tipped darts and let them fly. The men were dead before they hit the ground. It was a real shame, Duncan thought, but it had to be done. He couldn't have these guys blabbing to the boss.

Duncan cracked open the crate. The glowing metal lamp, stained from its centuries in the clay, was intact and waiting. He didn't need an army, real or terra-cotta. He was now in possession of the ultimate weapon.

27

AS THEY WAITED, REESE WENT through every drawer and cupboard in Professor Ellison's kitchen.

"I have never seen so much food outside of a grocery store," she said, amazed. "Potato chips, shrimp, Ding Dongs, fresh Bundt cake, herbs and spices I've never even heard of, frozen pizza bagels, one-pound tins of caviar, hot dogs. It doesn't even make any sense!"

Like the rest of the house, the kitchen was immense, immaculate, and imposing. The refrigerator and the stove were stainless steel. Parker and Fon-Rahm were dwarfed at a table that seated twelve. There were lush flowers and bowls of fresh fruit, but somehow the room still seemed cold and sterile. The kitchen at the Merritts' house was a jumble of pots and pans and random silverware. The refrigerator made so much noise they had nicknamed it the Beast. The stove was old and the sink didn't always drain right. It was small, but it was alive. It was Parker's favorite room in the house.

Reese got on her hands and knees and crawled deeper into a low cabinet. Her voice was muffled. "How would Professor Ellison ever eat all this stuff before it went bad? Maybe it's magic! Instead of shopping she just conjures up a ton of food every week. She has five different kinds of peanut butter! And look!" Reese backed out of the cupboard with a colorful box labeled in Cantonese. "Cookies from China! Do you want to try some, Parker?"

"I'm not hungry."

"You're not *hungry*? Come on, you're *always* hungry. One time I saw you eat an entire box of croutons."

"Yeah, well, I'm not hungry *now*."

"Ooooooooookay." Reese cracked open the cookie box and sat heavily next to Parker at the table. After a minute's silence she said, "I don't suppose you want to go over the plan again?"

Parker snorted. Professor Ellison had made them repeat the plan over and over again until they knew every step by heart. It wasn't complicated. They would see Vesiroth and Duncan and their army of Path goons as soon as they got anywhere near the house. The defenses would be triggered, hopefully taking out some of the Path members. While Fon-Rahm battled the Path, Vesiroth would probe the house and find that the weakest link was simply the front door. Working as a tag team, Reese and Parker would lead Vesiroth through the house and to the trap in the library, where Theo and Professor Ellison would be waiting with the final piece of the Helm as irresistible bait. Everyone had a part to play.

Reese took a curious bite out of a cookie. "So," she said with her mouth full, "I told my mom I was going to a lecture at the university. On number theory, whatever that is." Reese knew all about number theory. She just didn't want Parker to feel dumb. "Did you guys have any trouble getting away?"

"No. It was fine." In fact, it had been awful. Parker had come up empty when he searched for the other part of the Babel Stone in his dad's stuff, but he still didn't know what to believe. It seemed to Parker like his dad was acting more suspiciously every day. When Parker laid out an elaborate scenario about an all-day paintball party he and Theo were supposedly invited to, his mom bought it but J.T. asked a million questions. Who was going to be there? When would they be home? Who was driving them? When he couldn't take it anymore Parker blew up at J.T. and the dinner turned into a full-on screaming match. Why was J.T. always poking his nose into everything? In the end it had been a minor miracle that Parker and Theo were allowed out of the house at all.

Parker had stayed quiet since the moment they set foot in the professor's house. He and his cousin had barely spoken to each other before Theo left with Ellison. They could all see something was wrong.

"Well, I for one am in trouble if Vesiroth *doesn't* show up today," said Reese. "Ironic, isn't it? If he does come, it's possible he'll kill me, but if he doesn't show up, my mom will *definitely* kill me." She took a bite out of a brown cookie. "How do we know he won't wait a week? Or a month? Why is Professor Ellison so sure it's going to be today?"

"The professor has her ways." Fon-Rahm kept his eyes on

Parker. "Vesiroth is not the only one with confederates in the world of magic."

Reese said, "Great. Professor Ellison has spies." Parker's eyes jumped at the word, but Reese kept eating, oblivious. "I guess I should have expected that."

"I don't know why everybody's okay with her all of a sudden," said Parker. "Am I the only one who remembers what happened the last time we put our lives in her hands?"

Reese closed the box of cookies. "I don't know. With everything that's going on . . . you have to trust somebody."

Parker stared off. "No, you don't."

Reese looked to Parker and then to the genie. Something was not right. "Whatever. These cookies are terrible, by the way." She looked more carefully at the cartoon dog on the box. "Wait. Are these *dog biscuits?*"

As Parker stewed, Theo and Professor Ellison walked the endless halls.

"Careful where you step," the professor said. Theo looked down and saw a silver wire running between the walls about six inches off the ground. "I've prepared a few surprises for our friend Vesiroth and I'd hate to see them activated ahead of time."

"Booby traps? What about Parker and Reese? Aren't you worried they'll set one of these things off?"

"Parker and Reese will have to pay very close attention. It would almost be better if they were off somewhere and out of the way, don't you think?" Professor Ellison made a slight adjustment to the tripwire. Theo didn't even want to know what would have happened if he had broken it. "All we have to do is get him to the library. He'll be able to see the containment room from there, and he won't be able to resist the Helm."

"How does the trap work?"

Professor Ellison stopped walking and pointed at the library doors. "The entire room is a magic circle designed to separate a magician from the Nexus. It's an ancient spell and it took me days to prepare. Vesiroth taught it to me himself. The trick is, the wizard must step inside the ring voluntarily."

"What happens to him once he's in there?"

"He stays in there until someone lets him out."

"You mean he'll be a prisoner here? Forever?"

"Yes. Well, until I can find something else to do with him." She seemed far away.

"Professor Ellison? When I get good, I mean, really good at magic, will I live forever?"

"I hope not." She turned her eyes to her protégé. "Have you ever been to the Grand Canyon?"

The question threw Theo. "Um, no. My dad talks about taking us, but, you know, money's been tight and..." He realized that Ellison didn't care. "I saw a movie about it once."

"Fine. I want you to close your eyes and picture the Grand Canyon in your mind." Theo shut his eyes. "You're standing above it, and it goes on for hundreds of miles in every direction. It is far deeper than the largest building in the world is tall. It is a hole of almost immeasurable size. Can you see it?"

Theo nodded. He could.

"Now I want you to imagine that once every thousand years, you are allowed to throw one grain of sand into the Grand

Canyon. Do you think it will take a long time to fill the canyon with sand?"

"Well, yeah! It would take eternity."

"That's the thing, Theo. It won't. Eternity is doing that a hundred thousand times and then a hundred thousand times more and a hundred thousand times more. Our minds cannot even comprehend the brutality that is forever." Theo opened his eyes to find Professor Ellison looking at him with something that might be defined as affection. "I have lived a very, very long time. That is nothing compared to eternity, and it is still horrific. Everyone I have ever loved has died; every place I have ever known has changed beyond recognition. I have no friends. I have no family. I have no home. I won't live forever, thank the stars. I'm beginning to see the end even now, and in some ways, I welcome it." She put her hand on Theo's shoulder. "I wish for you a long life, Theo, and a good one. My hope is that you'll die an old man of a hundred and two and not a century more."

She let her hand linger for a moment on Theo's shoulder before she turned on her heel and started the long walk back to join the others.

Two black SUVs pulled to a stop by the side of the road within eyeshot of Professor Ellison's modest farmhouse. "We shall wait here," said Vesiroth, staring at the house from the front passenger seat of the lead truck.

The Path driver nodded and signaled to the truck behind them.

"If we're going in we might as well do it now," Duncan said from the backseat.

"Stop. Savor this moment. We may not face a foe like Tarinn again. Enjoy the calm before the storm."

"Whatever you say, boss." He popped his gum and looked out the window. "I still think it was a mistake to not bring more men. Us and three guys? I can't see how it would hurt to have backup."

"The members of the Path are loyal but weak. They would only be underfoot. I really only need the one." Vesiroth gave the taciturn driver a once-over. "But it's nice to have a few spares."

"The professor will be ready for us. If we did this in a week, or a month, she'd have let down her guard a little. Nobody can stay at red alert forever."

"You don't understand"—Vesiroth turned his scarred features to face Duncan—"because you have faced uncertainty before. I have not. Tarinn and Fon-Rahm wait in that house with the object I need to take control of the entire world. They know we're coming and they'll be ready for us. We have the power of righteousness on our side, plus I have arranged a little surprise for Fon-Rahm. It might be enough, but, then again, it might not. I remain weak. We may very well fail. The prospect fills me with excitement." His mouth twisted into a grim smile. "Whether we win or lose, this promises to be a day to remember."

28

THEO STARED AT THE MONITORS.
Vesiroth was out there, somewhere, waiting in the shadows,
dreaming of a world without war and a world without freedom.

"Anything?" As Parker walked into the room with Fon-Rahm
and Reese, he didn't even try to catch Theo's eye. Things were
still tense between the two cousins.

"Not yet." Theo rubbed his eyes. He took a quick look around
the massive room with its priceless works of art and its endless
dimensions. Were they really a match for Vesiroth? Fon-Rahm
was hurt, Professor Ellison seemed unsure for the first time since
he had known her, Reese was in way over her head, Parker was
refusing to see reality, and Theo himself was just a student. They
weren't exactly an unstoppable force. And what if Vesiroth had
learned everything he needed to know from his spy?

Theo leaned into one of the monitors. Did he just see something move? Yes! There, by the side of the house. Someone was sneaking up the lawn.

"Get Professor Ellison!" Theo yelled.

Reese and Parker were there in a heartbeat. "What is it?" Reese asked.

"It's starting. Look!"

Parker and Reese concentrated on the monitor. The figure took one more step toward the house and stopped. He looked down at his feet like something was wrong. Then vines erupted out of the ground and wrapped around his body.

"Yes! Got him!" Theo shouted.

Reese asked, "What will happen to him?"

"Well, if the last time was any indication, something really unpleasant."

"Wait a second." Parker squinted at the screen. "It's not Vesiroth, and anybody from the Path would be wearing a suit. That guy is…" Parker froze. "Holy crap."

Before Theo could hold him back, Parker was heading for the door. "Parker! Come back! This is all in the plan!"

"No, it isn't!" As he ran, Parker shouted, "Fon-Rahm! I wish I had a samurai sword!"

Parker rushed out the front door of the house, the sword materializing in his hands. He knew he was screwing up Professor Ellison's plans, but he also knew he didn't have a choice.

Fon-Rahm followed him out, on the lookout for any movement from the enemy. "Be careful, Parker. We do not know who this man is."

Parker reached the figure struggling on the lawn. "I know who it is!" The vines covered the man's face and wrapped him up from head to toe, but Parker would have recognized the shoes and the hair anywhere.

"Just stand still and don't move," Parker said. He raised the sword and let it rip, but he checked his swing right before he made contact. "Um, also I wish I knew how to use a samurai sword!" Fon-Rahm made it so, and the wisdom of thousands of hours of intense practice shot into Parker's brain. He tried the swing again. This time, the razor-sharp blade sliced through the woody green vines and stopped within atoms of making contact with something human. The leafy bonds fell away, revealing a stunned J.T.

"What...what just happened to me?" J.T. asked.

Parker cut away more vines creeping out of the ground. "You got caught. What are you doing here, Dad?"

"I followed you! I knew something was going on, but I never thought..." He stared at the genie in his flowing black robes.

Fon-Rahm said, "We must get inside the house."

J.T. asked, "Why? What's going on here, Parker? What's *he* doing here? What in the heck is he *wearing*?"

"We must hurry. Danger approaches." Fon-Rahm pointed. Duncan was lazily skateboarding down the driveway and toward the house.

"You *know* what's going on, Dad. Stop pretending."

"Parker, I..."

Duncan stopped, popped a bubble with his gum and waved. "Who's that little kid?"

"Later, Dad. Get inside. Now!"

Fon-Rahm and the two Quarrys ran full speed for the house.

J.T. looked over his shoulder just as Duncan thrust his arms out. Parker pushed his dad through the open door and down to the ground as a deadly cloud of razor-tipped arrows arced over their heads and embedded themselves into the floor of the house.

Fon-Rahm slammed the door shut. Duncan's next barrage bounced harmlessly off the house's exterior.

"The attack has begun," said Fon-Rahm.

Professor Ellison stared icily at the man on the floor. "And we're lucky these two idiots didn't give up the whole game."

Parker jumped up from the floor. "I had to save him. Vesiroth would have killed him if your vines didn't!"

J.T. finally stuck his head up. "Okay, I give up. What in holy heck is a Vesiroth?"

Duncan skated back to the road where Vesiroth was waiting. "Another five seconds and I would've had 'em."

The burned skin on Vesiroth's face constricted as he smiled. "Your arrows would have no effect on the first of the Jinn, and the boy is of no concern to me. This house, though . . ." He probed the air with his hands. "It's magnificent. My protégé camouflages its true dimensions with a cloaking spell. It's very clever. Tarinn hides among the peasants in plain sight."

"Whatever. You want me to lob some more blades at it?"

"That would be a waste of time and energy. We will not breach this house with your paltry gimmicks."

"Then what are we supposed to do, wait them out? That could take weeks."

"We will not have to. They will bring the Helm to us."

"Oh, yeah? Why would they do that?"

Vesiroth abruptly turned away from the house and began walking toward the black SUVs. "Have your men bring the package. It's time to see just how seriously Fon-Rahm takes his precious ideals."

J.T. stood up and took the house in. "Wow. This place looks a lot smaller from the outside."

Reese cleared her throat. "Mr. Quarry, um, this is our friend Professor Ellison. She works at the university with Theo's dad. And Mr. Rommy is..." Reese trailed off. Fon-Rahm was wearing his robes and floating six inches off the ground. J.T. had been attacked by sentient vines and then barely escaped a stream of arrows shot at them by a homicidal ten-year-old. There was no explaining this.

"Don't bother, Reese," Theo said. "He knows exactly what's happening."

"How would he know?" asked Reese.

Parker said, "He knows because he's a spy."

Professor Ellison turned from the window. "What's all this about a spy?"

Theo turned red. "Well, um, we, Parker and me, we found this thing, the Babel Stone? In the barn? And we think that somebody planted it on one of us, to, you know. Spy on us."

"The Babel Stone? And you didn't think this should be brought to my attention?" The professor's voice was ice. "The fate of the world is at stake here, Theo, or have you forgotten?"

"No! I know! It's just that we didn't know who the spy was, and you can be a little, you know. Harsh. We thought you would shut us out."

"As indeed I would have! You have put three thousand years of work at risk!"

J.T. said, "Wait. Did she say three *thousand* years?"

"Shut up, man." Professor Ellison glared at J.T. "What exactly did Vesiroth pay you to sell out the entire human race?"

"Wait. Wait." Reese said. "Hold on. This *can't* be true. He's Parker's *dad*."

Theo crossed his arms in anger. "Yeah, and he's been watching our every move for days, maybe weeks. He's been lying right to our faces."

"It's what he's best at," said Parker.

Reese, Fon-Rahm, Theo, Ellison, and his own son surrounded J.T. He did not like the look in their eyes.

"Okay. Okay." J.T. held his hands up. "I'm not sure what I've stumbled into here but I'm not a spy. I swear. I don't know who this Vesiroth is and I don't know what he wants and I don't care. I just wanted to make sure my son was safe. And he's clearly not." He puffed up his chest and stood toe to toe with Fon-Rahm. "What have you dragged Parker into, Rommy?"

"It is not as you believe, Mr. Quarry."

"Yeah? Because what I believe is that you've put my son's life in danger. That crazy kid outside is trying to kill him!"

Parker crossed his arms. "So you didn't plant the Babel Stone."

"I don't know what a Babel Stone is!"

"Why should I believe you, Dad? You've done nothing but lie to me my whole life!"

"Parker, I know I..." J.T. stopped. He wished he was alone with his son instead of surrounded by kids and strangers. "I may not have told you a hundred percent of the truth about absolutely everything, okay, but I'm not lying." He stared at the genie. "*I* would never do anything to hurt you. You're my son."

"Yeah, I know what that's worth."

"I haven't been a perfect father. Fine. But whatever else I am, I'm not a spy! You have to believe me!"

Parker didn't know what to believe. He loved his father, but someone was spying on them. If it wasn't J.T., who was it?

"Fon-Rahm!"

The voice came from outside. They all rushed to a window and looked out.

Vesiroth stood on the lawn, alone. His hands were crossed behind his back. If it weren't for his impeccable black suit and his scarred face, he could have just been a man out enjoying a sunny New Hampshire day.

"That's him? That's Vesiroth?" Reese said.

Theo said, "He doesn't look so tough. He's just a guy with a scarred face."

Parker shook his head. "He's a lot more than that."

Vesiroth called again. "I wait, first of the Jinn."

"Are you going to answer him?" Reese asked Fon-Rahm.

"I will if my master commands it."

J.T. said, "Your *master*?"

Vesiroth turned his face to the sun. "Come now, Fon-Rahm. Is it too much to ask that you have a conversation with your maker?" As he spoke, the vines beneath him shot up to encircle his legs. Vesiroth casually touched the silver spike at his neck. The vines instantly withered and died.

Parker nodded at his genie.

Fon-Rahm spoke. "I hear you, Vesiroth. What do you propose?"

"A trade."

"And what shall we trade, creator?"

"You will trade me the third piece of the Helm."

Reese shook her head. "Well, that's never going to happen."

Fon-Rahm said, "And what will you give me in return?"

Vesiroth gestured to someone behind him. A Path member brought a struggling Naomi to his boss, a knife at her throat.

"How about the life of this human girl?"

29

"GO AHEAD AND KILL HER," PROFESSOR
Ellison shouted.

"No!" said Reese. "You can't let Naomi die!"

"Why not? She was stupid enough to be taken hostage."

"It's not her fault! This doesn't have anything to do with her!"

Out the window they watched as Naomi struggled against the
Path member who held her. A knife glinted at her throat.

"We all know where Tarinn stands, Fon-Rahm," Vesiroth
said. "But you . . . you are a different proposition altogether. You
could destroy her if you wanted to. You could kill her and you
could give me what I want."

Professor Ellison turned her eyes to Fon-Rahm and huffed.
"I'd like to see you try."

"Tarinn has lived centuries, enough lifetimes for any fifty

people. This girl, though..." Vesiroth ran his hand through Naomi's hair. Naomi pulled away in revulsion. "She's so *new*. Doesn't she deserve a chance to live a full life?"

"Please, Fon-Rahm," Reese pleaded. "Please. Don't let my friend die!"

Everything that made Fon-Rahm what he was screamed out to save this innocent girl. But he more than anyone else knew that the wizard Vesiroth would stop at nothing to achieve his aims. In his hands the completed Helm would be an instrument of chaotic destruction. "Parker," he said, "I cannot give him the Helm, and I cannot let Naomi be destroyed."

Parker turned the problem over in his head, the weight of the entire world crushing his seventh-grade frame. Suddenly the riddle in the catacombs seemed like something out of a kids' book. "Dude, I have no idea what to do."

All eyes were on Fon-Rahm as he thought. Finally, the genie spoke. "Vesiroth! I cannot bring you what you ask for. But I offer something else in exchange for this girl's safe passage."

"Oh? And what else do you have that I want?"

"I will trade myself."

Parker felt like he had been kicked in the stomach. "You can't do that! I won't let you! I command you to stay!"

"That is a command I cannot obey, my master."

"You're a fool, Fon-Rahm." Professor Ellison snorted in disgust. "Vesiroth will kill you, or worse. You've played right into his hands."

"Perhaps," Fon-Rahm said. "But I have made my choice."

* * *

"Look at that," Vesiroth said to his squirming hostage. "It's almost as if Fon-Rahm truly cares whether you live or die."

"What good is he to us?" Duncan asked. "I thought the whole point was to get the Helm."

"He was never going to give us the Helm. I just wanted to see how softhearted he really is." He shouted to the house. "I am not interested in combat with you, Fon-Rahm. I know what you're capable of. I built you myself."

Fon-Rahm answered. "I will not harm you, creator. You have my word."

"You have a deal, Fon-Rahm. If you give yourself to me, I will guarantee this child safe passage." The scarred wizard cackled to Duncan. "Amazing, isn't it? My genie is willing to risk extinction to gain this ridiculous girl a few more hours of life." His eyes turned dark. "And now we get to make him squirm."

Parker shook his head and crossed his arms over his chest. "No. I can't let you do this. We just have to think of something else, that's all, some other idea . . ."

"You and I both know that there is no other way, Parker," Fon-Rahm said. "And now I must command *you*."

"What is it, Fon-Rahm?" Parker didn't want the genie to see he was about to cry.

"I command you to be brave." The genie rested his hand on Parker's shoulder. "What happens to me is of no importance. You must be steadfast and you must place your faith in Professor Ellison. If you remain strong, everything will be all right. Things will be..." He searched for the right words. "Totally tubular."

Parker stifled a laugh. As the genie went to the door, Parker wrapped him in a hug. "Be careful, Fon-Rahm. Be careful and come back to us."

Fon-Rahm looked deep into Parker's eyes. "As you wish, master." Then he opened the door and stepped outside.

Vesiroth saw the door open. "Let her go." The Path member released his grip and Naomi ran to Fon-Rahm. She embraced the genie as hard as she could.

"Mr. Rommy, what's happening? Who are these psychos? Why are you wearing this..."

She stopped talking and looked down. Her math teacher was floating six inches above the ground.

"I am not who you think me to be," he said. "But know that, in my way, I am your friend." Fon-Rahm released her. "Go to the house. I have business with my father."

Naomi ran to the house and into her best friend's arms.

"I'm so sorry, Naomi," said Reese, close to tears. "I'm so sorry I got you dragged into this."

Naomi just stared out the open doorway, watching in awe as Fon-Rahm floated to Vesiroth. "He's not even scared," she whispered. "He sacrificed himself for me and he's not even scared."

Fon-Rahm reached the scarred wizard. "My firstborn returns to me at last," said Vesiroth.

The genie stared straight ahead. "I am here as you bade me to be here."

"Yes, and as helpless as a kitten. It must gall you, Fon-Rahm. The might of ages pulses inside you and yet you must abide by your promise not to harm me."

"Do your worst, creator."

"Oh, don't worry," said Vesiroth with an evil grin. "I intend to."

30

FON-RAHM WAS THE ONE BEING tortured, but Parker felt every blow.

The mighty genie was hovering, helpless, two feet off the ground. Vesiroth's silver spike concentrated his power and delivered wave after wave of pure pain to Fon-Rahm's injured left arm while Duncan watched with a gleam in his eye.

"He should fight back!" Theo said.

"He promised Vesiroth that he wouldn't," said Reese, clasping the hand of her shell-shocked best friend, Naomi. "You know Fon-Rahm would never go back on his word, no matter what."

Professor Ellison shook her head. "His weakness put us all in danger. He could end this now with one bolt of lightning."

"You would do it, and I would, too." Parker buried his head

in his hands. He couldn't stand to see Fon-Rahm abused. "But Fon-Rahm wouldn't kill anyone, even Vesiroth, unless he absolutely had to. He's better than all of us."

J.T. just stood back, as if he was way, *way* out of their depth. "I knew there was something weird about that math teacher," he said.

Vesiroth yelled into the house. "This is your mighty Fon-Rahm, the first of the Jinn. He is supposed to be the most powerful creature on the planet, and to me he is a mere puppet." The wizard delivered another burst of concentrated agony to the genie. Fon-Rahm contorted in torment. "What chance do the rest of you have against me? No one need die here. Bring me the Helm and stand aside as I fulfill my destiny as mankind's savior."

"Do not . . . do not listen to him," said Fon-Rahm through the fog of his own anguish. "Keep the Helm safe. Bow to no man."

"Be quiet, Fon-Rahm. This is between Tarinn and me." Vesiroth raised his hand and cast another salvo of red-hot energy at Fon-Rahm.

"What are those things?" Theo asked, nodding out to the lawn. Parker got himself together and returned to the window. The Path members were assembling metal staffs of some kind, topped with globes of pure jade.

"I don't know," admitted the professor. "I've never seen anything like them."

"Last chance," shouted Vesiroth. "As much as I do enjoy spending time with family, my patience wears thin. Bring me the Helm or watch Fon-Rahm be destroyed."

"Don't let him kill you!" Reese called out, near tears. "Break your promise! He would never keep his! Fight back, Fon-Rahm! *Fight back!*"

Professor Ellison put her hand on Reese's shoulder. "He made his decision, dear. We might not agree with it, but you have to admit he's consistent."

The Path members held their assembled staffs at the ready.

"So be it," said Vesiroth. "This is what it looks like when an immortal dies." At Vesiroth's command the jade globes on the elaborate metal rods began to glow green. When the light from the staffs hit Fon-Rahm, the genie writhed in absolute agony. The bruise-colored web that marked the infection in his arm had spread to cover the genie's shoulders and half of his face. He was being pulled apart.

"I guess we know what those poles are for." Theo stared at the floor. "They're a genie-killing machine."

Parker closed his eyes. Fon-Rahm had told him once that it didn't matter if they were together or not. If Parker wanted something, all he had to do was wish for it. Parker wanted something. He wished for it.

And Fon-Rahm vanished in a puff of smoke.

"What . . . what is this?" stammered Vesiroth. There was empty air where Fon-Rahm once hung. The two Path members looked at the globes of their staffs, as if they had somehow managed to vaporize the genie by accident.

Parker yelled out, "Fon-Rahm promised not to hurt you, but he never promised he would stick around. I wished he would escape and he did."

"The child speaks! This is your doing, then?"

"Why not? I'm insolent and all that."

"You made him teleport?" Theo said, the hope draining from his face. "Parker, Fon-Rahm can't teleport in his condition! He could wind up in the middle of a volcano!"

"Anywhere's better than here." Parker wanted more than anything to be right. "All we can do is hope he's okay, wherever he is."

Outside, Vesiroth fumed. "Get me the pieces of my Helm," he snapped.

"I don't know, boss," said Duncan. "The Helm's super unpredictable."

The wizard grabbed the ten-year-old by the collar and threw him to the ground. "Get me my Helm!"

Duncan glared at his boss. For a split second it seemed as if he were going to defy him. Then he reached into a bag filled with weapons and handed the two separate pieces of the metal helmet up to Vesiroth.

The wizard snatched them and held them high enough for everyone in the house to see. "Do you see this, Tarinn? This is just a taste of what's to come." Vesiroth jammed the two pieces of pounded brass together. "Consider it a preview of your own death!"

When she saw the two pieces of the Helm in Vesiroth's hands, Professor Ellison snapped into action. "Okay. Theo, all of you. Come with me."

Reese and Theo chased after her into the bowels of the enormous house. Reese had to practically drag Naomi and J.T. along.

"Where are we going, Professor?" asked Theo. "Shouldn't we try to counteract Vesiroth's Helm somehow?"

Ellison never broke stride. "With what, pray tell? Are you hiding something special in your little bag that I don't know about?"

"Well, no, but—"

"Then please do not discuss things you know nothing about." She stopped abruptly at a door Theo had never seen before. He wasn't even sure what part of the house they were in. "Everyone," she said, holding the door open, "inside, quickly."

Reese poked her head warily into the room. It was unfurnished, just a blank white space in the middle of nowhere. "Why? What is this place?"

"It's a safe room, girl. The walls are thick and the room is cloaked. Vesiroth wouldn't be able to find it even if he knew what he was looking for, and he doesn't."

"But if we're in here—"

"Just get in. I'll explain everything to you when we're all inside."

Outside, Vesiroth put the two pieces of the Helm against his head. The black tentacles that emerged were thicker and more chaotic than ever, lashing out in all directions. Finally, they found the true dimensions of Professor Ellison's house. With a strange viciousness they attacked, probing for weak spots. They began to batter the outside of the house.

"Well, will you look at that?" said Duncan between chomps of his gum. The glamour hiding the house was failing under the onslaught. Glimpses of the house's true nature were flashing through.

* * *

Reese walked into the room. Parker, J.T., and Naomi followed her.

Professor Ellison stopped Theo before he stepped inside. "Thank you," she said as she slammed the door shut and locked it from the outside.

Parker pounded on the windowless door. "Professor Ellison! What are you doing?"

"I'm getting you out of the way," said the Professor. "Come on, Theo. You and I have work to do."

"But . . . we can't just leave them here!"

"Of course we can."

"What about the plan? We need Parker and Reese to get Vesiroth to the library and the containment room!"

"Luckily for all of us, I have prepared a contingency plan."

"You were never going to use them. This whole time you were going to lock them in there."

Professor Ellison stared into Theo's eyes. "Parker and Reese are not like us, Theo. They would just be in the way."

"Is it really a safe room? Are they really hidden from Vesiroth in there?"

The professor strode away. "Does it matter? If Vesiroth takes the house we're all dead anyway."

Theo hated to leave his friends behind, but he had work to do. He pressed his palm to the locked door for a brief moment. Then he turned and ran to catch up with his mentor.

Finally, Professor Ellison's glamour spell gave way and the house was laid bare for all to see. The quaint farmhouse was gone. In its place was an ugly gray nightmare of concrete and steel that stretched in all directions.

"Whoa," said Duncan. "That is one ugly building."

Vesiroth wasn't listening to him. He removed the pieces of the helmet from his head and handed them to Duncan. Then he approached the massive slab of metal that was the house's true front door. With the force of will that had been driving him for thousands of years he placed one hand on the door and one on the metal spike that hung at his neck.

The door began to melt.

Duncan put the pieces of the Helm into a black bag he hoisted over his shoulder. The clang of the brass shards against the glowing metal cylinders inside was masked by the sound of Professor Ellison's door falling off its hinges.

31

THE INTERNATIONAL SPACE STATION
orbits three hundred miles above the Earth and travels at almost
five miles per second. It has been called the most complicated
piece of machinery ever built by man, a miracle of engineering
that took years and the cooperation of multiple rival space agen-
cies from all over the world to build. The ISS was an achievement
for the ages, and, as Dr. Momoko Nakagawa had learned, there
was always something wrong with it.

Dr. Nakagawa checked the instruments once again and got the
same result. "That's a negative on the diagnostics test. It could
just be a blown sensor."

The voice on her headset agreed. "It's not mission critical.
Sergei can check it on his EVA tomorrow morning. Looks like
your drink is getting away."

Dr. Nakagawa shot her hand out and caught the silvery pouch before it floated into something important. This was her second week in orbit, but she was still getting used to zero gravity. "Thanks." She smiled at the camera. "I don't want to be the one to short out the electrical system in a hundred-billion-dollar spacecraft. I'm going to run the second cycle again and then I'm calling it a day." She stifled a yawn. The other five members of the crew were already asleep in the next module, but with video feeds to NASA's mission control center in Florida, she was never really alone.

"That's affirmative. Talk to you at oh-four-hundred."

Dr. Nakagawa pushed off from her computer and floated over to the window. Earth zipped by below, a blue marble in a sea of velvety blackness. Everything, the years of school, the missed parties, the countless hours spent in libraries and simulators, the hundreds of tests, it was all worth it for this view.

And then the lights flickered.

Dr. Nakagawa scrambled back to her computer. "Mission control? Did you see that?"

"We saw it. Just an electrical glitch."

"Affirmative. I should probably run a few checks just to make—"

"Um, Dr. Nakagawa?"

"Yes?"

"Your hair is standing on end."

Dr. Nakagawa ran a hand through her hair. Mission control was right. It was as if the air was suddenly filled with static electricity. "That's odd. I suppose it could be some kind of loop in the relays. . . ."

There was a flash of light and a burst of ozone.

"Oww! What..." Dr. Nakagawa rubbed at her eyes. When she finally got them open she saw a tall figure in flowing robes floating in front of her.

"Where am I?" Fon-Rahm asked. He was clutching his left arm and seemed disoriented.

"Um," said Dr. Nakagawa, "the International Space Station?"

Fon-Rahm looked out the window and saw his home planet from orbit. He had wound up as far from Parker as he could have possibly imagined. He clenched his jaw and turned back to Dr. Nakagawa. "I must return to the professor's house. How do I escape this metal room?"

The astronaut pointed blankly to an air lock behind the genie. She had the stunned look of someone caught in a very weird dream.

Fon-Rahm quickly examined the contraption. He opened the first air-lock door and closed it behind him. One more door was all that separated him from the vacuum of deep space. The genie flexed his arms to assess the damage Vesiroth had done to his body and without another word opened the thin aluminum door and launched himself into space with a flash of blue lightning.

It took Dr. Nakagawa a moment to gather her thoughts. "Mission control? Did you...see any of that?"

"You mean the guy in the blue robes who just appeared in our space station? No." The voice in Dr. Nakagawa's headset paused. "And neither did you."

"But..."

"Some things just get filed away. Come on, Doctor. Do you think NASA tells the public about everything we see in space?"

Vesiroth took an unsteady step into Professor Ellison's house.

He hadn't expected to use the Helm so early. That, combined with the energy it had taken to torture Fon-Rahm and melt Professor Ellison's front door, had left him depleted and weak. It was a tactical error. He had let his emotions get the better of him and now he was forced to lean on his second-in-command.

"Need a hand there, boss?" Duncan asked.

Vesiroth sneered. Was that a hint of contempt he heard in Duncan's voice? When he had the rest of the Helm he wouldn't need Duncan at all.

Duncan helped Vesiroth gingerly around the melted metal that was once Ellison's door and pointed to two of the three Path members. "Okay. You stay with us. And keep your staffs ready. We might need 'em." He strapped his skateboard to his back and pointed to the remaining man. "You go in and kill anything that moves."

Vesiroth, Duncan, and the other two zealots made their way deeper into the house. One of the Path members took a step forward, his globed staff raised, but Duncan held him back. "Watch where you step, genius," he said, gesturing to the silver wire stretched across the hall. "There are booby traps all over the place."

"We stop for nothing," said Vesiroth as he stepped over the wire. "We keep moving until we find the Helm and establish my throne."

"And keep on your toes, Vesiroth," said the disembodied voice of Professor Ellison. She was speaking through an intercom system that ran through the entire house. "I've had days to prepare."

Vesiroth smirked. "Ah, Tarinn. Afraid to face me?"

"I'm not stupid, if that's what you mean."

Professor Ellison and Theo were holed up in the house's control center, a lead-lined room set deep in the center of the building. The only door was disguised with a spell that made it virtually invisible. The room was stocked with state-of-the-art monitors that showed every angle of the sprawling house, inside and out. Theo kept one eye nervously on the video feed showing Parker, Reese, J.T., and Naomi. Ellison had other things to worry about.

"You look tired, Vesiroth," she said as she watched the wizard being helped along by Duncan. "It's not too late for you to turn around and go lick your wounds."

"I am strong enough to kill you, my dear."

Theo turned his attention to Vesiroth. The dark wizard was limping but he was still terrifying. The only other person Theo had met who was so clear of purpose was Professor Ellison herself. He knew that Vesiroth would kill him or Parker or half of humanity to get his way. He wondered, not for the first time, if they had made a huge mistake in luring him here.

"So you've said," said the professor. "Ah! And Duncan. Welcome. Feel free to make yourself at home. If you're very good, I'll read you a story when it's your bedtime."

"Keep talking, Ellison. Sooner or later it'll be you and me. . . ." Duncan halted abruptly, stopping Vesiroth and the two Path goons behind him. He examined the hallway for a moment before conjuring up a glimmering long sword and carefully tripping an electric eye rigged in the hall. A trap sprang, freeing massive magical sledgehammers to swing down from the ceiling and smash straight through the walls with a deafening crunch. If they had walked even two steps farther Duncan and his boss would have been crushed by thousands of pounds of swinging metal.

"Your preparations mean nothing to me, Tarinn." Vesiroth cackled. "You cannot hope to stop me."

"We'll see. In the meantime, don't look down."

"What..." Vesiroth and Duncan felt something shift below them and jumped forward as the floor dropped away, taking one of the Path members with it. He fell screaming down a hole that led straight into blackness and fire.

Duncan shifted his sword to his other hand and hefted the metal staff the man had been carrying. "You were right," he told Vesiroth. "We did need a spare."

They kept walking. Theo saw they were headed straight for the library.

J.T. threw his weight against the locked door once more. It didn't pop open, just like it didn't pop open the first six times he tried it.

"Give it up, Dad, the door's not going to open." Parker, Reese, and Naomi were sitting on the white floor, their backs against a wall.

"I'm going to give it one more shot," J.T. said. "I think I felt a little give that time."

"If anything gives, it's probably going to be your shoulder."

J.T. tried the door again. The seventh time wasn't a charm. He gave up and slumped down the wall next to his son. "Some friends you've got. Theo and that woman locked us in here and threw away the key."

"Don't say 'that woman' like you don't know who she is," said Reese. "Apparently you know all about everything."

"I'm not a spy! How many times do I have to tell you that?"

"Whatever." Reese clasped tightly to her friend's hand. Naomi still seemed shell-shocked. "None of this will matter if we can't find a way out of this room."

"There *is* no way out of this room," said Parker.

Reese said, "You don't know that. There might be a secret door, or a magic ceiling. Professor Ellison's too smart to not give herself options."

"I think my son's right." J.T. rubbed the shoulder he was using as a battering ram. "We're in here for the duration."

Parker closed his eyes and let his head bang against the wall. Then his eyes popped back open again.

"Um, guys," he said, inching away. "I think we all ought to move away from the wall. Like, really far away."

"Why?" asked J.T.

Reese stood and pulled Naomi gently into the center of the room. "When Parker says stuff like that, it's better to move first and ask questions later."

Then a fist crackling with blue electricity simply punched through the brick and metal of the wall. Fon-Rahm reached in and tore the bricks apart as if they were made of cotton candy.

"Jeez, Fon-Rahm!" Parker said with a grin. "What took you so long?"

Out in the hall, the Path member roaming on his own heard a small explosion. He swung around and headed in the general direction of the sound. He had been walking around for almost fifteen minutes and he had yet to shoot anybody. He was getting antsy.

* * *

Using his one good arm, Fon-Rahm helped Naomi and Reese across the ruined wall of the safe room. "We have no time to lose," the genie said. "I must find Vesiroth and join the battle."

"Fon-Rahm, you look terrible," Parker said. The blue-black infection had taken over almost every bit of the genie's visible skin. "The infection from your arm has spread *everywhere*."

"It matters not. I must go." The genie looked to J.T. "Mr. Quarry. I know I have given you many reasons to distrust me."

"That's true," J.T. said.

"I ask you to set that aside and put your faith in me now. You must lead this group out of this house and to safety."

Parker snorted. "You're not getting rid of me so easily, buddy. Where you go, I go."

The genie whirled on his master, mist coming from eyes that had suddenly turned as black as polished onyx. "You will do as I say!" Parker was shocked into silence. Fon-Rahm had never before spoken to him in anger.

"Fon-Rahm, what's gotten into you?" asked Reese. "Since when do you yell at Parker?"

"I . . . I am sorry," the genie said. His eyes returned to their usual light-blue color but his face was contorted with confusion. "I do not understand my own actions."

"It's the infection," said Parker. "It's taken over your entire body and now it's seeping into your mind. You have to stop using your magic before it kills you!"

The first of the Jinn shook his head. "I must act. We all know what is at stake." At this moment, he seemed more human than ever to Parker. "My mind grows thick with fog. You must command me to fight."

Parker knew he had no choice. He put his hands on his genie's arms. "Go. I command you to go. And, you know. Try not to get vaporized."

Fon-Rahm nodded gravely. "Ten-four," he said, before he closed his eyes and oriented himself in the massive house. Then the genie tucked his left arm into his body and charged in a straight line, blowing through walls and leaving a trail of utter destruction behind him.

32

VESIROTH, DUNCAN, AND THE PATH
member thought they had reached the library using their own wits.
In reality, they were herded like cattle through a slaughterhouse.

They easily dodged the column of flame that shot from
the library walls, but the wizard's patience was wearing thin.
He shouted, "You merely delay the inevitable. Show yourself,
Tarinn!"

"Um, boss?" Duncan said, snapping his gum. "I think we got
company." He directed the Path goon and his globed metal staff
to a position by a wall. "You might want to get behind something strong."

"I am Vesiroth, father of titans. I will not cower like a child."

Duncan shrugged and got on his skateboard. "Suit yourself."

At that moment the wall in front of them exploded. Fon-Rahm

stood in a swirl of blue mist, lightning crackling from his eyes and fingertips. Even with his left arm hanging uselessly by his side the genie was a wonder to behold. He was pure power in the shape of a man.

Before the dust even settled Duncan fired a barrage of edged boomerangs at the first of the Jinn. Fon-Rahm tracked their curved paths and cast a glow of electricity meant to melt them in midair. To his surprise, he couldn't hit the boomerangs at all. He finally ducked out of their way and used his good arm to send bolts of lightning back at Duncan. He missed by a good ten feet. He tried again and was even further off the mark.

"Might want to work on your aim, there, killer," Duncan said before he heel-flipped his board behind a row of bookshelves and out of Fon-Rahm's range.

Fon-Rahm was finding it hard to concentrate. It took everything he had to focus on his true target. "Vesiroth! This ends here!"

The dark sorcerer smiled at his creation. "Does our pact no longer stand, Fon-Rahm? I believe you promised you would not attempt to hurt me."

"I propose a new agreement," said the genie. "You give up your mad quest for the Helm and leave here at once."

"And what do I get?"

The first of the Jinn's black eyes misted over with smoke. "You get to survive."

Professor Ellison and Theo watched it all on cameras from their control room deep in the bowels of the house.

"We finally have Vesiroth right where we want him and that idiot genie shows up to fight him," Ellison said. "He'll ruin everything."

"There's something wrong with Fon-Rahm," Theo said. "His eyes look funny. He's not acting right."

"That's not our concern, Theo. Concentrate on the task at hand."

Theo didn't say anything. He turned his attention to another monitor that showed Parker, Reese, J.T., and Naomi in the hall outside their safe room. He made a silent wish to himself that they would leave the house and find their way to safety. Then he made another wish that he was going with them.

"All right. Let's get a move on, guys." J.T. looked down one direction of the endless hallway and then down the other. "I gotta admit, it'd be a lot easier to find our way out of here if this place wasn't the size of the Staples Center."

"I'm not following you anywhere," said Reese.

J.T.'s mouth tightened into a hurt frown. "Come on, Reese. You can trust me."

Reese just looked away.

"Parker! Tell her! Tell her I'm not a spy!"

"Dad, I want to believe you, but..." Parker stopped.

"Parker, look out!" Reese cried, pointing backward. The Path member had finally caught up to them. J.T. instinctively stood in front of his son. The Path henchman raised his rifle and prepared to shoot. Suddenly, a look of sheer terror crossed his face. He dropped his gun and clutched his fists to the side of his head.

Finally, the Path goon fell to the floor. He curled up in a ball and began to sob quietly to himself.

Parker, Reese, and J.T. turned to see Naomi Cook holding a tarnished gold ring high in the air. She looked terrified.

"I think maybe we found our spy," said J.T.

"Um, Professor Ellison? You should probably take a look at this."

Ellison reluctantly turned her attention to Theo's monitor and the drama unfolding among Parker, Reese, J.T., and Naomi. "Exactly how well do you know your little classmate Naomi?"

"Not real well, I guess. Why?"

"Because she appears to be carrying the Ring of Sorrows. I don't suppose you came across it in your studies?"

"Yeah, sure, the Ring of Sorrows. I think it, um . . ." Theo had no idea.

On a normal day Professor Ellison would have let her pupil sweat. This was not a normal day. "It's not important what the ring does. What's important is that I know for a fact who has it."

"Who has it?"

"The U.S. government."

Parker, Reese, and J.T. all stared at Naomi.

"You were *spying* on us?" asked Reese, crestfallen.

Naomi lowered the ring. "It wasn't my idea."

"Did Vesiroth send you?" said Parker.

"If Vesiroth sent me I wouldn't have saved you, would I?" Naomi looked down at the Path member. He was rocking back and forth on the floor and babbling to himself. "The ring is supposed to make you relive the worst thing that ever happened to you, over and over again. That's the first time I ever used something like this."

Parker was furious. "Yeah, sure it is!"

"It is! I never wanted to hurt anybody, not even the enemy!"

"Parker, back off," said J.T. He turned to Naomi. "Take a deep breath and try to calm down. You're shaking."

She was. "I'm not supposed to be here. They told me not to engage but I knew something bad was happening. I couldn't just let you guys walk into a war zone. I can't believe I was dumb enough to let Vesiroth grab me."

"Who sent you? Why are you watching us?"

"Come on, Parker, why do you think?" Naomi gestured to the destroyed walls. "Your friend the math teacher has *superpowers*. Did you think no one would notice? You had to know you couldn't fly under the radar forever. This thing is bigger than just you. It puts the whole planet at risk. We're just trying to do the right thing."

"And who is *we*, exactly?" asked Parker.

"I can't tell you. I'm sorry. But I can say that we're the good guys."

"Of course you are." Parker snorted. "Even Vesiroth thinks he's a good guy."

"Okay. Look, we can sort this all out once we get out of here."

Parker stared straight ahead. "I'm not leaving."

Reese said, "But you promised Fon-Rahm—"

"I know what I promised Fon-Rahm. But I won't leave him here to fight alone. He needs me, even if he doesn't realize it."

J.T. stepped between his son and the trail of rubble that marked Fon-Rahm's path through the house. "Parker, that's out of the question. I have to get you to safety,"

"You can't stop me, Dad. I have to do this."

"Fon-Rahm is a genie, Parker. He might be able to rip down walls with his bare hands but you're just a *kid*."

"It's hard to explain, but . . . he's my responsibility."

"But you can't—"

"I won't argue with you, Dad. I'm going. My friends need me."

J.T. looked at his son. Parker was steadfast and brave. "When I left you seemed so young and small. But now . . . Well, if you're going, I'm going with you."

"Dad—"

"You're *my* kid. I can't let that other guy take all the glory. Besides, buddy, at this point I basically have to. If I show up without you your mom's going to kill me anyways."

Parker felt a flush of pride for his dad. "Dad, I'm sorry I thought you were a spy. I'm sorry I didn't believe in you."

"I know. Don't worry about it, kiddo."

"Well, what about us?" asked Reese.

Parker glared at Naomi. "You have to keep an eye on Naomi."

"I just saved your life," Naomi said. "You still don't trust me?"

"Nope." Parker took a deep breath and climbed over the ruins of the wall. J.T. followed, and Parker broke into a jog as they charged into a battle that neither might survive.

When they were gone, Naomi turned to Reese. "I'm sorry I lied to you. I want you to know that I wasn't faking being friends with you. I think you're the coolest person I ever . . ."

Reese didn't seem to be listening. She picked up the fallen Path member's gun and gestured down the hall.

"Let's go," she said in a voice as cold as snow.

The Path member, dazed but alive, scrambled away from Vesiroth and Fon-Rahm and vanished into a sea of bookcases in search of Duncan. Fon-Rahm let him go and stood in front of Vesiroth. "What is your answer, wizard? Do you live or do you die?"

The wizard smiled as his fingers found the silver spike hanging from his neck. "Fon-Rahm! Finally I see myself in you, ruthless and cold-blooded. This world is no place for the weak, my child."

"I am not your child."

"Of course you are. You and your brothers are all my children, and you will all serve me in one way or another. That's what children are for."

"Do not make me destroy you."

"You were created from my essence, Fon-Rahm, and I know you better than you know yourself. You wouldn't kill me even if you could."

Fon-Rahm's entire body ached. His own energy was depleted and his thoughts were buried in a deep fog. If it came down to it, he really didn't know if he could beat Vesiroth in an all-out war. "Do not test me, creator."

"Ah, but, you see, a test is precisely what I had in mind. You've proven you're still capable of blasting down walls, but there's something amiss, isn't there? You're not quite yourself these days, firstborn. The question is, just how much of you is actually left?"

"Enough to end you."

Vesiroth nodded sagely. "Perhaps. But then again, it won't just be me, will it?"

"But who else . . ."

The answer dawned on Fon-Rahm. Vesiroth laughed as the genie stuck his good hand into the nearest bookcase. Fon-Rahm tore through the wood and paper to find Duncan with the Path member dead at his feet. The ten-year-old finished the rituals, making the last few turns to the ends of the last canister. The empty lamp landed with a clang on the floor, next to another canister just like it.

Through a cloud of thick and acrid smoke Fon-Rahm could see horrors on either side of Duncan. The genie called Kain had the torso and arms of a man, a face that resembled both Fon-Rahm's and Vesiroth's, and the segmented body of a giant millipede trailing behind him. His eyes were wide with rage and madness. The genie Resparia was a ghostly version of Fon-Rahm, translucent, flickering in and out of visibility as if he was not really there at all.

The two genies struggled against invisible tethers and let loose unearthly screams. Duncan stood between them, using all of his strength to keep them in line. Fon-Rahm saw at once what had happened.

Duncan had opened both lamps himself. He was now the master of two of the Jinn.

33

IT WAS EVERYTHING DUNCAN HAD
ever wanted.

The power. The absolute, unadulterated *power*. His genies were
a direct connection to the Nexus, a gate through which power
flowed like water. He had been readying himself for this moment
for centuries, and now that it was finally here Duncan knew that
without his two genies he would never feel complete again.

Parker and J.T. entered the library just in time to see Kain's
millipede body skitter disgustingly up a wall. The smell of
rancid meat hung in the air like a fog. "Look out, Fon-Rahm!"
Parker cried. Fon-Rahm ducked out of the way as Kain lunged.
The millipede genie opened his mouth and let out a horrible
screech.

Fon-Rahm whirled on his young master and J.T. "Parker! You swore to me that you would leave this place!"

"You know I couldn't let you do this alone!"

J.T. took one look at Kain and went pale. "Um, Parker, what exactly is that thing?"

"Nothing good."

Kain jolted toward Parker and J.T., but Fon-Rahm grabbed him by his wriggling body and threw him to the floor. In seconds, the two genies were locked together, Kain wrapping his segmented body around Fon-Rahm in an attempt to crush him, Fon-Rahm using his blue lightning to singe legs off of the hideous insect genie. It was a failing tactic. No matter how many legs Fon-Rahm burned away, there were always more.

In the midst of the chaos, Vesiroth seethed. "You dare?" he said, staring daggers at Duncan. "You defy my orders and take the Jinn for yourself? You hide a lamp from me? From *me*?"

"Yeah, sorry about that, boss," said Duncan, euphoric in his newfound role as genie-master. "Should have kept you in the loop." With that, he commanded, "Resparia! Be a bud and bring me Vesiroth's head, would you?"

The ghost genie vanished and appeared behind Vesiroth, his hands around the dark wizard's neck. Vesiroth tried to pry them off but his human hands went through the Jinn's wrists as if the genie was made of smoke.

"Why should you have the throne and not me?" Duncan asked Vesiroth. "So we can have a world at peace? A world without war? I *like* war." He sneered as Vesiroth struggled. "I'm really, really good at it."

* * *

As they walked, Naomi desperately tried to get through to her onetime best friend. They could hear the battle raging deeper in the house.

"We have to help them," she pleaded. "Please. I know you're mad at me. . . ."

"I'm not mad at you," Reese said calmly, the Path goon's rifle uncomfortable in her hands. "I just don't trust you."

"I'm sorry I lied. I really am. I thought I was doing the right thing. Hasn't that ever happened to you? Haven't you ever done the wrong thing for the right reason?"

Reese wavered. She was always second-guessing herself. Who wasn't?

"You have no idea what my life is like. This wasn't my choice. I was raised to do this. I never got to be a regular kid. I never had friends. And then I met *you*. . . ." Naomi looked at the floor. "Maybe you don't understand. Maybe making friends comes easy to you."

Reese whirled on Naomi. "Easy? Everybody thinks I'm a geek and a loser! My whole life I've either been too smart or too weird for friends. Parker and Theo are all I've got and I don't know if I would even have them if we had never found Fon-Rahm."

"You've got me."

Reese looked away.

"And Parker and Theo are *my* friends, too, and I say we go and help them," Naomi said. "That's what friends do."

Reese lowered the gun. Naomi was right. That was what friends did.

* * *

Fon-Rahm threw off the millipede genie and fried it with a blast of blue electricity. Kain landed on his hundreds of legs and hissed at the first of the Jinn. He didn't like the taste of lightning, and decided to go after an easier target. Kain planted his front claws and leaped straight at Parker and J.T. Parker shoved his father aside and used his residual knowledge of parkour to escape. By the time Kain reached Parker, the seventh grader was gone, using the table and the wall as launchpads for a series of impossible-to-follow acrobatics.

Fon-Rahm targeted the millipede genie and unleashed everything he had. The air in Professor Ellison's house was filled with arcing blue bolts that slammed into Kain one after another. The heat from the attack blistered the paint off of the ceiling and set fire to the furniture. Kain curled in on himself in pain, looking like the world's largest and most deadly potato bug.

And then Fon-Rahm collapsed, spent. Parker and J.T. rushed to his side.

"Fon-Rahm!" Parker cried. "Are you okay? Can you hear me?"

The genie could barely speak. "I ... I cannot ..."

"He's hurt bad, kid," Parker's dad said. "He's black-and-blue all over."

Parker said, "Fon-Rahm, it's okay. You can rest for a minute. Let Vesiroth and that psycho kid fight it out. With any luck, they'll kill each other and save us the trouble."

The genie stared at Parker like he could barely recognize him. "The infection, Parker. I can feel it in my mind. It is telling me ... telling me ..."

"Telling you what, buddy?"

Without warning, the genie lashed out his arm, backhanding

J.T. across the room. Parker's father hit the wall like a rag doll and slumped to the floor, unconscious. The genie bared his teeth at Parker, his eyes as black as his skin was sickly gray. "It is telling me to *kill you*."

34

VESIROTH STRUGGLED AGAINST RESPARIA. The dark sorcerer was the most dangerous wizard who had ever lived, but what could he do against a ghost? As Resparia choked the life from him, Vesiroth gurgled in a vain attempt to speak.

Duncan leaned closer to Vesiroth. "Sorry, boss, I can't quite make out what you're trying to say."

"You . . . you . . ."

"I *what*? I beat you without even breaking a sweat? I'm the greatest wizard that ever lived? Yeah, that sounds about right." He turned to the millipede genie. "Kain! I command you to make me twenty again!" A mist passed over Duncan. When it was gone, he was no longer a ten-year-old. He was a twenty-year-old man in the absolute prime of his life. "Looks like I didn't need your help after all." He flexed the muscles in his arms and cracked his neck. "That feels *so good*."

"You . . ."

"You know," Duncan said, "if I were you I would save my strength and enjoy my last, oh, say ten seconds of life. Adios, *boss*."

Vesiroth's hands found the silver pendant that hung from his neck. He grabbed it and concentrated all his will on the ghost genie. Resparia howled in pain and dropped the scarred wizard to the floor. Vesiroth gasped and locked a gaze of pure hatred onto Duncan. "You . . . have made a grave mistake."

Duncan frowned. "Kain! Stop blubbering and kill this old fool."

The millipede genie pulled himself from the floor and lunged. Without even taking his eyes off his betrayer Vesiroth grasped his pendant with one hand and held the other to Kain. A blast of pure energy knocked the genie back. The fury in Vesiroth's voice was blistering. "Did you really think you could use my own creations against me?"

He sent out another shock wave and pushed Kain to the other side of the room. That's when Duncan discovered the downside to genie ownership. He was tethered to Kain and Resparia both, and when the millipede genie was more than fifty yards away, a rush of white-hot pain shot through his head. Duncan put his hands to his temples in abject agony.

"Kain and Resparia are mindless beasts brought into being through a sheer force of will. My very life force courses through them . . ." Before the ghost genie could disappear, Vesiroth sent a blast that forced him away from Duncan. Duncan moaned in pain as Vesiroth picked up one of the jade-and-metal staffs dropped by the now-deceased members of the Path. "...until I decide that I want it *back*."

Parker vaulted away just as a bolt of blue lightning destroyed the place he just stood. "Fon-Rahm! What are you doing? I command you to stop!"

Fon-Rahm ignored his master's orders. Lightning radiated down his arms and off the tips of his fingers. He was aglow with blue electricity that pulsed like a heartbeat.

"Fon-Rahm, stop! It's me! It's Parker!"

Fon-Rahm didn't seem to care. Electricity crackled around him as he prepared to fry Parker. Parker closed his eyes, ready to die in a way he never would have thought possible, at the hands of a being he had always considered his friend.

"Leave him alone, Fon-Rahm!"

A chunk of concrete bounced off the back of Fon-Rahm's head. He whirled around to see Reese and Naomi standing in the wreckage of the room. Reese held another piece of rubble in her hands, ready to let fly. "What's gotten into you? Parker's your friend!"

Reese dropped her weapon when Fon-Rahm tipped back his head and let out a bloodcurdling roar.

"Parker!" yelled Naomi. "Run!"

Theo watched it all on the wall of monitors that flickered in Professor Ellison's control room.

"Well, I can't say it's all according to plan, but things actually seem to be working out quite well for us," the professor said. "Vesiroth and Duncan may well kill each other, and Fon-Rahm is taking himself out of the picture. Of course, things do seem rather bleak for Parker."

Theo jumped out of his seat. "You don't care about him at all, do you? Even after all the times he's saved you?"

"I care about more important things."

"Like yourself?"

"Be careful what you say next. Up until now you've only seen my maternal side. Don't make me raise my voice."

Theo shook his head. "All this magic. All this power. And what has it got you? What has it got any of us?" He looked his mentor dead in the eye. "I'm going out there to help my friends."

There was real anger in Professor Ellison's voice. "Do not disobey me, Theo. I will not warn you again!"

Theo went to the door and grabbed the handle.

"I'm going, Professor Ellison. If you want to stop me you're going to have to kill me. We both know you've had plenty of practice."

Theo pushed the door handle, half expecting to be cut down by a magic spell. When it didn't happen he opened the door and ran into the maze of the house.

Naomi could hardly believe her eyes. She knelt with Reese by J.T.'s side, trying to shield the unconscious man from the flying debris and the general mayhem of the surroundings. On one side of the gigantic room Parker ran from Fon-Rahm. On the other, Vesiroth used his blasts to keep Resparia and Kain away from Duncan. It was chaos. She said, "We have to get out of here. We have to get J.T. some place safe!"

"I thought you understood what was happening here." Reese

shook her head. "This is a battle between good and evil. If Vesiroth wins there *is* no place safe."

Naomi clenched her teeth. She felt helpless. She wanted more than anything to make a difference and prove to Reese that she was on the side of the angels.

Thanks to Parker's magically enhanced parkour skills, Fon-Rahm's zap missed the seventh grader's leg by less than six inches. Parker ran and yelled over his shoulder, his voice dripping with desperation. "Come on, Fon-Rahm, cut it out! Deep down you know it's me!"

The genie continued to silently stalk his former master, casting electric volleys and staring with sickly black eyes.

"If you really wanted to kill me I would already be dead!"

A blast of red-hot electricity scorched the air around Parker's head.

"That's enough!"

Parker stopped running. He was out of breath and covered with plaster dust. His parkour skills were almost gone, returned to the Nexus with his long-lost ability to speak French. "I'm not running from you anymore! I'm your friend!"

Fon-Rahm held his good arm out and blasted a hole through a bookcase not a foot away from Parker's head. Parker did not flinch.

"We defeated Xaru together. We battled the Path and we saved humanity. I taught you to eat junk food. You taught me that there are some people in this world who keep their word."

Fon-Rahm fired off another round of lightning. It tore chunks out of the ground at Parker's feet. Parker did not flinch.

"I taught you what it meant to be human. You taught me what it was to be a true friend."

Fon-Rahm let loose a storm of sparks that surrounded Parker like an aura of blue flame. Parker did not flinch.

"You won't kill me because we need each other. You're a part of me and I'm a part of you."

Fon-Rahm raised his good arm and then let it drop. The black in his eyes clouded over. He was winning the battle that raged inside him.

"Parker..." he said, his entire body trembling with the effort it took to speak. "I cannot control myself much longer. Please. *Run.*"

Parker did not flinch. He crossed his arms and stared down the genie. "No."

Naomi watched as Vesiroth took a metal rod in each hand and aimed one each at Resparia and Kain. The jade globes glowed bright green, and beams of light struck the evil genies, contorting the two creatures in a dance of pure pain.

"Kain! Resparia! Seventh and twelfth of the Jinn!" Vesiroth roared. "I, your creator, command your obedience!"

The genies spasmed in agony.

"He's killing them!" said Reese. "He's killing his own genies!"

Naomi didn't say anything. She just stared at the ground next to Vesiroth's feet. In the chaos the welded pieces of the Elicuum Helm had been ripped from Duncan's black bag. The artifact that would allow Vesiroth to enslave mankind was simply lying in the dust and torn pages of the destroyed library, waiting for someone to pick it up.

Vesiroth's voice burned. "You were created from my very life force, and I call upon the power of the Nexus to unmake you. Begone from this earth and exist no more!"

The rods shook in Vesiroth's hands. Kain and Resparia clasped their hands to their heads. As Resparia blinked in and out of existence and Kain's repulsively segmented body whipped around in a frenzied panic, Naomi saw her chance. She broke from Reese and sprinted toward Vesiroth.

"Naomi! No!" Reese shouted. "You don't understand!"

It was too late. Naomi got to the Helm just as the two genies, vibrating with the pain of the Nexus's pull, imploded in a storm of ash and smoke.

Vesiroth began to shake as the life force once contained in Kain and Resparia rushed back to its home. His metal staff crashed to the floor.

Duncan, his head aching and blood pouring from his nose, had been to this rodeo before and he knew he had to get out of the way pronto. He started to run but stopped when he saw Naomi reaching for the Helm. The Helm! With the Helm, Duncan would be invincible! He manifested a scimitar in each hand. "Hand it over, girl, or I'll slice you to pieces."

Reese knew it was true. She charged Duncan's back with a scream of her own, pushing him toward the energy field that was about to erupt from Vesiroth in a storm of chaos and destruction. Reese and Naomi left the Helm where it was and dove for cover.

"No," said Duncan, as he realized what was about to happen. "Please, no."

It was too late. Vesiroth threw his arms to his sides as a blast of untamed power burst from his very soul. Duncan was blown back by the wave of pure energy that scorched the walls, burned every book, shattered every piece of furniture, and torched every priceless piece of art in the room.

Reese threw herself on top of Naomi and closed her eyes tight. She had just killed another human being. She felt sick to her stomach.

When Fon-Rahm saw what was happening he instinctively activated a crackling blue field of electricity to protect himself and Parker. The entire house rumbled as walls fell and beams cracked. When it was over, Fon-Rahm looked at Parker with clear eyes.

"I knew it," said Parker, almost collapsing with relief. "You protected me. Nothing could change what you really are. Nothing could turn us against each other."

"Parker..." Fon-Rahm shook his head with growing horror. "I am sorry."

Parker's smile faded as Fon-Rahm's eyes slowly turned black.

The genie raised his right arm and prepared to incinerate the boy who had freed him from his prison of three thousand years. Before the fatal blow could be struck, Fon-Rahm cried out and fell to a heap in front of Parker.

Professor Ellison stood with Theo at her side. Her hands were raised, a fine green mist settling around her.

"What did you do?" Parker asked, dropping to his knees to tend to his fallen genie. "What did you do to him?"

"I told you there would be a price to pay when you cut your tether," Professor Ellison said. "I figured that as long as I was messing around in Fon-Rahm's mind I might as well put in a back door."

"What kind of back door? What did you do?"

"I installed a kill switch, dear boy. I always knew that I would have to put him down someday. I severed Fon-Rahm's connection to the Nexus. He no longer has any powers to grant wishes or throw bolts of lightning or fly." She stared at the prone genie. "Now he's just like the rest of us."

35

THE ROOM WAS DESTROYED. VESIROTH,
his tsunami of power spent, staggered to his feet. He knelt
unsteadily, pulled his two pieces of the Helm from the rubble,
and cleaned the dust away with slow, almost loving hands. It was
all he could do to keep from collapsing where he stood.

"You're done, Vesiroth," said Professor Ellison, serene and
regal in the wreckage of her own house. "It's over."

"I . . . am strong enough to finish you, Tarinn." Vesiroth clasped
his fingers around his silver spike and cast a wave of energy at
Ellison. The spell was so feeble that it barely moved the air. By
the time it reached the professor it was nothing but a stiff breeze.

"Be careful, Professor," said Theo, hiding behind her. "When
his power comes back he's going to be really mad."

"By then it will be too late." Ellison knew that her window was closing. If she wanted to trap Vesiroth she had to do it now. She walked backward, hoping the wizard would follow her to the containment room and the trap that would hold him for the rest of eternity.

Vesiroth staggered after her. He was so sluggish he could barely walk.

Parker cradled his genie's head in his hands. "Fon-Rahm? Can you hear me?"

"Yes, I hear you," said the first of the Jinn, blinking into the light with clear eyes. The magical infection that had taken control of his mind and body had vanished along with his Nexus-given power.

"Are you all right, buddy?"

"Yes, I feel..." He cocked his head to the side. "I feel as if the ground pulls at me. It is a most unusual sensation."

"That's gravity. That's what happens when you can't fly."

"I see. And this air that moves in and out of my body..."

"You're breathing, Fon-Rahm. You should probably keep doing that."

"Ah."

"Fon-Rahm, we have to fight Vesiroth."

Fon-Rahm held his right hand in front of his eyes and turned it over. He held it in the air and concentrated. A glowing mist did not flood from his eyes. Blue arcs of lightning did not materialize. Nothing happened at all.

"I am afraid I will be of little use, Parker." He dropped his hand. "I feel a drumbeat inside my chest. It grows stronger even as I contemplate the dangerous situation in which we find ourselves."

"That's a pulse, Fon-Rahm. You're feeling your heart beat."

"A heartbeat, of course. And why does its tempo increase?"

"Because, buddy," said Parker, patting the genie on his shoulder, "we're in a boatload of trouble."

Reese dug through the destruction until she found Duncan's broken body. "Is it possible he's still . . ." The hint of hope in her voice died when she pulled a piece of collapsed wall from his face and saw that in death he had reverted back to his cursed childhood. The sight of Duncan's ten-year-old face shocked her.

Naomi pulled her friend away from the rubble. "You had to do it. He didn't give you any choice."

Reese stared for a moment longer. Duncan's hand reached out as if to accuse her of murder. Reese clenched her jaw and pushed herself to her feet.

"Take it easy, Reese," Naomi said. "You should give yourself some time to recover."

Reese's voice was steel. "I don't have time to do anything but stop Vesiroth."

Vesiroth followed Ellison and Theo to the very end of the immense room. He kept casting his energy spells and they kept dying well before they could reach their target and inflict any damage.

"That's it, Vesiroth. Just a little farther." Ellison signaled to

Theo and they threw open a final set of closed doors. "Your prize awaits."

It was a small room, for Professor Ellison's house, at least. Windows stretched from the floor to the ceiling on three sides, revealing the gorgeous landscape of New Hampshire. The final piece of the Elicuum Helm floated in midair, suspended by a beam of pure light in the middle of the room.

Vesiroth was entranced. All he had to do was walk into the room and take it.

Theo and his mentor backed out of the way. They wanted to give the scarred wizard plenty of space. Theo whispered, "He won't do it, Professor Ellison. He must know it's a trap."

"He has just absorbed a tremendous amount of energy and he's not thinking clearly. Right now he wants one thing in the world and he will do anything to get it, including lie to himself."

"But even if he's trapped, the piece of the Helm will be stuck in here with him! He'll use it to break out!"

"Do you really think I didn't account for that?"

Vesiroth stood outside the room, wavering. He didn't appear to notice the sea of ancient runes painted on the room's floor, ceiling, and walls. He didn't see the circle drawn in red under the Helm. He was exhausted and barely on his feet. The pull of the Helm was the only thing holding him upright.

"Do it," the professor whispered. "Don't think about it. It's right in front of you. Reach out and take it."

Vesiroth raised his foot to enter the room, but at the last second he stopped. He stared at the hovering metal helmet with newfound suspicion.

Reese and Naomi, running hard, finally reached Theo and Professor Ellison. "What's happening?" asked Reese. "Why is he stopping?"

"I don't know," said Professor Ellison. "We need him to go in himself. It has to be his idea."

Reese bit her lower lip. "Do you trust me?" she asked Naomi. Naomi didn't hesitate. "Yes."

"Then follow my lead."

Reese dropped her head and ran. She and Naomi charged past Vesiroth and into the library.

"Reese! Naomi! Stop!" Theo cried out, but it was too late. The two girls were standing under the floating Helm in the middle of the room.

Vesiroth glared at them.

"Father," Reese said, "why do you stare at us so strangely?"

Vesiroth's face became a mask of confusion. Could it be? "My . . . daughters? Here?"

Reese's instincts screamed at her to take a step back, but she held her ground. "Of course, Father. It's us."

"My girls . . . I thought I had lost you. . . ."

"Never, Father."

"My daughters . . ."

"Won't you embrace us, Father?" Reese held out her arms to the terrifying wizard, and Naomi did the same.

Vesiroth walked into the room, all thoughts of the Helm gone. He had waited (was it years? decades?) for this moment. He couldn't quite remember why.

"Father, we missed you so much."

The wizard's footsteps echoed in the silence of the ruined house. He was going to be reunited with his daughters. Nothing else mattered.

"At last, we'll be together," Reese said.

And then the levitating shard of the Helm disappeared.

Vesiroth stopped, just a few feet shy of the circle that would sever his connection to the Nexus and entrap him forever. He stared at the empty air.

Reese shifted her feet. Naomi shot her a nervous glance.

"It's okay, Father," Reese said. "It's not important."

Vesiroth took another step, and the Helm was there again. He halted on the very edge of Professor Ellison's painted circle. "It's not real..." he said, examining the broken piece of the Helm. "It's..."

His eyes searched the room and found the professor's polished-glass hologram projector. He grabbed the metal spike at his throat and cast a spell of energy that knocked the box over and shattered it into a million pieces.

"A trick. A paltry magician's illusion." The wizard whirled on the girls. "You are not my daughters....My family is dead!" His eyes burned with madness and anger. He reached for his spike again and Naomi and Reese dove for cover. His blast found only the professor's circle.

"It's gone wrong," Professor Ellison told Theo as she rummaged through her bag. "And his power has returned."

"What are you going to do?"

"It's time to pull out the big guns, Gods help us." She pulled the real final shard of the Helm and held it to her own head.

But before the Helm could work its magic Professor Ellison was blown backward and off her feet. Theo turned to see Vesiroth, fuming.

"You sought to trick me, Tarinn? With illusions and little girls?"

Ellison tried to raise the broken Helm to her head. Another attack from Vesiroth threw her into a wall and sent the Helm flying.

"To think I doubted myself, when fate demands I succeed! I need no baubles and tricks to defeat the likes of you!"

He threw his own pieces of the Helm into the rubble and bore down on the professor. He wrapped his hands around her throat and hoisted her off the ground. Professor Ellison kicked and flailed at his arms but it was no use. She was done for and the war for humanity's freedom was lost.

"I was going to keep you alive to witness the glory of my kingdom. A world without war! A world of servants who would live in fear of my displeasure! A world in my own image!"

The professor's kicks and jabs grew weaker. She was dying.

Theo picked up the three broken pieces of the Helm. They had not been in the same room for hundreds of years. Theo gasped as they welded themselves together, making the Elicuum Helm complete once more.

"Perhaps it's better this way," said Vesiroth. "It would break my heart to see you a slave."

As the life drained from Professor Ellison's eyes, Theo placed the Elicuum Helm on his head.

36

THEO'S BRAIN WAS ON FIRE.

His neck snapped back. Intensely bright color and light flooded his mind in a burning rush and every thought he had of helping his friends was gone, killed as the Helm took over. He clawed at the metal in desperation. The pain was immense but no matter how hard he tried he couldn't get the helmet to come off. It was like the Helm had bonded with Theo's skull.

His scream made Vesiroth turn his attention away from Professor Ellison. He saw that Theo was wearing the Helm and his face twisted into a mask of anger.

"You..." The wizard dropped Ellison. She fell to the floor in a limp pile.

Theo was thrashing now, prying frantically at the brass with his fingers. The Helm wouldn't budge.

Vesiroth clutched his silver spike and held out his hand to hit Theo with a blast of energy. Suddenly, Theo's body became rigid. It was as if a powerful electric current was running through him, curving his spine and pulling his head back in an impossible angle. Before Vesiroth could get his spell off a black tentacle hurtled out of the Helm and straight into Vesiroth's chest. The scarred wizard flew back as if he had been shot.

More tentacles began to emerge from the helmet. Theo screamed again.

Parker didn't hear the scream so much as he felt it in the pit of his stomach.

"What was that?" he asked, looking to the battle on the other side of the immense library.

"Theo has donned the Helm," said Fon-Rahm.

"But the professor said..."

The two exchanged looks before Parker helped the once-powerful genie to his feet and they ran to join the others in the smoldering ruins that used to be the center of Professor Ellison's library.

Reese ran to her friend. "Theo!"

She didn't get anywhere near him. A black feeler from the Helm swatted her away. Naomi rushed to her side. "Reese. We have to get out of here. That thing has taken control of him."

"We can't leave Theo here," Reese said, dazed from the blow. "We have to save him."

Naomi shook her head. "I don't think we can."

As they spoke, the color in Theo's eyes disappeared, leaving blank white orbs. The tentacles from the Helm began to whip madly around the room, and Theo left the ground to float in midair.

Professor Ellison came to, choking but alive. Her protégé was rising into the air wearing the Helm. She saw Vesiroth collapsed facedown in the dust. The wizard wasn't moving. Ellison reached out to see if he was dead.

He grabbed her wrist.

Naomi and Reese dove for cover as the inky black tentacles from the Helm flailed around, destroying anything that was still standing in the library.

Parker and Fon-Rahm reached Theo too late. The Helm had complete control of his body and his mind.

Parker yelled, "Theo! You have to fight it! Theo!"

He reached for his cousin but Fon-Rahm held him back. "You must not interfere with the Helm. I fear there is nothing we can do for Theo now."

Parker ignored him. He was mesmerized by the vision of his cousin, levitating in midair, the power of the corrupted Helm shooting havoc in all directions.

"Theo!" he said. "Don't give in to it! Don't let it control you!"

"Parker! Get down!" Fon-Rahm tackled Parker to the ground as a tentacle raked the air where he once stood. Parker never took his eyes off of Theo.

Theo stretched out his arms. The Helm was a part of him now. A tentacle found Vesiroth on the ground and knocked him aside, freeing Professor Ellison. When he tried to run a black arm slashed Vesiroth from behind. The wizard staggered to his feet, but another tentacle grabbed him and lifted him off the ground.

Vesiroth grabbed for his silver spike. A tentacle pried his hand away. More black limbs emerged from the Helm to hold the wizard by his arms and legs, helplessly suspended in midair.

The power emanating from the Helm became a storm. Professor Ellison's papers and books were blown away from Theo. He was in the eye of a hurricane.

Parker had to yell to be heard over the roar. "There must be some way we can help him!"

Professor Ellison grabbed him from behind. "It appears the Helm can't take the power. It's only a matter of minutes before it goes critical. We have to get out while we still can!"

"What will happen then?" asked Naomi.

"I have no idea," said the professor. "But I don't want to be here to find out."

"I won't go," Parker said. "It's my fault all this is happening. I won't let Theo die."

"And what about Reese?" asked Fon-Rahm. "And me? And your father? Theo made his choice to save us all. If we stay, his sacrifice will mean nothing."

"But..."

"I am sorry, Parker. Sometimes there is no good outcome. All we can do is survive."

Naomi screamed as the tentacles began to whip Vesiroth around the ruins of the room, bouncing the wizard off of any solid object they could find. The wind howled.

Reese said, "I love him, too, Parker, but we have to leave! It's the only way!"

Parker took one last look at his cousin.

"I'm so sorry, Theo," he whispered. "I'm so, so sorry."

Then he ran to help his father off the floor.

They made it outside just in time.

Parker and Fon-Rahm dropped J.T. on the grass and turned back to see hundreds of black tentacles tearing the roof off of the house. Theo floated above the ruins, spinning lazily in the air. Lightning flashed in the gathering mist below him. Vesiroth was in the Helm's grasp and fighting helplessly against the black arms that held him.

Reese pointed. "The Helm! It's coming apart!"

The cracks in the Helm were glowing. The very air above the house began to vibrate as the corrupted relic started to shake itself to pieces.

"No," Parker said quietly. "Please. Not Theo."

Then the helmet cracked and a sphere of pure power pushed out from Theo. It was like a mini nuclear explosion that flattened everything in its way. Parker and his friends were knocked to the ground. All the twisted power of the Helm collapsed in on itself. With the sound of a thousand claps of thunder, the tentacles, Vesiroth, and Theo vanished into a tiny pinprick of black that hung for a moment in the air before finally blinking out of existence.

All was quiet. No birds chirped. No dogs barked.

The only sound came from Reese. She was quietly sobbing.

37

PARKER SAT UP AND BLINKED AT THE ruins that were once Professor Ellison's house. The massive structure, once hidden from human eyes by Ellison's spell, had been reduced to a huge pile of rubble. It reminded Parker of a picture in his history textbook that showed a block of London row houses obliterated by German bombs in World War II.

J.T. came groggily back to life, coughing out the dust that was thick in the air. Naomi and Reese gawked at the carnage, unwilling to accept what had just happened. Parker waited for a long minute before he pushed himself to his feet.

"Parker!" Professor Ellison stood unsteadily and brushed off Fon-Rahm's offer of help. "Where do you think you're going?"

"I have to look for Theo! He might still be alive in there!"

"Parker . . ." Fon-Rahm shook his head sadly. "No human could have survived that. Not even Theo."

"You don't know! He could have cast some sort of protection spell at the last second! He could have transported himself or . . . or something!"

"I'm sorry, Parker," Professor Ellison said. "But he's gone. He gave his life to save all of us."

"Well, you guys can sit here and do nothing if you want but I'm going in there to look for my friend!"

Before he got a chance an armada of black cars and SUVs surged down Professor Ellison's driveway, kicking up clouds of dirt as they surrounded the grounds.

"It's the Path!" shouted Reese. "They sent *everybody!*"

The lead truck skidded to a stop right in front of them.

"I still have my bag," said Professor Ellison as she girded herself for the battle to come. "And I for one am not going down without a fight." She selected two artifacts from her collection and held one in each hand. Whatever stepped out of the SUV would face a three-thousand-year-old wizard who had just lost someone she had become irrationally close to.

The door of the SUV opened and a woman stepped out. She wore a business suit and an earpiece connected to a radio on her belt. Her dark hair was pulled into a tight bun on the back of her head. As she strode closer Parker saw that she had a handgun in a shoulder holster under her coat.

Ellison was seconds away from blasting her before Naomi cried, "Don't hurt her!"

With Parker, Professor Ellison, Fon-Rahm, and J.T. looking

on, Naomi ran to the woman. The woman dropped down to scoop Naomi up into her arms. "Naomi!" she said, holding the girl close. "Oh, thank God you're all right. Thank God!"

A flood of armed men and women climbed out of the cars and trucks that circled Professor Ellison's property. Fon-Rahm said, "These people are not from the Path."

"Then who are they?" Reese asked.

The woman hugging Naomi broke free and wiped tears from her eyes in an effort to regain an air of no-nonsense professionalism. She pulled a leather wallet from her pocket and flipped it open to reveal a badge and an ID card. "I'm Agent Erica Cook."

"Erica Cook?" Reese asked Naomi. "Does that mean she's your..."

Naomi nodded. "She's my mom."

"I'm an idiot, is who I am," Agent Cook said, holding on to her daughter's hand. "I must have been insane to let the D.E.N.T. talk me into sending you into this mess."

"I give up," said Parker. "What's the D.E.N.T.?

"The Department of Extra-Normal Threats." Professor Ellison put her talismans back into the Louis Vuitton bag for another day. "I should have known they were getting close."

"Wait a second," said J.T. "Are you telling me that the United States government has a whole department devoted to *genies*?"

"Not just genies. Wizards, dragons, necromancers, anything magical that might pose a threat to national security. We've been watching your son for quite some time." Agent Cook turned to Parker. "We needed a field agent to infiltrate your group and my superiors convinced me that only someone your own age could gain your confidence."

Reese said, "So you made your own daughter do it? That's crazy!"

"She didn't *make* me do it," said Naomi. "I volunteered. No one knew what you guys were up to. We didn't know if you were good guys or bad guys. For all anybody in the D.E.N.T. knew, Parker could have been a terrorist."

"Yeah, I can understand that," said Reese.

Parker bristled. "I'm right here, you know."

"I've been arguing with my boss about this for weeks. I never should have agreed to send Naomi in the first place." Agent Cook squeezed Naomi's hand. "I'll never make that mistake again."

The questions went on and on but Parker was barely paying attention. He couldn't keep his eyes off the small army of D.E.N.T. agents who were combing through the debris field that used to be Professor Ellison's house.

"Parker, I need you to focus." Agent Cook snapped her fingers in front of Parker's face. The D.E.N.T. had bundled Naomi and Reese over to an SUV, where they sat swaddled in blankets, drinking bottled water. Professor Ellison and Fon-Rahm were being interrogated by other agents. J.T. was laid out on a stretcher with an IV, close enough that Parker could hear him complain that he felt just fine and that the only thing that hurt was his pride.

"It's no use pretending this is all going to go away, Parker. I don't want to play bad cop with you but you might as well face up to what's really happening here. You've started something big and you've freaked out a lot of very powerful people."

Parker leaned back onto the hood of the black sedan and stared at the sky. "Yeah, I know a few powerful people myself."

"I'm talking about the kind of people who can throw you in

jail, kid. I'm talking about the kind of people who can make your whole family wish you had cooperated with me. They'll try you as an adult. They'll ruin any prospects you might have for a successful future. They'll ruin your life."

"Okay, that's it!" J.T. pulled the needle from his arm, pushed the D.E.N.T. medics aside, and went to defend his son. The agents reached for their weapons but Agent Cook waved them off. "That's enough. Is my son under arrest?"

"Not yet, Mr. Quarry. If he plays ball he won't be arrested at all."

"Well, if you want him you're going to have to go through me." Parker jumped off the car's hood. "Dad, don't!"

"Parker, I wasn't there for you before but I'm going to be here for you now."

"It's not going to do any good if you get in trouble, too!"

"Mr. Quarry's already in trouble."

"What do you mean?" Parker asked.

Agent Cook crossed her arms. "We checked with California. Your father wasn't supposed to leave the state. He's going back to prison for violating his parole."

"Yeah, right!" Parker snorted. "You guys just didn't do your homework. He got *permission* to leave. Tell her, Dad." J.T. stayed silent. "Dad, tell her. Please! Tell her you didn't run out on your parole!"

"She's right, Parker. I wasn't supposed to leave."

Parked felt himself deflate. He had lost Fon-Rahm, he had lost Theo, and now he was losing his father, too. "Dad, why?"

J.T. looked at the grass. "Your mom told me . . ." He stopped and started again. "You and your mom were making a new start here in New Hampshire. Without me. I thought that once I was in the rearview mirror you would just forget about me. I just hoped that maybe we could all make a fresh start, together. I love you, Parker, and I love your mother. I screwed up once and I just couldn't stand the thought of losing you forever."

"But it's not fair!" Parker leaned in to his dad and screamed right in his face. "I finally got you back! We were a family again! Besides, you never did anything wrong in the first place!"

"Yes, I did." J.T. put his hand on his son's shoulder. "I did everything the police and the lawyers said I did."

"But that's not possible! You never would have ripped off those old people. It was just a mistake. It was just bad bookkeeping and all that other stuff. You didn't mean it. It wasn't your fault."

"I lied to you, son. I just couldn't bring myself to tell you that I was a criminal."

All the energy drained out of Parker. He sat hard on the car's front bumper.

"I wanted to be a player. I wanted money and everything that comes with it and I started taking shortcuts and before I knew it I was doing things...things I'm ashamed of. I stole the money. I lied and I lied and I just kept digging a deeper and deeper hole for myself. I deserved to go to jail. I deserved to lose you and Kathleen." He let out a deep breath. "I can't change the past, Parker, but I can make sure I don't make the same mistakes again. I have learned so much from you. The way you stand up for your friends, the way you fight for what you believe in. I know I promised you I would change before but this time...I don't even have to promise. I'm already changed. Because of you."

Parker wiped his eyes. He wasn't crying. He wasn't.

"Son, I need you to do something for me."

Parker sniffled. "What?"

"I need you to tell Agent Cook everything you know about Rommy, about Professor Ellison, about all of it."

"But Dad, this is *our* thing! They'll screw it all up!"

"Maybe, but Naomi was right about trying to keep something this big a secret. It's going to get out eventually. You might as well spill it."

Parker stared at Agent Cook in defiance.

"I know you've got issues with authority, Parker," J.T. continued. "Believe me, I know. But I can't stand the thought of you getting into real trouble. Promise me you'll cooperate. Promise."

Parker looked away. "I promise."

J.T. nodded and looked over to where Fon-Rahm was speaking with other feds. "You know, maybe that math teacher's not so bad. He's some kind of magical being that an evil wizard cooked up in a lab, sure, but he seems pretty solid. You could have worse role models in your life."

"I have the best role model in the world, Dad. I have you."

Parker hugged his father. J.T. savored the moment. He knew it would have to last him a long time.

A D.E.N.T. agent ran up to Agent Cook. "We've searched all through the remains of the house, ma'am. We found a few bodies . . ."

Parker's heart sank.

". . . but judging from the suits and weapons found nearby, we think they were members of the Path. There's no sign of Theo Merritt or your mystery wizard."

"Vesiroth," Parker said softly. "His name is Vesiroth. I'll tell you all about him."

As Parker spilled his guts to Agent Cook, Naomi sat with Reese on the grass.

"What do you think is going to happen now?" Reese asked.

"The D.E.N.T. will take care of everything. They'll cover all this up"—she gestured toward the destroyed house—"with a story about military tests or something. If there's one thing the D.E.N.T. is good at, it's keeping things out of the papers."

"No, I meant what do you think is going to happen with *you*?"

"Oh." Naomi ran her hands through her hair. "I'm going home."

Reese nodded. "Where's home?"

"Washington. Well, right outside Washington, in Virginia. My dad's down there. He writes these really technical manuals for medical equipment."

"Is he nice?"

"Yeah. I mean, he's a huge nerd, but he's pretty great."

"I'm glad." Reese picked at a blade of grass.

"I just want to have a normal life. No more spying. No more lies. I want to have real friends."

"Well, you've got one."

One side of Naomi's mouth curled up. It was almost a smile.

"Do you think your folks will let you come and visit?" Reese asked.

"I don't know, Reese," Naomi said, looking out over the house where she'd lost her friend Theo. "New Hampshire is kind of dangerous."

38

"HE LOVED THE NEW ENGLAND Patriots and the Boston Red Sox," the reverend said. "He spent hours practicing with a glove and a bat so that he might someday take his place as a left fielder in the shadow of the Green Monster. He had an infectious laugh and a love of life that showed whenever he ran, or jumped, or smiled. Theo Merritt was an athlete. He was a student. He was a son. He was a friend."

Martha Merritt let out a choked sob. Her husband, uncomfortable in his only suit, hugged her tight. His face was blank. He had missed a spot shaving. He wanted more than anything to learn that this was all a mistake or a bad dream that would vanish when he woke up. He wanted everyone to be wrong.

The memorial service was being held outside, on the very spot in which Theo had disappeared. When the parents of Cahill heard about Theo's death they clucked and warned their own kids, again, not to swim in the Conway quarry. It was a death trap. A total of seven kids had drowned there since 1978. Theo's body had never even come up. Divers had scoured the bottom of the quarry for days before calling off the search. It was just too deep.

Almost all of Theo's classmates from Robert Frost Junior High were there. Parker could hear the girls sobbing behind him. Sure, he thought, they never cared about him when he was alive, but now that he's *dead* . . .

He shifted in his wobbly folding chair. He wanted desperately to take off his stupid tie and put on a T-shirt. His mother sat on one side of him, holding so tightly to his hand he was afraid it would fall asleep. Even if it did, he wouldn't complain. He would just sit there with a numb hand. He could take it.

Reese sat with her parents. Parker caught her eye, but only for a second. She turned back to the reverend and focused on his stupid speech.

"Theo was kind, and gentle, always ready to help out around the house or carry someone's bags from the store or blah blah blah blah blah . . ."

Parker tuned him out. The guy didn't know anything about Theo. The Merritts never even went to church. They'd gotten the reverend to talk because Cahill was a small town and this was the kind of thing that reverends did. He didn't know the real Theo. Hardly anybody did. How could they?

Parker resisted the urge to turn around and look for Fon-Rahm. The genie (was he still a genie? What do you call a genie without any powers?) was standing near the back of the crowd, silent and alone. Parker knew that Professor Ellison was there, too, somewhere. She pretended she didn't care about anybody but Parker had a sneaking suspicion that she blamed herself for Theo's death. Parker knew how she felt.

Kathleen let go of Parker's hand to wipe her eyes with a tissue but clutched it again as soon as she was done. As if the loss of her nephew wasn't enough, her husband was back in a California prison. Everything good in her life seemed to have vanished overnight.

The drowning story had been cooked up by the D.E.N.T. The nation would panic if word got out about what really happened at Professor Ellison's house. Markets would crash, economies would fall, a new arms race centered on magic would consume the world. No one could know just how close mankind had come to falling under Vesiroth's rule. In order to keep the incident under wraps, Agent Cook had concocted a cover story: Parker and Theo had lied to their parents and had snuck down to the Conway quarry to go swimming. In an effort to impress his cousin, Theo had taken a dive off the quarry's highest point. He hit the water and disappeared. The police and rescue crews used searchlights and boats but they had turned up nothing.

It was a solid story, but it took a heavy toll on Parker. He knew that his aunt and uncle blamed him for Theo's death. He wanted so badly to tell them the truth, but he had to keep his mouth shut. Agent Cook had told him that sticking to this narrative would be the hardest thing he would ever do. She was right. It was awful. Parker felt like it was killing him.

* * *

The service was finally over. Parker, his hands shoved deep into the pockets of his new sport coat, stood talking to Reese, Fon-Rahm, Professor Ellison, and Maksimilian, who had cut short a complicated and shady scam in Eastern Europe to pay tribute to a boy he had considered a friend. "They all think it's my fault," Parker said as classmates and adults walked back to the cars, avoiding his eyes. "They think I let Theo drown because I was scared."

"I wish they would have let me be a part of the story," said Reese. "There's no reason I couldn't have gone swimming with you guys. We were together all the time."

"There was no point in both of us feeling like crap for the rest of our lives."

She nodded. Her dress was simple and black. For the first time in years there was no added color in her hair. She wanted to blend in with all the other mourners. She wanted to be unseen.

"I always liked the lad," Maks said. He had tidied up for the occasion. "I would say he reminded me of myself when I was that age but I was never that brave. I should have stayed and helped. If I had been there . . ." He trailed off and looked up into the sky. "Maybe I could have made a difference."

"I warned him not to touch the Helm. He never listened to me. I told him to . . ." Professor Ellison stopped talking. For a second, Reese thought the professor was going to tell them all that she loved Theo like the son she never had. She was going to turn away from them so that they wouldn't see her tears. She was going to drop the walls around her heart she had been building for three thousand years and let them see that underneath the spells and the relics she was a human being who needed other people around her, just like anyone. Instead, Professor Ellison sniffed and regained her aura of haughty superiority. "All that time I invested in him was for naught," she said. "All that potential squandered."

Reese felt anger rising inside of her like a volcano. She was going to really give the professor a piece of her mind when Parker said, "You might act like you don't care, Professor, but you and I both know what Theo meant to you."

Professor Ellison looked into Parker's eyes. "I will not forget him. If I live another three thousand years I will not forget him."

She turned to Maks. "I suppose we still have work to do. The war goes on."

Maks nodded. As he and the professor walked away, he turned back to Parker, Reese, and Fon-Rahm. "There's not a lot of magic left in the world, you know." Maks pulled the flask from his pocket. "Less and less every day. Maybe it's for the best, no? Maybe we're the problem. Maybe the whole thing"—he gestured to include everything around them—"would work better without us." He put his flask back untouched, gave Professor Ellison his arm, and walked with her to the parking lot.

Finally, it was just Parker, Reese, and Fon-Rahm, standing silently on the rim of the quarry. They all knew a piece was missing. They all knew there was nothing they could do to get that piece back.

"I have failed you, Parker," said Fon-Rahm. "Your father is . . . gone, Theo is no longer with us, and without magic I am a newborn finding his way in a strange world. I would give anything to be able to grant you wishes now. I would give anything to ease your suffering."

Parker shook his head. "There are some things magic can't do, Fon-Rahm."

"I've been having nightmares," Reese said. "About Duncan. He knows he's about to die. He reaches out for me but I just push him away. Then we both get swept into Vesiroth's energy field and right before Vesiroth kills me I wake up."

"Duncan would have killed you," Parker said. "He wouldn't have given it a second's thought."

"It doesn't make it any better."

"So what are we supposed to do now? Just pick up where we left off? Go to classes, watch TV, and pretend that we don't know what's really going on?"

"The war is over for us," said Fon-Rahm. "My creator is vanquished and my connection to the Nexus is gone. Professor Ellison no longer needs our help."

"But there are still lamps out there. There are still genies waiting to be released. When they get out..."

"When they get out someone else will have to fight them. It is up to us to simply live our lives as best as we can."

"I don't know if I can do that."

"I don't see how we have a choice," said Reese.

Fon-Rahm nodded. "We will move forward and we will remember. Theo gave his life to protect us. We owe him that much."

"If I had just one more wish I wouldn't ask for anything for myself." Parker stared into the inky black water in the quarry beneath them. "I would wish that Theo was still alive."

EPILOGUE

THEO OPENED HIS EYES.

He was in a bed in what was clearly a hospital, but it wasn't like any hospital Theo had ever seen before. The paint on the walls was peeling off and the equipment seemed like it was all fifty years old. He could smell mold. Sunlight came through a window, but Theo could see the iron bars outside the glass.

He threw back the sheets and swung his feet over the side of the bed. He was wearing his regular clothes. He gave the room a quick once-over and spotted his shoes underneath a green metal chair. He tried to walk over to grab them but his knees buckled and he fell to the worn-out floor.

"You shouldn't exert yourself. I imagine you're still quite shaken from your ordeal."

Theo felt his blood run cold. Vesiroth stood in the doorway.

The seventh grader tried to force his legs to work. He fought to his feet and frantically wracked his brain for a plan. He had no magical objects on him and he didn't have the strength to call on the power that had caused so much havoc at the Merrimack River. He wished he had paid more attention to Professor Ellison's lessons.

"Still spoiling for a fight, are we?" Vesiroth said. "I do admire your spirit."

Theo willed himself to stand and stumbled toward the window. Maybe he could pry it open and run to safety. He got to the glass and stared out. He was on the upper floor of a building set in the center of a field of ice. There was nothing to be seen for miles besides gleaming drifts of frozen wasteland. He was in the middle of nowhere.

"Where am I?" he asked, still staring at the snow.

"Siberia. I've been using this old hospital as a base of operations since my...reunion with the world. No one ever comes here. It was shut down when they discovered abnormally high radiation levels. Of course, I had the place thoroughly scrubbed. It's perfectly safe."

Theo didn't feel safe. "What am I doing here? What happened?"

"You really don't remember?" The scarred wizard strolled into the room and sat on the bed. His suit was impeccable.

"Of course I remember!" Theo frowned. What did he remember? His brain was buzzing. He was at Professor Ellison's house, waiting for the war everyone knew was coming. They had some kind of a plan to trap Vesiroth. Something about a shield? No, a *helmet*...

"You put on the Elicuum Helm and you unleashed a power

you couldn't control. You destroyed your professor friend's house. It was really quite a show."

Theo put a hand to his head. Why couldn't he remember?

"The Helm fractured and the resulting explosion tore a hole in the Nexus itself. Can you imagine it? You and I were absorbed into the very fabric of the most powerful force in existence. We were floating in the cocoon of the Nexus for days. It took all of my strength to find you and break us both free. We wound up in the Sahara, but you wouldn't recall that. You were barely alive. I had agents of the Path come for us, and now we're here. The two of us have survived something no one else in history has ever experienced. Not even the Elders were exposed to the very essence of the Nexus."

"But...I tried to trap you. Why did you save me?"

"Isn't it obvious, Theo?" A ghastly grin spread over Vesiroth's scarred face. "The Nexus isn't finished with us yet."